TWENTY-ONE (21)

CLARISSA WILD

TWENTY-ONE PLAYLIST

"My Mamma Said" by Aqua
"Coldest Winter" by Kanye West
"30 Minutes" by T.A.T.U.
"I Am Become Death" by Ben Salisbury & Geoff
Barrow
"Casual Affair" by Panic! At the Disco
"Counting Bodies Like Sheep To The Rhythm Of
The War Drums" by A Perfect Circle
"Psycho" by Muse
"I Don't Wanna Be In Love" by Dark Waves
"Come Say Hello" by Superhumanoids
"Skin" by Rihanna
"Good For You" by Selena Gomez
"High By The Beach" by Lana Del Rey
"Dark In My Imagination" by Of Verona
"Machine Stop" by Duologue
"Cybergoth" by The Enigma (TNG)
"Shut Up And Swallow" by Combichrist
"This Night" by Black Lab
"My Songs Know What You Did In The Dark" by
Fall Out Boy
"Never Let Me Go" by Florence + The Machine

GLOSSARY

Cosa Nostra: This business of ours (Illegal operations)

Omertà: Oath or 'code of silence'

Papà: Papa, dad, daddy

Mamma: Mom, mother

Madre: Mother

Don: Boss

Pinched: Getting caught by the police or feds

Bambina: Girl

Bambino: Boy

A mother is she who can take the place of all others
but whose place no one else can take.
- Cardinal Mermillod

PROLOGUE

ANGEL

My name might be Angel, but I'm far from a saint.

In fact, I'm a fucking killing machine.

I was born and bred for one purpose; murdering those who stand in the way of *Cosa Nostra*.

I know nothing other than blood and vengeance. This is what I live for, and what I'd die for if it were up to my father. If it were up to me ... well, let's just say I enjoy the benefits enough to continue doing what I do best.

Kill.

I pace around in the pig's cell, tossing a knife in my hand, careful not to let the blade touch my skin. His screams pierce my ears, but they won't wipe the smile off my face. The bound pig who's just pissed all over the chair is much too amusing.

"Did you have to piss that badly?" I ask, laughing. "Maybe I should've let you out for a break, huh?"

The pig repeatedly nods as sweat drips down his red and bloody face. His hands shiver, or at least, what's left of them. Maybe two or three fingers.

"Or should I chop the rest of your fingers off just for wetting the floor?"

This makes him screech out loud.

I'm so glad I stuffed his mouth with his own underwear. I can't be bothered with listening to his sad cries. I'm not here to feel pity, nor am I interested in what he has to say.

He's the asshole who ratted me out to the police using that picture of my license plate. Instead of keeping his mouth shut and stopping our family from prosecution, he decided it would be best to expose my little operation. Suffice to say that he didn't get to enjoy the benefits too long.

He thought the police would offer him protection. Instead, my father bribed them so they'd hand him over to us. Personally. Like a fucking roasted apple-stuffed pig offered on a platter.

His ass belongs to me now. Literally. I think I should just hang it on my wall, like a fucking trophy. It's what he deserves.

He pisses me off, that's what. I walk toward the guy

6

and hold out my knife close to his eye.

"Or maybe I should take your eye instead? You know … an eye for an eye or something."

He shakes his head vehemently, tears running down his bloody cheeks.

"Seriously? You're gonna cry like a fucking pussy now?" I punch him in the face with my fist and make sure to hold the knife on the other side where his head flings. The laceration it creates from left to right across his nose makes him whelp.

I shake my head at his pitiful appearance.

"Please …" he murmurs into the cloth.

"What?" I lean in, grabbing his chin so I can take a good look at him. "You think begging me will help you?" I growl. "You should have thought of that before you became a rat. Too late, motherfucker." I cut into his hand for good measure. "Not much left of this now, is there?" I muse, looking at his sad three little fingers. "Should I let you keep these?"

"Yes!" he says.

"Hmm … but that wouldn't be much fun now, would it?" I say.

And then I cut another one off.

There is no rhyme or reason to what I'm doing.

Hell, I don't even feel anything while I'm carving this pig.

Maybe that makes me fucked up in the head, but hey, what can you do? I was born like this, and I don't see anything wrong with getting revenge on the fucker who took my freedom away from me.

He thinks he still has a chance. That he can beg his way out of this.

Too bad, he doesn't realize that ain't how this organization works.

He took the *Omertà*. He knew what it meant.

Break the silence and you die.

Pick a fight with me, and you get a slow and painful death added on top of your sentence.

It's my job either to intimidate and shake down a victim for information or to kill. It depends on what the job entails. We get them from clients who hire our company to do their filthy work. I don't mind because I get a kick out of every kill I make.

I step away from the pig and watch him quiver in his seat before I throw another knife at him.

When it hits the middle of his chest, I yell, "Bull's-eye! That's twenty-five points. So close to zero now. And you know what that means?"

He closes his eyes momentarily, almost as if he's praying or something.

"Hey, fuckwad, I'm talking to you," I say, spitting on him. "Look at me." I push another knife underneath his chin to force him to look at me. "You and I … we're almost done. That means death is next."

He lets out an exasperated sigh, almost as if he's relieved.

I cock my head and squint. "Would you like that, huh? Do you want me to kill you?"

"Please …"

"Anything but the pain, huh?" I smile. "I guess nothing's worse than being my toy. Maybe I should have some mercy."

He nods, pleading with his eyes.

"Or maybe not," I muse.

And then I slice off another one of his fingers.

I continue cutting until he's rid of them all, left with nothing but stumps. I stop only when the blood has painted his body and the floor beneath him red, squirting all over my shirt until he's completely emptied out and his head hangs lifelessly against his chest.

I lift it up by his hair, forcing him to look at me with the last shred of energy he has left. "Do you think I'll go to hell for this?"

He nods.

I grin. "Yeah, I think so too. But you know, the fun part will be when I meet you there. Bye for now."

With one quick jab, I shove the knife in the back of his neck, pushing through until it pierces the front. Gurgling sounds leave his mouth as he chokes on his own blood gushing down his esophagus. I leave him gasping for his very last breath while I get up.

As I open the door of his cell with blood on my hands and face, I glance back at my victory. This pig won't ever snitch again.

Covered in his own blood, he sits on the chair like a doll stolen of life right in front of him. I can't be bothered with cleaning up the mess he made; I'll leave that up to the maids. They'll have to do it quickly, though, because this cell needs to be ready tomorrow for the next victim … a very special one I probably won't forget anytime soon.

With a grin on my face, I leave the cell, already pumped for what's in store.

Twenty-one days of pain.

*****

SKY

My mamma named me after the thing she loved to stare at the most. Every day, she would tell me I would grow up to be someone special. Something bigger than this world. Something I could never imagine.

I envied her ability to see beyond what our eyes could see … to witness the beauty of this world, even if horrible people tainted it.

She, out of all people, knew all too well what kind of monsters hid in the dark.

And yet, she faced it anyway so she could do what was right.

She was always right.

I never understood what she meant when she'd told me I would one day find out the true meaning behind my name. Why she named me after the vastness that enveloped our world. She'd spin me around in her arms and called me her world … her Sky.

One day, she'd say, I'd understand what it meant.

But then the day came that I was no longer her world. She'd stopped spinning and so had I. Everything had ceased to exist.

And then my sky came crashing down on top of me.

DAY 1

SKY

My cake goes untouched as I stare at the fork in my hand. I can't swallow another bite. I thought I could celebrate, that I could forget my worries for just a few minutes despite my parents not being here with me. Even though it's my birthday, it feels as though I've aged fifty years in one day.

Drops of rain clatter against the windows when the phone rings again. My heart beats in my throat, and I immediately pick it up from the table. The sound of the melody sends a shiver down my spine because the last time I heard it, my papà cried over the phone. Threats were issued. People were shouting and screaming. And then a few gunshots.

The line was cut off.

My heart stopped at that moment, and I rushed to gather everything.

However, my body is still weak; my muscles are barely able to support my fragile body. My thin frame wasn't ready to carry such a hefty burden, and now it would have to run.

I knew then that I would never make it out in time. I would never be able to outrun them.

As I hold the phone to my ear, I listen to the heartbreaking sound of my papà's unsteady breathing.

"Papà, are you okay?" I whisper.

The sudden feeling of my best friend's hand on my shoulder almost makes me jump up, but I appreciate her support.

My papà groans. "I'm sorry, bambina. They tortured me. I'm so sorry."

"Papà, what did you do?" I say. My friend and I exchange worried looks.

He coughs, spitting up something. Probably blood. "I told them where you're staying. I'm sorry."

Lightning strikes at the moment my heart stops beating.

"They're coming. Run. Hide."

This is it. I knew this moment would come, but I am prepared ... prepared to sacrifice everything I have.

I look at my friend, and she nods silently. We both know what we must do.

"I'll go grab everything," she says.

She grabs my hand and squeezes it tight before leaving the room. I sigh and return my attention toward the phone. "I understand."

"I'm so sorry, bambina. I'm so sorry …" My papà begins to cry, and it makes me shake in my boots. The raindrops outside cascade in rivers down the window, casting a dark shadow over the bedroom.

"I love you, bambina," he says after a while.

"I love you too, Papà." My voice fluctuates, emotions taking over as I almost crush the phone in my hand, so I decide to end the call.

A lightning strike tears my eyes away from the window. Being so close to danger makes me realize just how much my desire to protect has grown.

I have to make sure those men never get close to my secret.

Never.

Even if it costs me my freedom. My life.

I will sacrifice everything.

"I have everything."

I turn around at the sound of her voice. Smiling, I say, "Thank you, Jamie. I'm sorry you had to endure me at your place."

"Nonsense, you were always welcome and that will never change," she says as I walk toward her.

I hug her tight, and we exchange looks and sighs. It's tough to say good-bye; neither of us wants to say the words, even though we both know that fate has caught up with me.

"Are you ready?" I ask her.

"Yes, but are you sure?" she says, grabbing my shoulders.

"Yes. I won't be able to outrun them. Not like this." I look down at my body, which still feels broken and tired of fighting after a month has passed.

"I could help you," she says.

I shake my head. "No. I'd only drag you down. I want you to be okay, so you have to go without me."

"All right," she says after taking a big breath.

Suddenly, a loud screech is audible outside. I rush to the window and stare outside. Three, maybe four, black cars park outside the building with the lights still on.

"They're here!" I shout.

I grab everything and give it to her, loading her up with as much as she can carry. "Be quick," I say, as I push her toward the window.

"You want me to climb?" she asks.

"They're already here. It's too late to go through the door."

She puts everything in her bag and ties it around her shoulders, making sure everything is safe and secure. "All right. I'll take the fire escape."

"Make sure they don't see you," I say as I open the window.

Rain gushes down the drains, and the moment I stick out my head, I'm already drenched. "There. Use that ladder." I point outside.

She nods and then gives me one more look. Even in times as dire as these, I still can't help but give her a hug. It's my way to thank her because the help she's offering is invaluable.

"Be safe," she whispers in my ear. "Come back. You know where I'll be."

I nod and pat her on the back, but then I hear people stomping up the stairs. They're coming. She has to get out now.

"Go!" I yell.

I help her through the window, holding on to her until she's on the ledge. With her agile body, she's quick to slide along the side and safely jump to the fire escape. My heart beats in my throat as I watch her climb down the ladder and run to the other side of the building, into the back alley, and across the street to safety. She knows this city like no other; it's her birthplace, so I know she'll be safe. She knows how to get around.

I, on the other hand, am trapped in her apartment with nothing but a few kitchen knives to protect myself. But I won't go down without a fight.

I run to the kitchen and sift through all the drawers until I find what I'm looking for. Armed with a big chef's knife, I turn and walk around the table just when I hear them ram the door and it flies open. They didn't even ring the doorbell ... I guess the time for negotiations has passed.

Sliding along the wall of the kitchen, I close the door slightly by giving it a push. Only a small gap remains. I fish a makeup mirror out of one of the drawers and hold it up so I can peek through and watch them enter the apartment. Men with black masks covering their faces and guns in their hands search the rooms, throwing everything upside down. The couch tilted and kicked, tables shoved, and chairs crushed by the sheer force of their attack. They look like people who won't give up searching for me until I'm dead underneath their very boots.

I swallow away the fear and look for an opening. The moment they move into the bedroom, I see a chance. I pull open the door and bolt through the hallway toward the front door. My body shakes, adrenaline pushing me forward, sweat drops trickling down my back as I run to my freedom.

The sound of a metallic click behind me makes me stop and turn on my heels.

One of them has stayed behind and now has his gun aimed straight at me.

"Going somewhere, love?"

A hand appears out of nowhere, covering my mouth.

I squeal.

He wraps his other hand around my waist, preventing me from moving. One quick jab to my stomach and the knife drops from my hand. A pungent smell enters my nose, filling my lungs. My muscles grow weaker the more I inhale. I tell myself not to breathe, but I can't stop my gasps while I'm under this amount of stress. It's too late. I've already succumbed to the poison.

"Take her." One of the men flicks his fingers. "Let's go."

The man forces me out of the apartment, and the more I struggle, the stronger his grip around my waist becomes. They drag me through the hallway while I scream and kick as hard as I can, trying to alert the neighborhood of what's happening here.

"Shut up!" the one holding me spits in my ear.

He pulls me downstairs, my feet smacking down the steps as I struggle to keep up. Due to the drug, my muscles have almost stopped working to the point of me feeling so dizzy I want to puke, but I have no energy left. I force my eyes to stay open as they take me downstairs and outside into the pouring rain. That's when it all dawns on me.

I might not make it out of this alive.

In my head, I apologize to Jamie for already breaking my promise, but I tell myself it's for the best. As they open the door to their black SUV and lift me up, I take one last look at the gray sky above me. I wonder if this will be the last time I ever see it.

Then a blow to the back of the head knocks me down into the backseat.

The last thing I hear is a whisper in the dark. "It'll all be over soon …"

***

A never-ending darkness shrouds me, the surrounding void like space, swallowing me whole. Eyes open or eyes shut, it doesn't make a difference to the vast emptiness around me. It seeps into my bones like poison, clouding my mind from the memories that I had.

Where am I?

My body feels cold, and my limbs solid, as if they're not mine. I notice myself breathing, however. The only thing I hear is the steady, rhythmic beating of my heart. The only sound in this dark hole. Thud, thud … thud.

For a moment, I doubt my own existence.

Who am I, even?

A drop of water falling onto a surface pulls me back into reality. I'm here, but how?

My fingers tighten and relax in an attempt to regain control. My muscles feel stiff, but slowly, the sensation is returning to the tips of my fingers, giving me a small bit of hope that I might find out what happened to me.

With slow movements, I let my hand slide only a few inches, but it's enough to determine that I'm lying on a concrete floor. My head begins to hurt, and with every passing second, the pain increases. I move my fingers to my head and touch the back of my scalp. The searing pain stops me and I realize I'm wounded.

When I touch my face, I gasp. There is a bag over

my head with a gaping hole near my mouth and nose through which I can breathe. Immediately, I try to hook a finger underneath the bag near my neck in an attempt to remove it, but to no avail, as it's securely tied. It takes me minutes to adjust to the feeling of the bag constantly in and around my face.

A buzz moves through my body, bringing my limbs back to life. And even though I'm regaining my sense of touch, my vision is still impaired. However, my eyes feel fine as I touch them, so it must just be the lack of light.

I push my elbows underneath me and lean up. A sudden queasiness overtakes me, making me feel dizzy. I tally up the sensations that I'm feeling. Nausea, loss of motor skills, buzzing nerves, botched memory … it all leads to one conclusion: I was drugged.

Stabilizing myself on the floor, I focus on regaining control over my body before moving again. I dig into my mind to find clues as to how I ended up here. The pain that's slowly creeping to the surface of my skin distracts me, but I still manage to catch a glimpse of a memory in the back of my mind.

Men with black masks and weapons dragging me out of a room. A cloth with a sharp odor pushed against my nose and mouth. Drowsiness engulfing me. Doors of a black SUV sliding to the side. A blow to the back of my head. All lights going out.

My skin pricks with anxiety, and I shiver to shake off the fear. It doesn't help because I know deep down that there is more to come.

I can't help but repeat one question in my mind. Why me?

Every victim of abduction asks this same question.

Except I already know the answer.

It was only a matter of time before they came for me.

My papà once told me that goodness always came at a price. Now, more than ever, do I realize the truth in his words.

However, I don't regret making the decision for even a second.

So here, I find myself in a darkness so deep it consumes me whole.

And still the light of rebellion sparks inside my heart, fueling a fire I haven't felt before. An uncontrollable need overwhelms me to defy whoever is keeping me here.

But I will wait. Lying in the cold, harsh, emptiness of this space, I will await my captor's arrival and take whatever he's going to give me. Punishment. Pain. I'll endure it all.

Because that's what a good person does when they've made their choice.

They bear the burden of their choice because it's the only thing they can do.

***

I don't know how many hours pass before a noise wakes me. I can't remember when and how I fell asleep, but I must've been very tired from the ordeal. A metallic door is slid open, a crack of light splitting through the opening. The burlap bag over my head makes it difficult to see, but when I narrow my eyes and focus, I can still determine where I am.

Only now do I see how small my cell really is.

The vast emptiness I thought would overwhelm me turns out to be not much more than the size of a bedroom. A quick look at the walls reveals iron rings and shackles of all shapes and sizes; used to hook a chain around and snare whoever needs to be contained and subdued.

In other words, me.

Squinting, I watch as a man steps inside, and I focus solely on his presence. Even though the door is open and freedom taunts me from the other side, I stay put and watch. No matter how much I'd try, I'd never be able to flee. Not like this, with my muscles weak and my body aching. There are probably guards waiting outside, wondering whether I'm going to try anything.

So, I won't. I'll sit right here on this cold, hard concrete, observing my captor as he walks into the room with a certain aloofness. His footsteps are bold, his body brawny, half of his face hiding behind a mask.

His footsteps sound more like sand scraping off a harsh surface as he circles around me like a snake ready to attack its prey. He left the door open like a silent

22

seducer, a tool to entice me to run. I look up at my captor, giving him a deadly stare, and even though I can't see him, I know he can feel my determination.

I won't be tempted to flee like a wounded deer.

Not when I know that this is merely a distraction; like a lollipop dangled in front of a child while the adult knows full well he's never going to give it to the child, and the child knows he can never reach far enough to grasp it.

I refuse to be that child.

My captor walks some more, and then returns to the door to close it.

His experiment failed.

I controlled my emotions.

He doesn't know whom he's up against.

In the darkness, I hear him come closer, the only sound being his steady breath and soft steps. He's still testing me. Seeing if I'll give in to the fear. Alone with him, the predator, in a cage filled with blackness. But I'm not afraid of the dark.

My soul has already been tainted and defiled. Nothing he does can hurt me. I was already pushed past the breaking point once ... and I survived.

"Up."

The sound of his voice suddenly breaking through the façade makes me take in a breath. It's familiar and yet so unknown; the way he speaks to me with full authority, resoluteness resounding in every spoken letter, even if there are but a few.

I crawl up from the ground slowly, steadily maintaining my posture. My aching back and pounding head won't stop me from attempting to keep my dignity as I stand up straight and stare ahead.

My captor's steps are everywhere, resounding in the darkness like echoes that disappear into the night. He's confusing me, and I try to concentrate on the sound of my own heartbeat instead.

Suddenly, he's right in front of me, and the air is sucked out of my lungs. I struggle not to let my breath come out in short gasps because I won't let his tactics work on me.

His breathing sounds like that of a bull, short and loud, as if he's readying for a charge.

But he doesn't move. He just stands there, gazing at me.

"Do you know where you are?" he asks with a low, gruff voice that brings goosebumps to my body.

I compose myself before I answer. "No."

"Good." I can hear a faint smile behind that word.

After a while, he says, "Do you know why you're here?"

I don't answer. I refuse to. Why would I? He is only here to intimidate and hurt me. I gain no benefit by answering his questions. As a matter of fact, I think he owes me some answers instead.

"Why am I here?" I ask.

He's silent for a few seconds, and then I hear a smug laugh.

"Bold. I like that." Suddenly, he puts his hands on my chest and shoves me. I fall down backward on the hard floor, bruising my butt.

"Ow …"

"Push me and I push you," he says.

"Who are you?" I ask, putting emphasis on every word as if they're the last that'll come from my mouth.

He muffles another laugh. "Who am I? I am the man who will break you."

I shake my head, still lying on the floor as if I'm taunting him. Maybe I am. I want him to speak, and for that to happen, I have to be the one asking the questions, not the other way around.

"Where am I?"

"Where you belong," he growls, and then he takes a step forward, grabs my arm, and pulls me up from the floor.

"Why—"

Smack. His hand hits me, silencing me.

"You do not talk unless spoken to."

I turn my head away. I will not bow to his violence. If he hits me, my body will remain rigid, unmoving. Not an inch of pain will exude from me.

"You may be wondering why you're here, but you forget the most important question. What have *you* done to be here?"

My lip quivers, so I force it to stop. I can't show weakness. Not now, not ever.

He grabs my face. "You don't seem to remember,

so let me refresh your memory," he says. "You stole something. It's time to give it back. You have twenty-one days to come up with an answer." He pulls me closer with a pinch. "Lie and I'll know. Do you understand?"

I nod while blankly staring at his mask. If I'm to obey to survive, I'll do just that, but no one can take away my pride.

He releases my face and pushes me away. "It's time for you to pay back what you owe."

Fear ripples through my veins. "Pay what back?" I say, taking a step forward.

He shoves me so hard my back hits the wall and the impact rips the air from my chest. I sink to my knees against it.

"Don't think I will go easy on you. Just because I know about you doesn't mean I won't rip you apart if you don't tell me the truth."

"What truth?" I gasp. "What do you know about me?"

He turns around but waits, standing still in the darkness with only the sound of his ragged breaths filling the room.

"You tell me," he says, his voice softer than before, almost as if he doesn't know the reason.

Frowning, I look up at him, and for some reason, the way he cracks his knuckles feels so familiar.

But then the feeling immediately disappears as he starts walking toward the door.

"Wait, you haven't told me why I'm here yet. How am I supposed to know what to tell you?"

I can hear him knock on the door. Then there's a pause. "Oh … you'll know soon enough."

The forewarning brings chills to my skin.

The door opens with a squeak and in comes the blinding light again. It's so bright; my captor's clothes almost look pale as snow. But then I realize that's only because I haven't seen any light in such a long time … and I won't be seeing it anytime soon.

His last spoken words remain with me for the rest of the day, echoing in my mind over and over again. "Welcome to your own personal hell."

DAY 2

SKY

The darkness makes me feel like I've gone blind. Minutes, hours, no matter how much time passes, it feels like an eternity stuck in hell. My captor was right. If he doesn't kill me first, this place will.

A cold draft makes me shiver, and I curl up into a ball on the harsh floor that provides little comfort to my aching bones. My clothes are soaked and stained. Last night, I had to pee in a corner, dirtying a part of my clothes. I feel worse than an animal in here; at least they have hay and maybe even light.

I have nothing but my own thoughts to keep me company, and they're driving me insane.

Memories from the day before float through my mind. My captor ... how he came to test me, to see if I was a runner or a fighter. I'm neither. I witness the world as an outsider instead of stepping in to partake.

But I have no other choice.

Much is at stake. It's the reason why I'm here.

The question of 'why' isn't because I don't know why I'm here. It's because I don't know why someone would do this to another person. Evil goes far beyond what I could ever imagine. All because of a choice.

Would I make the same choice if I knew then what would happen? I don't know, but it doesn't matter. I can't change the past, no matter how much I think about it.

The door suddenly makes a screeching sound, and I shoot up from my place to see who enters. A woman. Not one, but three. One by one, they shuffle into my cell like mindless drones. I wonder who they are, if they work for him, if they know that I'm a captive here ... if they even care.

A small, glowing light switches on, and I cover my face with my hand to block it out. I'm not used to it, and my eyes have trouble adjusting. As I blink, I notice the women coming toward me with buckets filled with water.

I crouch back and push myself toward the wall. "Stay away!" I yell.

They don't listen. One of them grips my arms and hauls me up from the floor.

"Let go!" I say. "Who are you? What are you doing?"

She pulls me toward her and takes the bag off my head. As my eyes try to adjust to the light, she curls her fingers underneath my dress. She pulls it up; almost ripping it as she violently drags it over my head.

"No!" I yell, but they ignore me.

Another woman unhooks my bra and the other tears down my panties. I struggle to block my privates with my hands, ashamed of being forced to stand naked in a dark cell. But the moment I cower, a bucket of ice-cold water is thrown over my head.

I shriek from the sharp pain of the water flowing across the wound on my head and running down my body. Blood mixed with sweat and water pools underneath my feet, causing the floor to feel slippery. I almost fall over from the way they twist me.

The women dip a few sponges into a different bucket filled with bubbly water and then lather the soap all over my body. I try to fight them off, but I'm still weak from my wounds and I almost tumble over from the water underneath my feet. As they wash me like a dirty pig, not giving me an ounce of acknowledgment, I fight the impending tears. This debasement is too much, but I will not crumble. Even when a tear or two escapes from my eyes, I will not falter in my resolve. They may have stripped me bare, dehumanized me, and taken everything I am away from me, but I am still here and I will not give up on life.

When they're done, my skin glistens and my body smells fresh and clean, even though it's only on the surface. Underneath, I feel violated and dirtier than ever before.

The women clean up the mess, brushing the water toward a drain in the middle of the room. I'm left standing in the middle, watching them work like robots. For a moment, I wonder if they're even real. If they question what they're doing. If they feel bad for doing this to me.

If they're capable of this, someone must've taught them. Someone who's in control, who demands complete obedience. If these people even listen to him, what kind of power does this man have?

Shivering, I watch the women get up, patting down their wet, ragged dresses. One of them comes toward me with a black cloth that looks more like a bag. And then she puts it over my head.

I scream as she tightens the bag with a tie-wrap around my neck. The others hold my hands down as the woman pinches the cloth near my mouth and cuts out a piece, leaving a hole through which I can breathe.

Tears stain my eyes, but I won't let them roll. "Why are you doing this?"

It must be because of *him*.

When she's done, the women let me go. I immediately try to rip the bag off my head but to no avail. She tied it around my neck so tight that I can't even fit a finger between the tie-wrap and the cloth. My face hides behind a mask, just like that man, except my mask cannot be removed.

At least not by me ... my freedom has been taken from me like I'm a criminal needing restraint.

As they scurry out the door, I blow out my last, cold breath before the light is switched off again and I'm left naked and alone in the dark.

The person in charge is no man ... he's a monster.

***

Hours pass before the door to my cell opens again. I want to stand up for myself and show them my pride, but my muscles are tense and sore from the cold that I've endured. I can't remember the last time I didn't feel goosebumps all over my body as I touch my own skin in an effort to awaken my muscles.

From the slow, bulky steps I hear, I can tell it's the same man from the day before. My captor, the man without a name. I wonder if he's wearing the mask again. And if so, is it because I might recognize him?

Something crinkles, like a stack of paper being sifted through. He's holding it, I can hear. As he steps closer, I manage to get up on my feet, covering my privates with my hands as much as possible. When he's in front of me, something harsh and stinging slaps against my outer thigh, causing me to cringe.

"Hands at your waist," he growls.

I do what he says, but the thing in his hand is still

stroking my thigh, like a gentle reminder of what will happen if I don't listen.

"Can you feel this?" he asks.

"Yes."

"Do you know what it is?"

"No."

He takes in a short breath. "Rope. You'll probably ask me why I have it with me, but I think you and I both know the answer to that question."

The promise in his voice fills my veins with despair. I swallow away the lump in my throat. "What do you want from me?" I ask after a while.

The small light in the back of my cell turns on. If I didn't believe in the devil before, then I do now because he's standing right in front of me.

He's barely distinguishable in the dark, as my eyes have to look through the threads of the cloth bound around my head. His mask gives me the creeps as he turns around and walks toward the wall, ignoring my question. I wonder if I should stay put or walk after him.

The ropes in his hand clatter against his pants, a firm reminder of what could happen. What will happen. Could I grasp them quickly and use them to strangle him? No, it wouldn't help. Even if I did kill him, I could never escape the guards outside. He knows this as well as I do, which is why he's so confident in his stride. He knows there's no way out for me. His death won't help me escape. But I know what will.

I take a step forward, and then another, until I'm right behind him and he turns around to look at me with that scary mask. Even with the bag on my head, I can still see him.

He doesn't speak. Instead, he grabs my wrist and forces me toward the wall near the metal ring. Just the sound of it banging against the wall as he pulls the rope through it and ties it to my wrist makes my heart beat in my throat. The pressure is rising and I struggle to breathe as he ties my other wrist to a second metal ring. Even my legs are bound.

On display and left to his mercy, I sniff and stop breathing. Controlling my breath is the only way I have to show him that I won't give in. My body isn't mine to govern anymore, but he cannot take my dignity away from me.

He takes a few steps back and gazes at me from a distance, shuffling around the room as if he's inspecting whether he did his job correctly. But then he unbuckles his belt and slowly slips it out of the loops, the sound making my skin crawl. He folds it in his hand and comes closer.

"Do you know what happens when you don't tell me what I want to know?" he says.

I shake my head.

The pain is sharp, like a smack with the hand but harder, as the belt comes down on my inner thigh.

"Do you want this?" he asks.

I don't reply.

"Speak up," he growls, hitting me again.

I endure the pain by grinding my teeth, and I block everything out by closing my eyes. *I won't give in. I won't give in.* I repeat this mantra over and over in my head. It's the only thing I can do. The only *right* thing.

"Tell me the truth!" he yells.

The belt comes down on my breasts, and the painful lash provokes a tear to form in my eye. I blink it away.

"I won't," I say. "I'll never tell you."

"Oh, so you do know what I'm talking about?" he says, putting his hands against his sides.

I slam my lips together and stare at him without saying a word.

"Fine. If you won't tell me, then I guess I'll have to beat it out of you."

"It won't work," I say.

The next one hits me so hard I hiss.

"How hard do you want me to hit?" he asks. "Because this isn't even half of what I can do."

I ignore him and focus on handling the pain as each strike reverberates through my entire body. I tell myself it's worth it. It's all worth it. My pain. My suffering. My fate. Everything.

"How far are you willing to go?" he says, striking me again. "Would you suffer for your secret?" He hits me again, and even he is hissing as the belt comes down on my belly. "Would you die for your secret?"

Again, the belt comes down. It's gotten so painful that I struggle to contain my screams. I don't want to give him the satisfaction of hearing me in pain.

"Tell me!" he growls, his belt swift and merciless.

"You said you know everything about me. But you don't, do you?" I say, looking up at him. I won't lower my head, not for him. "That's why you're beating me with a belt. You don't want me to tell you because you want to hear it come from my mouth … You want me to tell you because you really don't know."

For a second, everything is quiet. The only sounds are our breaths and my groans as I try not to move because the pain is almost unbearable.

And then he whips me again, much harder than before.

I scream out loud this time, unable to keep it inside.

He comes so close; I can smell his intense cologne, which intoxicates me to the point of almost passing out.

"That scream …" he whispers into my ear, groaning as if he's excited. "I'll hear many, many more of them. So many … your voice will become nothing but a rasp."

"I don't care," I say.

"What do you care about then?" he asks, cocking his head.

I frown, rubbing my dry lips together in an attempt to stop myself from speaking. I know what he wants to hear, but I won't say it. Not a chance.

"Hmm ... I thought so." A faint smile is audible. "You know, I pegged you for a girl who cared about her own wellbeing more than this."

"There are some things more important in life," I mutter.

"What's that?" he says, standing directly in front of me, turning his ear toward me. "I didn't quite catch that."

"Screw ... You ..." I say.

When I cough, he hits me with the belt, causing me to buck and heave.

"You don't speak unless told," he says. "But I'll help you remember each time you forget."

I take audible breaths, trying to contain the pain and keep from coughing up blood. Blood is weakness, and weakness is something I can't afford right now.

"You know ... I wish you'd just tell me," he says. "That would make this all so much easier."

"So you can kill me afterward," I muse.

I can hear his amusement. "Maybe. Maybe not. Who knows?"

"You do," I reply, lifting my head to look at him.

For a moment, I think I can almost see something through the tiny slits in his masks. Dark brown eyes filled with confusion. Denial.

Wait.

"Oh ..." I mumble.

"What?" he growls, and then he flicks the belt. "Shut your mouth."

He hits me again, but the strike doesn't faze me.

At this moment, for a fraction of a second, he showed me his feelings. Just one tiny slip-up, but it was enough for me to see through his façade.

He isn't the one in charge.

There is someone bigger, more powerful behind the man in the mask.

Someone to whom he answers. Someone who wants him to do his dirty work for him. The person who's really after me. And I know exactly who it is.

DAY 3

SKY

My body aches when I breathe, so my inhales are sparse. Swelling on parts of my skin has made moving quite the ordeal. My toes can only barely touch the surface of the floor, and I desperately tiptoe around to keep myself up. Hanging on the wall, my limbs feel numb. I don't even know how long I've been hanging here, and the more I try to keep my focus, the more I'm starting to lose it. Seconds turn into hours, and the small amount of oxygen that can enter through this hole near my mouth is not enough to stay awake. Sooner or later, my muscles will give out on me, and then I'll be hanging like a martyr.

It's all for a good cause.

Every punch. Every lash. Every painful bruise. It's all worth it.

Sometimes I think to myself 'who on earth would say that?' But then again, only those who've been through the same thing I have would know. My secret is worth everything, and I would hand my own life over on a platter if it would keep my secret safe.

***

ANGEL

I will make her submit.

Whether it takes one day or twenty-one, she will give me what I want.

But dammit, this girl angers me.

I admit, I have anger issues, but this girl definitely manages to get under my skin. Her incessant unwillingness to yield isn't something I normally accept. Not many have the luxury of living through that, which makes her all the more special.

I don't know why, but it felt like there was something about her. The way she moved … her voice … it captured my interest. Despite the masks and the bonds that separate us, I'm curious to find out why she continues to resist.

I should punish her for not telling me the truth until she finally does, just as I've always done. That's my job, that's why I exist, and that's what I'll do.

Except, she's not like the other girls … she doesn't whimper at the sight of me and she doesn't beg for mercy. It both excites and riles me up to no end.

I wonder what her reasons are. Maybe she knows more than they've told me. I'm sure she hasn't seen my face, and I haven't had enough time with her yet to see hers. But something tells me I don't want to see it.

My father always tells me it would only serve to distract me from my job, and that I should focus on maximizing the pain to get it done quicker.

I don't think this one will be as easy as all the others were. She seems rather reluctant to spill, which means I'll have to work extra hard to make her talk.

I walk to my father's office on the third floor and knock two times.

"Come in." His gruff, darkened voice never fails to make me grimace.

He's standing near the window with a glass of cognac, sipping it slowly as if he's taking in the scenery outside. When I close the door behind me and clear my throat, he turns his head and nods.

"Angel. Good to see you. How are things going with our little problem?"

"Not that good," I say, licking my lips.

He frowns, cocking his head. "Let's sit down for a moment." He points at the chair in front of his desk and then sits down in his own leather chair, leisurely leaning back.

"What does 'not that good' mean?" he asks.

I take a deep breath. "Well, for one, this one doesn't break easily."

"Hit harder," he says, taking another sip, as if it means nothing to him.

"She doesn't respond to my threats the way the others do."

He smiles as if he's ridiculing me. "Then hit harder."

I narrow my eyes. "I don't think you understand what I'm saying here."

"Oh, I do ..." He sets his glass down in front of him, taking extra good care of the placement, before dragging his eyes back up to me. "Do you have a problem with her?"

I just glare at him, not even giving him an inch to go on. He's testing me, seeing if I've reached my limits. My father does this with everyone. Not even his son is spared. If he spots one weakness, we're out, and that's not with retirement funds, but rather in a bag containing your own heart.

After all, he is Joseph "Joe" DeLuca. In other words, he is the Don of this fucking company that I work for—and would die for, if it were up to him. Our family trade isn't exactly kosher; we kill people for a living. People pay us to do their dirty work, and when my father's angry, he'll even kill people just for the fun of it. Except, this time, he's letting me do his dirty work.

I don't have the right to refuse. He'd pull a gun on me in a second.

This business works because its employees are tough as a nut, unbreakable, and I should be no less. Does my father really think that one simple girl can make me weak?

"Are you mocking me?" I say.

"I am simply asking you if you can do your job," he says.

I sit back in my chair as well, giving him the same deadly stare as he's giving me. "Why do you want to torture her?"

At first, he just seems confused, but then he slowly starts to laugh. "Boy, are you growing a conscience? Is this what they teach you in prison?"

Prison. He talks about it as if it's kindergarten, but I almost lost my mind back in that small cell I shared with Phoenix. Fuck, that's not something I'd like to think about, that's for sure. I felt so fucking useless after the police caught me and then shipped me off to jail. And to think I actually spent so much time locked up together with Phoenix Sullivan is crazy.

He would rip out my guts if he ever saw me again.

After what I did … I don't blame him.

Still, I didn't come back here for my own father to lecture me.

"And here I thought you'd finally learned your

lesson," he says.

"I know what I'm doing. Shut up."

"Or what? Are you going to kill me?"

"Just shut up," I growl.

"Do you think you can threaten me, Angel? Me, out of all people?" He rubs his scruffy chin as if it's one big joke to him.

"Hey, I didn't come back here just so you could punish me. That place was a hellhole I'd rather not go back to, so stop talking about it."

His chair slides back and he stands up with ferocity. "And you seem to forget that it was me who got you out of there in the first place!" he yells.

I get up too now. "You only wanted me out so you could use me like some executioner!"

"You ungrateful son of a bitch," he growls. "I should've left you to rot in that place."

"I am your motherfucking son!" I slam his desk with furor. "And I will not let you treat me this way."

"What are you gonna do about it?"

In a fit of rage, I pull my gun out from under my belt and hold it up to his face. My finger hovers over the trigger as I come face to face with the man who I love. Who I despise. Who is my equal and my superior in every way.

A devilish smile appears on his face. "Ha-ha, that's my boy."

I frown, not moving an inch.

"Well done."

"What?" I mutter.

"I'm proud of you."

"Why?" I grumble, lowering the gun slowly.

"Because you're the son I'm looking for."

He grins and then sits back down on his chair as if nothing happened. He waves at mine too and says, "Sit, sit."

I flop back down, still confused as to what the hell is going on.

"I just wanted to see if you still had it in you."

"What? Killing?"

"Exactly." A sparkle in his eye that screams danger makes me clench my teeth. "A man who won't hold back when he needs to do the job. Precisely what I need."

I tilt my head and lower my brows. My father has always been a mystery to me. I wish I could understand him, but I don't. Always testing me as if I'm some sort of science project … he's amused by me, I can tell. And it pisses me off so much that I still almost fire the gun at him.

Almost.

The only thing stopping me from executing him on the spot is the fact that he is my father.

I was born from his cells. He is inside me as much as I am inside him. We are two sides of the same blade, but he made me according to his rules. His will is law.

"Am I just a machine to you? A killer? Something to use as you see fit?"

"Oh, please, Angel, not this again." He waves it off as if my words are nothing.

"No, really, I wanna know."

He leans forward, placing the tips of his fingers against each other. "What you are is what I made you. You'd best remember that. There are a million other people desperate to be in your shoes right now."

"I doubt it."

"You're an heir to this business, Angel. The *only* heir. And that makes you a target as well. You may have forgotten this during the time you spent in jail, but let me reassure you … there are plenty of opportunities for others to take over the reins. All they have to do is do what you just tried." He makes a cutting gesture near his neck. "And then this business is finished."

"What makes you think I still care?"

He licks his lips and smiles faintly. "Because you don't want to die," he says.

"Right …"

It's quiet for a while, and my father picks up his glass of cognac to take another sip.

"So, are we clear?"

"Clear as can be." I sigh.

There is no arguing with him. There is nothing inside him but wrath, and I'm his son, so I am to behave the same. There is no other way to keep the company and our lives intact.

"Great. Now, is there still a problem?" he asks.

"No." I look him directly in the eyes.

He gives me a fake smile. "Good."

"I just want to know why? What are you looking for?"

"That's none of your concern." He grabs a cigar from the box on his desk and puts it in his mouth. "Want one?" he asks.

"No, thanks," I say.

He shrugs. "You should really learn to enjoy life a little more."

"Enjoying life doesn't equal smoking a cigar."

"No, but it does calm you down, which is obviously something you need."

"I prefer killing a few people," I say with a smug smile.

Maybe I mean it. Maybe I don't. Who knows? Only me, and it's best to keep it that way. I'll give my father what he wants … for now. I don't care what he has to tell me; I'm not in the mood for jokes.

"Actually, I would much prefer to get out of this house," I say, blowing out a big breath.

"Yes, well, unfortunately, that won't be possible for a while considering I had to bribe the fucking cops to get them off your ass. Not all of them are that easy, so you have to stay under the radar. Fuck me, it was a giant mess to clean up … I can't believe one fucking bambina was behind everything. It cost me a fortune to buy out both of them."

"I know," I say, rolling my eyes. He's just trying to

make me feel bad.

"Believe me, I hate it as much as you do, but you can't do anything stupid right now. I paid them too much and we made a deal that our business would be more ... discreet from now on, so you have to take it easy for a while, Angel."

"Which means being locked in a mansion doing your dirty work."

He smirks. "Exactly."

"So much fun ..."

"I know you prefer the hunt, but this can be fun, too."

"I didn't say it wasn't. I just prefer freedom over exchanging one jail for another."

"At least the best cooks in the country serve you breakfast, lunch, and dinner every single day as well as wine and beer. I'd say that beats prison any time."

I shrug. I don't do it for the food or the drinks. I don't stay here because of that. I stay here because I have to ... because it's my job to stay out of the hands of the Feds.

"For now, it'll have to do," my father says.

"I can't wait to get back into the field again."

"Angel," he says, after lighting his cigar. "You were made for this. You know that. Your muscles are your best asset, not your speed. This is what you trained for all those years."

"Not girls. I don't remember that part."

"Bambinas, bambinos, what does it matter? As long

as it talks." He waves with his cigar. "As long as you can make your father proud. Now that … that is what matters," he muses.

"I'm not a machine."

"You were born to do this, Angel. Born and bred. Like a fucking horse."

His harsh words leave a sour taste in my mouth.

"If you think this is hard, keep in mind that the bambina you're punishing isn't innocent. She stole something from me, and I want it *back*. She has to pay for what she did," he spits. "Now, do your fucking job. Hurt her, fuck her, I don't give a damn. Just get it done. Understood?"

I nod, keeping my emotions locked down tight as I get up from the chair like a robot and walk toward the door.

"And remember … no mercy. Don't give her any food until she's talked."

I look over my shoulder. "What about …"

"*Nothing*," he says. "You give her nothing except pain."

"And you're sure this will work?"

"It will or else she'll die."

"I hope for your sake it's worth it," I say.

I'm not sure I'll listen to him. No way can I make her talk without giving her food somewhere along the line.

"Use everything you've learned. Any method you can think of. I want what's *mine*." He slams the desk with his fist. "Make her talk."

"I won't rest until it's done," I say, and then I close the door behind me.

I could disagree with his methods, but it would lead me nowhere. He is my father, after all ... And the sole reason he brought me into this world was to bring pain to his enemies. It's what he expects me to do, what he loves about me ... my power and brutality. So I'll do what he says and he'll see that I can be more than just a killing machine. I am his son and he'd better be damn proud of me when I'm finished with her. If not, then I'm going to kill him, too.

DAY 4

SKY

Sweat drips down my forehead, the sound deafening when the drops hit the floor. I can't handle the silence … the darkness, but I have no choice. It's been hours since my captor last came to visit me, and I wonder what he's planning … what he meant when he said twenty-one days.

Will it be the end of me?

Will he kill me if I don't tell him what he wants to know?

I just hope I have the courage to hold out until that day comes.

My bones ache as I hang from the wall. My tongue

feels dry as I attempt to wet my cracked lips and try to ignore my growling stomach. The thought of him whipping me again pains me more than the ache in my arms. However, nothing—*nothing*—compares to the pain I felt a few months ago ... the day my mamma died.

They say you'll get over it and that you'll learn to accept and move on, but I haven't. Not in a million years. My mamma didn't deserve to die. No one does ... but she didn't go on her own.

She was murdered.

Killed because she tried to save another.

My mamma was a courageous lady. Much more courageous than I am.

She worked for a bureau that saved women from abuse. But it isn't just any bureau because my mamma actually infiltrated the places where they held these women against their will. Illegal trades. Drug lords. Mafia. Everywhere—you name it, and she was there. She helped these women escape and get their lives back. And it worked; my mamma actually made a difference. I remember being so proud of her all the time, and my papa, too. But I was also scared ... because I knew that day would come when she wouldn't come home.

When that day finally arrived, I died a little inside.

One of the mafia bosses found out my mamma had taken a captive woman with her, and the moment they fled, he came after them with everything he had. My mamma sent me a text while she was driving the very car later found set on fire in a ditch.

My mamma and the woman never made it out alive.

The police couldn't find any evidence of foul play, but I know what happened. I know the truth. They chased her and drove her off a cliff. And even though they tried to tell me a different story, I know she would've never killed herself on purpose. That wasn't her.

They murdered her and got away with it.

This world is as corrupt as it can be.

I thought the police would help me, but when they didn't, I showed them the text my mamma had sent me. It even included a picture of the license plate of the car that was chasing her.

They couldn't ignore me anymore, which made me believe it was finally over.

Or so I thought.

All I did was try to find justice for my mamma, but I opened a hellhole in its place.

And now I'm here, hanging on the wall like a rag doll waiting to be toyed with and thrown around the room.

But it's worth every ounce of dignity I have left.

Suddenly, the door to my cell opens, and my ears perk up at the sound.

The new, thin cloth the women strapped around my head instead of the burlap bag allows for much more light to enter my eyes. I'm not used to the brightness and that makes my eyes narrow. The same guy as before steps inside, his mask no longer a method to instill fear in my heart. Now I recognize him for who he is.

A coward. Someone who hides his identity behind his mask.

Someone who's afraid to show his true self.

Which means if I found out who he was, I'd have power over him.

This thought alone makes me laugh. Out loud. Maniacally. "Have you come to torture me again?"

The door falls closed behind him, and I'm left in the dark with only a monster to keep me company.

I can hear him walk toward me. His steps are a painful reminder that he's here, in the flesh, and that I'm still naked, vulnerable, and left to his mercy. I swallow down the nerves and prepare myself for the pain.

"Do you have an answer for me?" he asks.

"An answer to what?"

"My question."

I lick my lips, trying to think of something, but I come up blank.

"Tell me the truth," he says. "That's all I ask." I hear him making a tsk sound. "It's not a lot. You could tell me now, and I would stop this immediately."

I frown. "What kind of guarantees would I have?"

"My word."

His word … is worthless.

He's my captor. How could I ever trust his word?

"Your word means nothing to me," I say.

"Hmm … pity you'd say that," he muses. "I was hoping this would go easier."

"You're a monster," I mutter under my heavy breath.

"You can call me whatever you like. It won't change a thing. And since you won't give me what I want, I will give myself what I want …" The dark, gruff undertone in his voice brings goosebumps to my skin.

"Are you going to hurt me now?" I mumble, trying to project a strong voice but it's still brittle.

Suddenly, he's in front of me. The small, glowing light on the wall turns on. I can feel his hot breath against my skin and his mask grazing my neck. I can see everything.

"On the contrary …" he murmurs in my ear.

I close my eyes, expecting a blow. I don't want to see.

But then he does something I didn't prepare for.

He pinches my nipples and rolls them between his index finger and thumb. I struggle to keep the sounds inside my mouth from pouring out.

"Do you consider this torture?" he whispers.

His fingers expertly twist and turn my nipples until they sizzle and send a buzzing feeling through my body. I groan, trying to suppress the unwanted arousal that comes with nipple play. My breasts have always been sensitive, but I've never been touched so crudely before.

"Tell me," he mutters.

And then he bites my earlobe, gently nibbling on it.

"Please don't," I say with a hoarse voice.

I don't know why I say anything. I know he won't stop, regardless of what I say or do.

But I can't help it either. My stomach clenches and fear surges through my body.

All this over a simple touch.

He grips my breast and kneads it coarsely, sucking on my earlobe as if it's his prize. "So soft ... so innocent," he murmurs.

His lips spread on my neck, licking my skin and leaving a hot, wet mark wherever he goes. Heat surges through my body accompanied by lightning fast zaps of terror. I move to avoid his touch, but there's nowhere I can go, no way I can escape his grasp. He has me exactly where he wants ... and he knows it.

It's precisely what he wants me to know.

I'm his to do with as he pleases.

For as long as I refuse to speak, I can't resist. And now he will take from me what I am most reluctant to give away ...

"Please ..." I mutter as he drags his lips along my collarbone, setting my body on fire.

"Please what? Stop?" He muffles a laugh. "Or do you mean, continue?"

One hand keeps tugging at my nipple while the other freely explores my body, cupping my ass to squeeze it tight. I let out a high-pitched noise when he slaps my still tender ass.

"Don't …" I grumble.

"Don't what?" He pinches harder.

I bite my lip in an effort to stop more noises from spilling out.

"So sensitive," he murmurs. "You know, I think I'll actually enjoy these twenty-one days I get to spend with you. After all … you're completely *mine*."

The way he says that word, mine, so utterly devoted to the way he pronounces it, makes me shiver to the point of sucking in a breath I didn't know I needed.

"Afraid?" he asks.

I hesitantly nod. I didn't want to admit it, but maybe if I give him just a tiny bit of truth, he might go a little easier on me.

"Good. You should be."

And then he slaps my breast, causing a moan to escape my mouth.

"Oh … that sound again," he growls. "Love it."

Tears stain my eyes. "Not this. Please …"

"Not what?" he muses, cocking his head. "Do you prefer this instead?" He starts tugging my nipples again.

"Neither!" I cry out.

"Well, you've gotta choose." He hums as if it's all a game to him.

I sniff, pushing away the tears. "It doesn't matter. I won't tell you anything."

"Oh, then I guess you won't mind if I pick this," he

muses.

And then suddenly his mouth is on mine, kissing me full on the lips.

I'm stunned. His mouth ... it's on mine, and my mind is completely calm. The storm that was brewing in my body and mind has evaporated and a serenity I haven't felt in quite a while replaces it. His kiss is so magnetizing that I don't even know how to react anymore. Only after a little while do I realize what I'm doing.

I'm letting him kiss me.

I'm not even fighting it.

I should be.

So out of plight, I bite him.

He flinches and backs away. Keeping his gaze on me at all times, he brings his finger to his lip and presses down, licking up the blood drop that surfaces.

"Hmm ..."

Is that a hmm of approval or a hmm of dislike? I don't know, which makes me even more nervous. But a better question is ... why did I let him kiss me like that? Why didn't I fight it right from the beginning? It was as if my body responded to his lips with a need so fierce, it just stopped functioning.

Why?

I wish I knew the answer.

"Don't look so fazed. It's just a kiss."

"Stop," I say.

He smiles. "You should really consider not saying

that word. My temper flares, and you don't want that. But I'll remind you now that you have no say in this. I decide what happens. And the more you resist, the harder it will become to stay alive."

"What if I don't want to?" I say.

He presses another kiss on my lips; this time softer, more determined, to confuse my heart and me. I don't know how much time passes because his mouth definitely puts a spell on me.

I don't understand ... why does he have this effect on me?

When he takes his lips off me, he smirks. "Because you're desperate to live. I can hear it in the way you talk ... that fire you try so desperately to keep hidden." He bites his lip, and even though I can't see his complete face, just the intense gaze he gives me makes me weaker than I already was.

"Now, tell me. What do you choose?" he murmurs, letting his fingers slide up and down my body. I shake my head, determined to ward off the signals of my body.

"You want this ..." he murmurs, pressing a kiss to my chin.

I shake my head again.

"I know you do ..." He presses his body to mine, and I can feel his hard-on pushing against the fabric of his pants.

"Stop, please," I mutter.

"Or what?"

"I'd rather take the pain over this."

There. It's out.

I tried to fight it, but I couldn't.

I'm weak. Unwilling. But my body is more resistant to breaking than my mind.

He can hurt my body, but I'll keep him away from my mind for as long as I can.

I can take the pain, but I can't take the pleasure.

He cocks his head, leaning back so he can look me in the eyes. My eyes fall to the floor, seeking a way to escape from this reality, but he grips my chin and forces me to look at him.

"You would choose pain over excitement? You'd choose whips over my cock?"

I smash my lips together because I want to keep the words from spilling out.

He can't know my only weakness.

Not this.

It's the one thing I know he'll use against me.

But then a smile forms on his lips and a familiar glint glows in his eyes.

I don't have to tell him. He already knows.

He deciphered my riddle just from looking at me. My one, excruciating memory.

"I'm not the only one to touch you like this," he mutters.

I try to keep my composure, but my lip trembles in fright of the conclusion he's drawing.

He cups my face and says, "Tell me what

happened."

"Why?" I wince. "Why do you care all of the sudden?"

His fingers tighten around my jaw. "Do not mistake my questions for kindness. Tell me who touched your body without your permission. *Now.*" His voice is so controlling that it makes me quiver. I've never felt this subjugated to a man's words, let alone his touch. It's as if he's already staked his claim on me, even though he's only had me in his possession for a couple of days.

How many days has it been?

"Tell me!" he shouts. "Was it here?"

"No …" I mutter, shaking my head.

"Then what?"

"Months ago … I …" I can't even say it.

Just the memory of what happened makes my pupils dilate and my body shiver with coldness as it brings me back to that one horrible night.

That one night that changed everything.

***

1 year ago

I haven't felt safe in a long time.

Not since my mamma died and her killer was brought to justice.

Wherever I walk, I feel followed. Stalked. Watched.

From the corners of my eyes, I see them looking at me, and each and every time I am outside, I run to my house like a girl possessed. Fear is dominating my life.

I thought I did the right thing by giving the police the evidence they needed, but I didn't know it would come at a price … my sanity.

My life is on the line, and I know it.

They're coming for me now.

I struggle to breathe as I run up the hill toward my house after picking up a late-night package for my papà. He needs his medicine, and he completely forgot to get it. He only has me left, so it's my job to keep him safe and healthy. His COPD is really getting to him lately, and he's so scared every time he can't breathe. Always so scared to die a horrible death.

I hope I never have to go through something like that.

After mamma had died, I dropped out of college and started taking care of my papà. I don't regret it, not even for one second, because I know I'm doing something right. My mamma would be proud of me if she were still here.

I have to make sure I get home, so I keep going as I always do.

But the moment I spot a guy in a hoodie walking after me, I know this is going to cost me.

I start running, but the guy behind me is sprinting, too. Then out of nowhere, a second one comes along. And then a third.

I turn a corner on an unfamiliar road to try to outrun them. I can't go to my house with them following me; they'd find my dad and then … no, I can't lose him, too.

So I try to shake them in the alley, only to find out it's a dead-end.

Out of breath and completely terrified, I turn around and face my pursuers. All three men stand at the entrance, watching my every move. Then one pulls out a knife.

I back away, trying to find a door or a window. Anything to escape. Except, there is nothing but concrete and my heart beating out of my chest.

"Get away from me," I yell. "Leave me alone!"

But they continue their slow saunter toward me, one in front of the others. There's an undeniable smirk on his scarred face and the gray scruff on his jaw tells me he is of my papà's age. However, his eyes, and those of his henchmen, hide behind dark glasses.

"We've been waiting for this …" he says.

His voice brings a chill to my bones.

I scream, but his hand muffles my cry for help as he wraps it around my neck and takes me down in a chokehold. With his body on top of mine, I struggle to breathe.

"No!" I squeal.

"You thought you could get away with what you did? Think again. Hold her," the man says, and then his buddies grab my hands and push them above my head.

With my last remaining adrenaline, I kick and shove, giving it my all to push them off me.

"You like to play with grownups, you can have it," he growls, and the men hovering above me laugh. "This is gonna be a lot of fun. For me, of course. Not for you."

"Get off me!" I scream.

And then he punches me in the face.

My head is spinning, and my vision is blurry as the man gets on top of me and pulls up my skirt. In a second, he's yanked down my panties and zipped down his pants.

My eyes widen at the sight of him. "No!"

"Shut up," he says, and he slaps my face again. "Hold her down. I want this to go nice and easy," he growls. "Hit her if she makes a sound."

I scream at the top of my lungs, but my body is no match for him. However, I can still use my teeth, and so I bite down on the hand of my attacker as hard as I can.

When he bleeds, so do I.

He strikes my jaw with lightning force and blood drips from my mouth.

"You little bitch!" he spits.

He spins me around, smacking me facedown on the concrete as he pushes my legs apart.

The pain that follows is unbearable.

"Fucking bitch, you had to go and do that?" he yells, pulling my hair and dropping my face on the ground again. "I'm gonna kill you!"

"What about us?" the guys say.

"Later. I go first," growls the man on top of me.

For a few minutes, I struggle, but my body becomes weaker with every strike ... with every thrust. I quickly realize there is no getting away from this, no matter how hard I try. I just have to accept it, make it as easy as possible, and pray for mercy so they'll let me live.

It's the weakest thing a person can do ... but also the only thing I can do to stay alive.

When the man finishes with me, I feel numb—both on the inside and outside. I no longer feel it when they stomp on my head or move me around like a ragdoll. They play with me for minutes, maybe hours, who knows, in all kinds of positions, in all kind of ways. One after the other. I feel like I'm nothing more than a vapid memory of a real, living girl, instead of a puppet subjected to their cruelty.

Tears stream down my face in an endless pool of sorrow. I force myself to switch off. To break away from this world and leave my mind so I can be at peace with my decision.

I have to live through this. I have to.

For my mamma.

For justice.

For myself.

I deserve to live. Even if they're doing this to me. Even if they say I deserve it all.

I don't deserve anything but my life ... and the right to kill them when it's all over.

***

Present

"I begged them to let me live," I murmur, swallowing back the impending tears.

His lips part and he takes a step back, clearly shaken up by my story.

I tell him exactly what I remember. What I have lodged in the back of my memory like a rotting pile of crap. I wish I could clean it up, but it will never go away. I hope it might stop him from doing what he was thinking of doing. So maybe his own conscience comes out to play ... I know he has one. I've seen it in his eyes. That single second where he took pity on me was the moment I realized I could make him stop on his own accord.

There is only one thing I omitted from my story.

After the ordeal, the man who took me first threw his jacket on me and spit on my face, but I managed to capture a glimpse of a peculiar tattoo marked on his arm. A swirling dragon with its tongue sticking out. I don't remember their faces, but if I ever see that tattoo again, I will grab the nearest weapon and lodge it in the socket of his eye.

The jacket made me feel filthy, but I knew what I had been given was priceless. There was a small note in the pocket with a signature and a few words scribbled on it. The words didn't matter to me as they were meaningless, but that signature ... I would keep it hidden and use it as a tool to find whoever was behind the attack. I'd cross match every signature I could find if I had to.

One day I would find him and make him regret he ever existed.

But I don't tell my captor any of this for one single reason.

He's connected to them.

I know it because those men who came after my papà just five days ago are the same ones who trapped me in the alley that day. I could hear their voices humming through the telephone as my papà told me they were coming for me.

This man in front of me is part of their heinous crimes. Whether he knows it or not.

My captor steps backward and looks at me with a cocked head.

"Who did this to you?" he says.

"A man with a dragon tattoo on his left arm."

At first, he just stares at me in disbelief.

Then he says, "No. I don't believe you."

"You wanted the truth," I say. "This is it. Maybe it's not what you wanted after all." I smirk.

It must be tough to hear that one of his friends did

that to me. Or maybe not, considering he was about to apply the same tactics to me, albeit less harsh and more focused on confusing me. It doesn't change the fact that he tried. But maybe he doesn't care.

He grinds his teeth, the look in his eyes seething as he gets in my face and growls, "You're mine. I don't give a damn what you tell me. You're still mine to do with as I please. You'd better remember that."

"You can't hurt me," I hiss as he grabs the bag and tilts my head up. "I'm already beyond broken."

He comes closer, his tongue dipping out to lick my skin, and then he forces me to look at him again. "We'll see about that."

Suddenly, he turns around and storms out of the cell, grunting and kicking the door as it closes.

It's then that I know I was right.

Maybe I'll get to live through this after all.

And then I'll finally get to punish the ones who did this to me.

DAY 5

ANGEL

Waking up and getting dressed seems like a difficult, tedious task after yesterday. On most days, I'm excited to get up and start my work, whether it's getting information out of a prisoner or going out into the field to kill.

Except, since I talked to the girl in the dungeon yesterday, my only thoughts were that I would fucking murder the guy who had touched her like that.

I don't normally talk with targets about anything other than what they're supposed to tell me. But for some reason, her choosing pain over pleasure piqued my curiosity. I wanted to know why … I never want to know why.

I shake my head and blow out a breath as I go out the door and walk to the other side of the mansion where I'd parked my car. It's a long drive to the underground dungeon she's at, so I'll have some time to think about what I'm going to do next.

There's no time to get sentimental. I might want her for myself, but that doesn't mean I can go easy on her. My desire to claim her as my own and kill anyone who gets in my way took me by surprise, but I won't let it ruin the task I've been given. Too much is at stake here.

My life with the company is in jeopardy if I don't do as instructed.

I messed up once, and it cost me. I won't mess this up again.

But damn … just thinking about yesterday gets me all riled up.

I'm supposed to get this girl to talk, but she's already been tainted by someone else. It pisses me off so much; I'm racing through the woods on a dirt road while the branches leave marks on the glass of my car.

I don't give a shit.

All I have on my mind is her, and what I'm going to do once I get to her location in the depths of the forest. Breaking her is going to require a completely different tactic than what I usually employ, but I know what to do now. I'll have to recapture her body, mind, and heart for her to talk. Erase the memories she once had until all that's left is me.

Only me.

I am the only one who should be on her mind.

And if she doesn't forget, I'll kill the guy who did this with my bare fucking hands just to make a point. I had the chance yesterday …

The moment she mentioned the tattoo, I knew who it was.

He already soiled her before I even got a chance.

Fucking prick. One day … I swear to fucking god, one day I'm gonna kill the son of a bitch.

But first, I have a job to complete.

***

Yesterday

I jump out of my car and storm into the house, screaming, "Dad!"

There's no response, but I know he can hear me. My bellowing voice alone has the power to quake the glasses on the table, and my stomps make the glasses fall to the ground as I barge up the stairs to his office.

As I open his door, I yell, "You fucked her?!"

It was him.

That tattoo, I would recognize the description anywhere. There's no mistaking—he's the one who did it.

My father looks up with raised brows as if he's insulted, and I slam the door, infuriated by his carelessness.

"You fucking used her! And you didn't fucking tell me?" I scream.

"Sit. Down." My father points at the chair in front of his desk.

"No, I will not fucking sit down! This was not part of the plan."

"Plan? There is no plan. There is only a job, which is what I tell you to do. Now sit down." His stern voice makes me grunt out loud, but I sit down anyway because I need to know why.

"Why did you do it?" I say.

"Why?" He laughs as if it's all some sort of joke, but I'm fucking serious. "I should ask you the same question. Why are you barging into my office like that? Over a stupid bambina?"

"She's my fucking prisoner! You had no fucking right to touch her."

"I have every right." He looks up at me with threatening eyes. "She is, after all, a prisoner of mine. Not yours."

"You gave me this job, and now I find out you're not even telling me the whole story. How the fuck am I supposed to work with that, huh?" I slam my fist on the table. "She's a fucking broken mess, and it's all thanks to you." I swipe his papers off, making sure he's completely focused on me instead.

72

"*Thanks to me* you're sitting here instead of rotting away in jail, so be grateful for once."

"Grateful? You fucking ruined her!"

"I gave her what she deserved," he says, "which is more than you've done so far." He clears his throat.

"What?" I wince. "What's that supposed to mean?"

"You're getting worked up over the fact that a couple of my men and I used that bambina? Have you lost your damn mind?" He cocks his head. "She's a prisoner. A worthless peon. She's only here to talk. Nothing more."

"I can't *break* a girl who's already broken."

"Then try harder."

I grind my teeth and look away because I can't stand that ugly look on his face. It makes me want to rip it off.

"Whatever is bothering you, forget about it. What's done is done," he says.

"Couldn't you just have given me a regular job? You know, the ones we get from clients?"

"No. This is personal to me, and I needed someone like you on the case. You're doing this for me. No one else."

"So you got me out of jail to do what? Drag some information out of a girl? Seriously, what is it that you're looking for exactly?"

He gazes at me with a stern look. "Like I said before, it's none of your goddamn business."

I shrug. "Fine, but if I make her talk, she'll tell me

exactly what you're hiding right now, so I don't understand why you try to keep this little charade up."

He sits straight and taps the desk with his fingers. "You want the truth? I don't trust you with that information."

I nod, frowning. "Thought so."

"You asked for it. There it is."

"I'm your fucking son." Out of anger, I grab a couple of his pens and throw them at the wall as if they were darts.

"And you messed up. And I'm sure you'll mess up again if I tell you what I want to know. It's best if you find out for yourself. At least then I'll know exactly what she has to tell me, even though it'll come from your mouth." He sighs as if that's a bad thing.

"Yeah, well, you could've told me what you did to her."

"Why? It wouldn't have changed a thing."

"It does," I say.

"Something tells me there's more going on than just your ineptitude to make her talk."

"She's my job. Of course, there's something going on. I hate it when I can't do my job properly, and I hate it when someone else has been there before me."

"It sounds more like you're developing feelings for her," he says, stopping his thrumming.

I look up at him. "No."

He leans forward. "Make no mistake, boy. I can see through you like glass. You think I don't notice how

74

worked up you get over that bambina? Don't for a second think this is more than just a job. A kill. If she doesn't talk within twenty-one days, you kill her. The end."

I sit back and watch him, biting my lip, because the more I think about it, the more I despise the feeling that he's hiding something from me. My father, out of all people, doesn't want me to know anything about the girl I'm supposed to punish. Something's up here.

"You want me to do it? Fine, I'll do it. But I'll do it my way." I get up from my seat, and as I prepare to leave, my father's thundering voice resonates through the room.

"*Don't* remove the bag or blindfold from her face. Do you hear me?"

I gaze down at the carpet, my fingers forming a fist as I consider ignoring all his rules.

His rules are law, and they could get me killed, but something tells me I'll regret it far more if I don't listen to my gut feeling.

"Keep your mask on, at all times," he barks.

I don't reply. I just walk out the door and close it behind me without acknowledging his demands. He knows as well as I do that I won't listen to him anymore.

I will do my job the way I want to do it. No one's gonna stop me, and if they try, I'll give them the same kind of cruelty that I'm supposed to give her.

***

SKY

Present

It took me weeks to tell my papà about what happened to me back in that alley.

One might wonder why I waited for such a long time, but it wasn't as if I had meant to hide it from him. I just couldn't tell him.

What daughter would be able to tell her papà that someone took her against her will?

It would kill him.

Maybe not literally, but it would certainly break his heart.

Or it would actually give him a heart attack.

I didn't want to risk the chance, but after some time, I realized I couldn't go on like that. I couldn't keep the secret from him, knowing it left such scars on my heart. He sensed it, always asking if I was okay. I wasn't okay; I just didn't want him to worry.

After weeks, I finally gathered the courage to tell him.

He fell down in front of me, crying like a baby. It tore my heart out.

I felt more sorry for him to know what I'd been

through than for myself for experiencing the whole ordeal.

My papà tried to make me go to the police, but I refused. I knew that if I told them anything, the men who abused me would soon come after me again. It didn't take a genius to figure out they had their connections. After all, they found me in that alley, and they knew I had given the cops evidence of my mamma's murder.

No, the police could not be trusted, and neither could any other government official. I became so wary of them that I didn't even want to go to a hospital. I spent most of my days in bed—being physically ill, tired, and hungry all the time but never in the mood to eat.

I felt miserable, or so I thought.

I didn't know the meaning of the word until I was thrown in this cell.

Every hour or two, they come with water and feed it to me with a spoon, probably only to keep me alive and not much else. Sometimes they bring me chicken soup; I savor the taste, as it's the only food I've been given since I came here.

The women tend to the wound on my head with a wet cloth and water, throwing it over my head, and then leaving me naked, hanging on the wall. The worst part of it all is that I wish they would stay. Loneliness is ripping me apart to the point of craving any attention, from anyone, regardless of who they are or what they do to me. I just want them to be near me. To talk to me. To acknowledge that I'm here and that I'm human … and that I'm suffering.

It takes all my energy not to let them notice, though. It's tough, knowing that when they finish, they'll leave me alone in this cold, dark cell again.

The only thing pulling me through is the thought that it'll all be over after twenty-one days.

Twenty-one days to keep me here and make me talk.

But then the door to my cell opens again, and I stop thinking about it completely, focusing only on the sound of footsteps shuffling into the room.

"It's you," I say with a brittle voice, trying not to sound surprised.

The door closes behind him, but the light in the middle of the room immediately springs on, making me blink. Even through the blindfold, the soft light is too harsh for my eyes.

"I'm not going to tell you anything," I say beforehand.

I know that's what he's after, but I won't give it to him. Not a chance in the world.

He has a chair with him, which he sets down in the middle of the room. Then he comes toward me and gazes at me before taking off the bands around my wrists. The moment the straps fall down, my body feels weightless. Lifted off the floor by a cloud. So heavenly. And then I fall down to the ground, breathing erratic breaths, coughing while trying to cope with the pain. My wrists only barely made it out without being dislodged, but it still sizzles.

He walks back to the chair and sits down, leaning back as he stares at me.

Why is he just sitting there?

I'm completely free. I could attack him at any given moment, and yet it doesn't seem to faze him.

Maybe he knows that I probably wouldn't.

It's futile. Both he and I know it.

This is just his way of affirming it.

"Thank you," I say, clearing my throat. "For taking me down."

I don't know if I said it because I meant it or because I thought it would make him go easier on me. It's worth a try.

"Don't thank me," he growls.

I guess my attempt failed. But he's still staring at me, his fingers entwined. I can only see a bit of what's happening, but from the way he's looking at me, I know he's waiting for me to do something ... to say something.

"I won't ..." I wheeze. "I won't tell you anything."

For a second, I think I spot a faint smile.

"You already did. Yesterday," he says.

I swallow away the lump in my throat. "That was different." A cough escapes my lips. It's tough to talk when my throat feels dry and my lips are chapped.

He muffles a laugh. "You keep being stubborn. I

don't understand you. Even after you spoke, you still try to keep up that you won't speak to me."

"A girl's gotta do what a girl's gotta do," I huff.

He shakes his head. "Stupid."

"I'm not stupid," I say.

"I know that." He cocks his head. "But your decisions are."

"I do what's right. At least one of us can say that without lying."

He curls his hands into fists, cracking his knuckles. When he gets up from the chair, I get the feeling he's going to hit me with his belt, so I cower in the corner and wrap my arms around my body to protect myself.

But then he does the strangest thing.

He cups my chin and lifts up my head, fishing a small bottle of water from his pocket, which he opens and then feeds me. I gulp it down gleefully until the very last drop, licking my lips afterward. He watches me like a hawk, his eyes following my tongue as if it's a trophy he won … and he won it yesterday. I can see it from the glimmer in his eyes, and the way his tongue dips out carefully to lick the bottom side of his lip … he already thinks my mouth belongs to him.

It's only a question of time before the rest follows.

I didn't expect him to give me water. In fact, I didn't think he'd give me anything at all, which is why I'm so surprised. A rush of energy surges through my body, and for some reason, I connect it to him. As if I'm supposed to be happy about this, which is absurd, but I know why I feel it … Because it's more than I've ever gotten from him; it feels like I should be grateful. Maybe this is his intention—to break me and then rebuild me to trust only him.

Ridiculous and yet a realistic possibility.

"Thank you," I say again, but he only frowns at me.

Does it piss him off that I'm thankful for the water? Is that not what he wanted? Does he want me to hate him? I don't understand him at all, and yet, looking at him feels so familiar. As if I should know more than I currently do.

"Stop thanking me. I'm not here to save you."

"Then why are you giving me water? Why did you untie me?"

Through my blindfold, I can still see his eyes narrow. "Don't mistake what I do for kindness. I am *not* nice."

I lean back and turn away my head. "I never believed you were. Not even for a second. Not since you hit me with your belt." I push away the thoughts about feeling the welts. I've not even looked at my body since. I can't stomach the thought of seeing the marks, knowing that he put them there and that he's now pretending to care.

"I give you water to make sure you live. The ladies who come in here every day give you food so you don't die. That's it. That's the only reason I took you off the wall. To make sure you don't die on me before you tell me the truth."

My lip quivers. "I won't give you what you want. You can stop now. Just kill me and get it over with."

He grabs my neck, squeezing as he pulls me up from the ground. "You don't get to decide when you die. Do you even know why you're given twenty-one days? It's not about some sort of weird connection, but because we wanted to give you the time to think about it. Answer us before the days are up or you die. The remaining days are a gift."

"Don't talk to me about gifts when you just told me I can't thank you! I'm not grateful to be put in here by you," I hiss, clawing at his hands to get them off my neck, but he won't budge.

He's much stronger than I am, and I'm losing the fight and my breath.

"I'm here to punish you. To make you see the error of your ways *and* to give you the possibility to escape it all."

"What?" I gasp.

"If you tell me now, you won't need to stay here and I won't hurt you anymore."

"You just dangled freedom in front of me like it's a fucking joke," I say. "No, I won't talk!"

"Don't you see? I don't want you to die," he growls. "I don't *want* to have to kill you."

"But you will if you have to," I say, "which makes you despicable."

His lips are jammed together, almost as if he's trying to maintain his composure.

"Stop trying to stay fearless. You can't stop this any more than I can."

"Yes, you can," I say. "I know you can."

He leans in so close I can feel his hot breath on my skin. "You know nothing about me. Nothing."

"I know you flinched when I mentioned the tattoo yesterday," I say, tilting my head.

He's quiet for a second, studying my face, before narrowing his eyes. I can see that much through the blindfold. I wonder if he can see me, too.

"Shut your mouth," he says.

"Or what? You'll hit me again?"

He growls out loud. "I've heard enough."

"First, you want me to talk, and now, you want me to shut up? Make a choice," I muse, taunting him.

I want him out of his comfort zone. It's time that something happened, something other than just physical pain. I want to know what's hiding underneath that mask of his so I can crack it open and worm my way inside.

I don't give a damn what it takes, but I will escape this place.

He might say that I'll die, but I'll believe it when I see it.

"You're infuriating. You know that?" he says.

"Says the one who has me by the throat."

"I'm trying to get through to you, dammit!" His forehead leans against mine as he battles his will. "You will only survive if you tell me what I want to know."

"Then I will not survive," I say.

He licks his lips, frowning at me. "Is it that easy for you to throw your life away?"

"If I have to."

He sighs out loud, still gripping my neck in a way that could snap it within a second. Except, I'm still alive, although barely able to breathe … he hasn't killed me. Yet.

I find the conflict I spot in his eyes puzzling. It's almost as if he doesn't *want* to do this, but he must.

"You're no ordinary girl, are you?" he muses.

I don't know how to answer, so I opt for nothing at all.

"There's something about you …" he murmurs, almost as if he's in a conversation with himself.

And then, out of nowhere, he smashes his lips on mine.

It catches me by surprise, and my eyes flutter open behind the blindfold. He kisses me deeply and with so much curiosity that it makes my heart beat in my throat. His kiss is tantalizing, scorching hot, and yet, so subtle, almost as if he's tasting me. As if he's desperate to find out why I respond the way I do … or to find out who I really am.

But why do I feel like I recognize this kiss?

I felt the same the last time he kissed me … as if his lips had been on mine before I came to this cell. But how?

He licks my lips, pulling all thoughts from my mind,

and shows me I'm his. With his strong fingers around my neck, I'm helpless, defenseless, and yet, I don't feel threatened. Not even for a second. The only thing I feel is wantonness and a growing pull between us.

In the past few days, I've never felt more alive than now.

There's something about him …

And then he pulls his lips from mine.

For a second, all he does is look at me. I can see that much through the blindfold around my eyes. And the way he stands there, with his warm hand gripping my throat as if my body is his to own, has me weak in the knees.

Pathetic. And yet, I can't help but feel aroused.

My body is weak, senseless. I shouldn't have allowed him to kiss me again.

But it seems as though he's the one who's even angrier with himself for allowing this to happen.

"You …" he mumbles. "Tell me your name."

I can feel his breath on my chin as he stands in front of me, waiting for my answer.

I swallow back the nerves, wondering why he asks. Doesn't he know? He's the one who keeps me here, and yet he would ask me for a name? Is it a test?

Regardless, I can't give in now.

I ignore his request.

"Tell me your name," he hisses close to my face.

"And what then? If I give it to you, then will you kill me?"

He smiles as if he finds it funny that I say it out loud.

Suddenly, his hand is on my face and he rips off the blindfold.

He sucks in a breath, and I can hear him step back.

As the blindfold drops to the floor, I struggle to open my eyes. They've become so accustomed to the darkness that it's hard to stomach the light.

When I'm finally able to keep my eyelids up, I see him stumbling backward, almost tripping over the chair in the middle of the room.

"It can't be," he mumbles, his face still hidden behind the mask.

Is he surprised? It doesn't sound as if he planned for this to happen. Does he know me?

More importantly, do I know him?

The words that leave his lips next make me question who he really is.

He mumbles, "Sky?"

DAY 6

ANGEL

I'm a coward.

A motherfucking coward.

The moment I saw it was her, I ran.

Fuck, I should've known it when I kissed her for the first time because it felt so familiar. Her lips brought back memories that I thought I'd long forgotten. Things that I thought I could forget, but ultimately stayed in the forefront of my thoughts.

It's exactly the reason I kissed her a second time.

I needed to know.

And now I do.

Sky Valenti ... she's the girl I thought I could be

with for more than just a one-night stand. Our meeting was a fluke, a random occurrence that pulled us together. Something so out of the blue ... so extraordinary. She's the girl who saw the darkness in my heart without me even telling her. I let her go because I knew I couldn't give her the life she deserved. Without me, she'd be safer, even though neither of us wanted to separate. Still, they were the best nights I'd had in a long time.

Fuck ... and now she's in there. How did this happen?

Sky ... why did it have to be you?

Out of all people, you are the one my father targets?

I make a fist and stomp the steering wheel, which makes the car dangerously drift through the woods.

I can't fucking believe it's her. She's the one my father's been after. The one with the answer he seeks. *And* she's the girl he took without permission.

I could kill him.

Literally, I could because I almost did.

The only thing that stopped me was the threat of my life.

I'm furious but not stupid.

After I had taken off that blindfold, I stormed out the building and went straight back to my dad. We needed to have a serious talk.

***

Yesterday

I storm into his room, not giving a fuck about knocking. "You fucking kidnapped Sky?"

"Angel, do we have to do this now?" My father cocks his head.

"Yes, now!" I say, slamming the door behind me.

He's lounging in his chair, his personal barber shaving him old school with a straight razor blade. His face looks ridiculous with all that foam on it, and it makes me even angrier to look at him knowing he doesn't give a shit about why I'm here.

"Her, out of all people?" I scream. "It had to be her you were after? You tried to keep it a secret from me, didn't you? That's why you had her blindfolded!"

"I did it for your own good." He clears his throat, taking his sweet time to respond. "First, I told you not to remove the blindfold. Second, she owes me, so she deserves this. I don't care if you know her."

"You fucking son of a bitch." I walk to him and push aside his barber, grabbing my father by the collar. "You fucking touched her. She's the girl you used. I won't let you get away with this."

He wraps his hands around my wrists and glares at me while shoving me away. "*She's* the one who got you thrown in jail."

"How do you know?" I yell.

"Because it was her *madre* you killed!"

This shuts me up completely.

I step back and let it all sink in, as my father straightens himself and grabs a cloth to wipe off the excess foam.

"I did that because you told me to …" I say.

"Yes, but I did not expect her daughter to go after you."

"Fucking hell." I kick his desk in rage.

"Calm down, boy."

"No, I will not calm down! Can't you fucking see? I knew her. I fucking knew her as something more than the prisoner she is now. She's broken as fuck, and it's all your fault."

"No, it's your responsibility too," he says, nodding at his barber to dismiss him. "In case you've forgotten, you're the one who was negligent. Leaving on your regular license plate instead of the many alternatives we have."

"It was a minor mistake."

"A minor mistake that got her to identify you as the killer."

"She doesn't even know it's me. The cops came to fucking pick me up from this house for crying out loud."

"Just because she didn't know it was you doesn't mean she wasn't the one who got your ass in jail."

I grind my teeth, leaning down on the desk so I can think about this. How the heck did this get so complicated all of a sudden?

"It doesn't matter, boy. What's done is done. You'll still have to pull the information out of her."

I look up at him, making a face. "How could I? After this? Knowing it's her?"

"Did you take off your mask near her?"

I frown. "No."

"Then there's no issue. She won't have any idea. The only thing that matters is that you get her to talk."

"I can't," I say, shaking my head. "She's … she's …"

"Just. A. Bambina." My father's brows draw together, forming a stern gaze. "You might have had a few nights with her, but that doesn't mean a thing compared to what's at stake here. This company is more important than your petty relationships. It's time you got that through your head."

"To you it is," I say.

"And it should be to you as well. Do you want us to fail?"

"No."

"You know you'd go back to prison when that happens, right? Or worse, you'd be dead. A rotting corpse on the streets." He grabs a water bottle and chugs it down until it's empty.

I let out a big breath. "I fucking hate this."

"I don't care," he says. "Do your fucking job … or I'll come and do it myself."

Frowning, I engage in a death stare with him, well aware of the threat he just gave me.

I only have one choice. Give him what he wants or he'll go get it himself.

It doesn't take a scientist to know what I'll choose.

I'm not gonna let him put his hands on her ever again.

I'd rather die than see that happen.

But I know he won't stop until he has what he wants, so there's no other choice for me but to continue with my job ... which is pressuring her into telling me whatever secret she hides.

"Here," my father says. He grabs another water bottle from the mini fridge in the corner and tosses it to me. "Drink. Freshen up. Do whatever you need to do, just get back in there and get it done."

He winks and gives me a fake smile. It comes so easy to him; it's as if he doesn't have a heart at all. And neither will I when I'm finished with her.

***

Present

As I enter the compound, I think of what I'm going to do next. I have to change my plans if I'm going to get through to her *and* keep my sanity intact. Time to take her punishment to a whole different level.

The women are just walking toward her cell, so I stop them. "I will do it."

They look at me, confused, but then nod and the one holding the bowl of soup hands it over to me. "And bring me some bread," I add.

She quickly scurries off to grab it for me from the small kitchen in the corner of the underground cellar. This place isn't huge, but at least it's hidden from outside view. No scanner can penetrate the ground this far down, and since we keep these women on a tight leash, nobody spills any information about this prison. Not that these women would be able to; their tongues have been cut off. A personal gift from my father. At least, that's the way he sees it. They get to live their lives here in peace, under the protection of our company, so long as they do whatever we say. They are fed, have a clean bed, and can shower whenever they want. According to my father, that's luxurious enough.

I don't say a word about it. I've grown accustomed to the women, even though to outsiders this would be cruel. I've been too exposed to savagery to feel anything for them. Hell, I've instigated and participated in plenty of savage acts myself.

As the woman comes back with the bread, I walk toward the door, but they stand behind me with questioning eyes, as if to ask me what I'm going to do. Of course, they don't understand. Good things like food and showers are brought by the women, so the prisoner doesn't associate me with good things. They only associate me with bad things, like whips and pain, so they'll fear me whenever I come into the room. It's a method of extracting information in a heartbeat, but I know now that tactic won't work on Sky.

I glance over my shoulder and growl, "Leave me."

The women hurry off to their rooms as I grab the mask that hangs from the wall and put it on. Before I open the door using the number pad and the retinal scanner, I turn on the light to make sure I can actually see something.

As I step inside, I notice Sky curled up in the left-hand corner, hugging her legs as if it's the only thing she can hold on to. The chair in the middle of the room has been torn apart. Completely ripped to shreds as if she used it as a weapon. Probably to wedge open the door.

I smile and call over my shoulder, "Bring me another chair."

Sky seems surprised by the fact that I give them orders as one of the women comes into the cell and puts down a new chair for me. Nothing's going to stop me from watching her, though. No matter how many chairs she rips apart, I will continue to place one there until she learns the meaning behind it … I'll always be watching her. There is no escaping this truth.

"Go to your room and stay there until I'm done," I say to the woman, and she nods and leaves us in peace.

Now I can focus on Sky, who's shivering as she watches me like a hawk. The moment I come closer, she backs away, crawling into the other corner as if to escape me. I hold out the bowl of soup and cock my head. "Want this?"

She looks at it as if she hasn't eaten in days.

Maybe she hasn't.

I never asked the women, and neither did I care. Not before I knew it was her who was in this cell. I distance myself from victims so I can do my job, but this is different. I already know her. It's too late to be a cold-hearted brute. I've already become personally involved just by kissing her and realizing it was Sky.

The longer I hold out the bowl, the more Sky looks at me with those big eyes that pierce a hole in my armor. I should go over there and give it to her, but that would defeat the purpose of this exercise.

So I shrug and sit down on the chair instead. The bowl is burning my hand as I hold it, waiting for her to make a move. Very slowly, she comes out of her corner on hands and legs, much like an animal would do if it were in distress.

Has she been reduced to that already? Or is she faking it to confuse me?

Whatever the case, I have to remain seated.

I need her to come to me, so she'll learn to trust me and only me ... so she'll learn to obey me.

"You want this?" I hold the bowl out in front of me so she can smell it.

I can see her nose go up, and she crawls even closer. In the light, I can clearly see the red stripes all over her body, remnants of my belt. I'd be lying if I said it didn't turn me on to see my marks on her skin.

It means she's mine. Mine to do with as I please.

And now, it pleases me to feed her.

"I don't bite," I muse, lifting my eyebrow. "Unless you misbehave."

She sits down in front of me with a flushed face, barely able to contain her thirst as she leans in closer. I hold up the spoon close to her mouth. "Open."

She does as I say and lets the spoon pass her lips, the hot soup pouring onto her tongue. Watching her gulp it down is like watching porn. So smooth … like it comes naturally to her.

When she swallows, I say, "Good girl."

I can already imagine she's swallowing my cum.

Her eyes narrow at the words 'good girl,' and we exchange silent threats through simple looks. As I put the spoon back into the bowl, she holds out her hand, but I pull back the bowl so it's above my head. "Ah-ah."

She frowns, sitting back down again.

"My rules," I say.

She sighs out loud but then nods in agreement.

I smile at her as I dip the spoon into the soup and push it past her lips again. We continue this ritual until the bowl is half-empty, which is when she notices the bread I brought with me lying on the armrest of the chair.

I pick up the bread and watch her round, azure eyes follow it as I tear off a piece, dip it into the soup, and bring it to her mouth. For a split second, I think I hear a soft hum coming from her mouth before she swallows. The sound alone brings goosebumps to my skin … and a twitch in my cock.

As I feed her the soup and bread, taking my time and having patience with her slow chewing, I feel like we're connecting on a level I've not experienced before. A dependency is growing between us, although I'm not exactly sure which one of us is bound to the other.

The bread and soup are gone within minutes, even though it feels like hours. Our eyes are locked in what seems an endless storm of silent screams. It would be worse if she could see behind the mask.

"Why did you come to give me food? The women …" she mutters.

I place a finger on her lip and silence her. "Don't ask questions."

"But—"

I grab her chin and force my lips on hers.

I admit, I'm selfish, but I couldn't last another second watching those pouty lips and sweet, helpless eyes without claiming her as my own. I want to taste her mouth, the very essence of her being, for as long as it remains. I don't know what choice she'll make, so every single second of those twenty-one days is precious.

With every kiss, a fire grows inside me. It intensifies the burning desire to take her frail body out of this place and lay it down on my bed where I'll lave her with my tongue until she's pure again.

But I know that's wishful thinking.

The world isn't as easy as it seems.

As I take my lips off her, she falls forward a little, almost as if she was expecting more, and when she opens her eyes, a familiar flush adorns her face. I remember it from last time, months ago, when she was still untainted, and I was hopelessly falling for her.

"They didn't come because I didn't want them to. Be thankful I came with bread."

"Thank you … I guess."

Her head drops forward, so I lift her chin with my index finger. "Tell me … What are you hiding?"

Her confused face immediately turns into disgust as she turns her head away. "I'm not going to tell you. You can't bribe me with a little extra bread or by personally feeding me. Do I look that easy to you?"

Grinding my teeth, I stare at her, insulted as hell. "How dare you."

I came here so she'd see it would be better to tell me instead of keeping things a secret so that she'd be able to live. I wanted to show her she could have more, if only she gave me something to work with, and yet she's not willing to give me *anything*.

Anger overtakes me as I smash the bowl on the ground, causing her to dash back into the corner.

"I am showing you that I can give you more if only you'd give me a simple truth, but you still resist." I walk over to her in a fit of rage, grabbing her by the neck to pull her up from the ground. "I'm *not* your enemy here!"

"You're the one who chained me to the wall, who takes and takes without ever thinking of the consequences."

"I live with the consequences every day of my fucking life," I seethe. "It's time you learned to accept yours."

"I can see that ..." she huffs.

I know she's being sarcastic, which pisses me off even more. She's Sky, for fuck's sake; the girl I'm not supposed to hurt. And yet here I am, hurting her because that's my fucking job. I have no other choice, and she's making it even more difficult on purpose. Dammit.

"Don't you fucking see I'm the only one here who cares even the slightest bit?"

"No, I think you're just scared of what will happen when I don't tell you," she gargles between heaves.

My eyes widen.

Am I that easy to read?

I realize I'm cutting off her oxygen, so I release her. She immediately grabs her throat and coughs. I take a step back, wondering how in the hell I am supposed to do this if I can't even keep my own thoughts to myself. She sees right through me.

Grunting, I turn around and leave the cell.

I can't take another minute of looking at her when she acts like this. It makes me want to do things to her that are beyond repairing. I need to take control over my own emotions first before I can take control of hers.

Clearing my throat, I alert the women and tell them to clean up the cell.

If she won't budge from getting more than she earned, I'll give her more than she bargained for.

I'll come back tomorrow and show her she can't say no to me.

DAY 7

ANGEL

I first met her in a dream, and in a dream, I met her again last night.

The first time I saw her was when one of my father's maids was outside on the stairs, drinking a cup of coffee, and I happened to look over her shoulder at a picture of the most beautiful girl I'd ever seen. She had a round face, plump lips, and gorgeous blue eyes, hiding partially behind long auburn hair. The picture quickly disappeared as the maid tucked her mobile phone in her pocket, and I walked down the steps. I can still vividly see the narrow-eyed glare the maid gave me as I left the property.

Back then, I would've never guessed she was an informant. Someone who'd infiltrated my father's company just to sabotage it. I just thought she was angry with me for peeking at her daughter. Yes, I knew it was her daughter because they looked the same; like two drops of water from the same bucket. Except, her daughter was my age and seemed so pure, so happy. That one picture is what sold me for life.

I was a cocky bastard. A hard-to-get player who only lived for pussy, ass, and money. I used girls, and they used me. I lived in the limelight while shadowing as a killer for my father's company. It was how he raised me—what he had in mind the moment I was born. That's what the company does, after all. We kill on request. Occasionally, we torture people, too. Sometimes we capture people and keep them prisoner for as long as the job requires.

It's not hard to understand why I was so caught up in it.

But then that girl came along ...

I don't know what did me in, but she ... she was everything I wanted. Everything I could never have.

The first time I saw her in real life—not on paper or digitally, but alive and right in front of me—was in a club. I was there to dance and pick up girls, but the moment I spotted her, I knew I wanted to take her home more than any girl I'd ever met.

She was beautiful, perfect even. Her sleek figure and big, round eyes were what drew me in like a magnet. I wanted to dance with her all night, and then take her home where I'd show her all the corners of my room.

I was awestruck by how she danced, so sensual and yet so classy. Just one look was all it took to sell my soul to the devil.

She'd captured something no other girl had ever managed to capture. With just one look, she'd stolen my heart.

And then to find out that I'd meet her here, in the club where I go every night ... what were the odds?

As intended, I prowled around her like a lion, claiming her and the space around her, marking her as mine with just a look. Our hands gripped and from that moment, everything else seemed to disappear. The dance was fierce, laced with sexual tension, sweat mingling with dangerous desires.

I knew it that if I took her home, one night wouldn't be enough.

I'd be hooked on her forever.

It didn't matter if she was a good sucker; that she had a hot body and a slick pussy. It was her presence, her interaction with me, and how she looked at me that unraveled me. If I had one taste, I was an addict for life.

Knowing all that, I still couldn't resist, and neither could she.

As if we were locked in each other's arms, we melded together to form one whole. We struggled to breathe between frantic kisses and lusty licks, making our way back to my home in a cab. The driver must've thought we were drunk or on drugs, but the only drug I was on was her.

I needed her.

I wanted her.

I had to have her.

Even if it were only for one night, I'd take it because she was perfection.

She was the kind of girl you read about in books, or see on the television, but never meet in real life.

And here she was, stumbling into my arms like a lost lamb … falling right into the wolf's trap.

I was reckless, egotistic. But I couldn't stop myself from taking her.

It was the best night I ever had.

I didn't think she'd want more; I figured she'd be gone by the morning, and that I'd never see her again. But when I found her getting breakfast in the kitchen, my heart was sold.

One day turned into a week.

Day and night.

It was like we couldn't stop.

I'd never experienced anything like that. Something so completely feral, so animalistic, and yet so unavoidable. We were the perfect match.

But then the day came when she had to leave.

The same day our maid, her mother, mysteriously disappeared from our service.

I should've strung it all together, but I was too high on her, still flying on that cloud, to notice the similarities. I just thought she'd left because her mother wanted to take a job in another city and she didn't want to tell me the bad news.

Boy, was I wrong.

I was too stupid, too preoccupied with my thoughts to even realize what my father had asked of me one day later. It was a personal request, one that came directly from him, which didn't happen often.

I was tasked with killing a woman who was fleeing in a car along with another suspect. I didn't think much of it, and I never checked to see who it was. Hell, I was too intoxicated by what had happened the week before that I didn't even change my license plate.

I drove her off the cliff. The car spun into cartwheels, which caused sparks to light the fuel.

It completely burned out.

I didn't know she'd seen my license plate and that she'd sent a picture of it to someone else. Nor did I know it was her mother until it was too late.

Until they came to shackle me and take me to jail.

Even in jail, I didn't realize it was Sky who had received the picture. That it was her who pointed out my car amongst all others.

But it turned out that Sky had never attempted to see for herself who the real killer of her mother was. She probably couldn't stomach the thought of seeing him alive, let alone find out it was the man she'd been sleeping with for an entire week.

She still probably doesn't know I killed her mother.

***

SKY

The women are washing me again, but this time they use actual soap. It smells nice, considering I've been smelling nothing good lately. They even brush my teeth. With the exception of the bread, this is the only extra treatment I've been given since I arrived, and I wonder why.

They even help me dry off and when they're done, they leave nothing on the floor, so it's spick-and-span. I wonder what the occasion is.

I don't have to wait long to find out.

When the door opens, I already suck in a breath, expecting the worst. The only time someone enters my cell is in the morning when the women feed me, and when *he* visits me.

He comes and goes whenever he pleases. He never comes at the same time, which is probably to confuse me.

At times, he just stares at me, sitting silently in the chair as if he thinks I'll come forward with the truth out of the blue. Other times, he chokes me, expecting me to blurt it out so he'll let me go. And then there are the times when he spanks me or belts me. Those are the times I'm the most confused ... because I feel he wants more from me than just answers.

I can tell because each time, I feel him press his hard-on into my skin.

And worst of all ... I can feel my own core tightening every time it happens.

I hate it.

I hate how conflicted he makes me feel. One moment, I think he's going to release me, and then with the snap of a finger, it could turn into an ugly murder.

I wish I could figure out what his deal is.

As the door closes behind him, I can already feel the room temperature rise. The small, buzzing light in the corner illuminates his mask and the scorching eyes inside. He walks toward me with a casual shrug, hands in the pocket of his sweatpants, black long sleeve shirt hanging loosely over the side. His pecs and biceps are clearly visible through the thin fabric, and for a second, I think I spot his cock swinging left and right in his pants as he walks.

I don't even know why I'm fascinated by how he looks, but his looks alone would draw attention from anyone, regardless of their situation. With a hot body like his, he just has that effect.

I swallow, trying to hide my heated cheeks behind my freshly washed, wet hair. I stand still in a corner, watching his every move as I hold my body with my hands, covering up whatever I can. I still don't have any clothes—not since they took them from me—but I've gotten quite used to the feel of naked skin. I just haven't gotten used to his piercing eyes soaking me up. There's an unmistakable smirk on his face, almost as if he enjoys looking at me being naked.

For some reason, that thought makes me flush even more.

As he stops to stand in front of me, he grabs my chin and makes me look at his mask. "So, have you considered talking yet?" he says, cocking his head at me.

I frown. "You keep asking that, but I won't change my mind."

His lip curls up into a smile. "Pity."

Suddenly, he grabs me by the waist and lifts me over his shoulder. I squeal as he brings me to the wall where the shackles are.

"No, not those things," I scream.

"Should've said yes…" He hums, putting me down.

I fight him, but he's too strong for my fragile body as he grabs my wrists and pins them to the wall. "You don't want to make an enemy out of me, Sky."

"How do you know my name?" I say.

"Maybe I'll tell you …" He leans in. "Or maybe I won't." And then he clicks the metal into place, locking my wrist in.

"No!" I yell. "Please, don't do this. Don't hang me

up again. I can't take it."

"Oh, you have no idea what kind of plans I have …" My senses go on full alert at hearing the deep, gruff undertone in his voice. He shackles my free wrist as well and then my ankles. My body is up for display right in front of him, and it makes me want to burst into tears. I admit, I pretend to be strong, but who wouldn't when faced with the impossible? Pain makes me do strange things. It makes me beg him to stop.

He narrows his eyes at me as I continue my attempts to fight the chains.

"Don't you see you caused this?"

"I didn't ask you to hang me up on the wall like some deer."

"You didn't give me what I want either, so now I'm going to take from you what I want even more." His tongue dips out to wet his lips, and he bites the bottom one for just a second. For some reason, my eyes zoom in on it, and they forget for just a second what's going on here.

"You'll like it … don't worry," he muses, stepping even closer so he can smell me.

I turn my head to the side while he sniffs me, trying to lean away, but it only makes him come closer. He places a soft kiss on my neck, his tongue drawing a line upward toward my ear. Right before he nibbles my ear, he hovers in front of it, and for a second, I think I can hear him smile.

He hisses, "I love your smell. Your taste. You make

me so fucking hard."

Suddenly, his hand is on my breast—kneading, tugging, and twisting. Everything and anywhere, all at the same time. Sensory overload makes me gasp, and when my mouth opens, he covers it with his. He takes my breath quite literally, kissing me until my moan is silenced; kissing me with everything he has. His taste is familiar, intoxicating, and for a second, I forget that I'm even hanging here. His tongue expertly licks the roof of my mouth, his lips brushing mine with equal fervor.

"This is what I'll take from you," he murmurs into my mouth.

His free hand slides down my body and past my inner thighs, pushing my legs apart as he starts rubbing me. I feel humiliated. Used. Shameful, for actually feeling my pussy thump from having him touch me.

"Hmm … you like it when I touch you." It's not even a question.

"No …" I say, shaking my head.

He grins. "Yes, you do." He pushes a finger on top of my clit. "Right here."

I moan when he rubs it with his index finger and then brings his thumb into the play to roll my clit. My wetness builds as my core clenches, desperate to fight off the arousal, but my body is a fool for his touch.

My mind has been deprived for too long, and when he offers me this release, I'm too weak to fight it. It crosses my mind that perhaps, if I give this to him, he'll be more gentle with me. Maybe, if I give him anything he wants, he'll let me go.

It might be a futile thought, but it's here, and it's not going anywhere.

"Don't think I'm doing this for your pleasure, Sky." He groans. "Oh, no. I'm doing this because I want to watch you writhe from my finger."

Still twisting and pulling my nipples with one hand, he's driving me crazy with lust, as the other expertly builds the desire between my legs.

"I'm going to watch you come, and you're going to enjoy it, and then hate yourself for liking it. And tomorrow, we'll do the same thing. And then again … and again …"

"Stop …" I moan.

Who am I kidding? He's not going to, and I'm not even sure I want him to stop anymore.

He has me under a spell, and I'm helpless to fight it.

I feared his touch so much because I became accustomed to the pain, but this is pure bliss. I thought my body couldn't handle this so soon after what happened to me, but it feels so different. So wrong … but so good. Like this was meant to happen.

As if it already did.

My eyes flash open and they meet his in a tempestuous staring match. I focus on his eyes, the color, the way they watch me as I come apart in his arms. They seem familiar, like I've seen them before.

"Not giving me answers means getting used by me, Sky. In whatever way possible," he muses. His finger slides up and down my pussy. "But I can feel you don't mind that. You say you hate this more than the pain, but I disagree. Your pussy is fucking wet from my touch."

I shake my head, my lips quivering, but he grabs my chin and smashes his lips on mine again.

Suddenly, I can feel his thumb entering me, making me moan out loud, but his mouth absorbs the sounds. His kisses numb the memories that lurk in the back of my mind, memories I tried to push away. But this ... this is so overpowering, almost as if he's trying to help me push them away.

When he takes his lips from mine, he says, "So, I guess this isn't really punishment now, is it?" He smiles as he dips another finger in and out of pussy. "One way or another, you're gonna talk, or I'm gonna keep taking your body."

He fucks me with his fingers, licking his lips at the sight of me panting. I'm having trouble composing myself as the pressure rises within.

"Coming already, Sky?" He chuckles. "You've not been fucked like this for a long time, have you?"

I refuse to answer. My personal life is none of his business, and even though I told him about what happened to me in that alley, I won't let it destroy me. It's different, completely different from what I experienced before. He isn't gentle with me, but he isn't evil either. My body is responding to his touch in a way I can't explain, and I think he knows, judging from the smug look on his face.

"Yes ... come all over my finger."

"No!" I moan.

"I wanna feel how you'd milk me if my cock were inside you," he murmurs against my lips.

The sizzling pain caused by him twisting my nipples brings me to new heights, and I can feel the orgasm building deep inside me. Even if I wanted to, I can't stop it. Especially when he gazes at me like that, with a look that claims ownership over my body, mind, and soul.

Suddenly, he pulls his fingers out, right before I'm about to climax. My entire body is shaking, and my clit is thumping like never before.

"What ..." I mumble.

He lowers his head and grabs my chin. "You didn't think I'd give that to you without you begging me now, did you?"

I frown. "I hate you."

There's a devilish smile on his face. "No, you hate what I do to you and how it makes you feel. You can't handle the fact that your body wants me."

"That's a lie!" I spit.

His grip on my face strengthens. "You can't handle the truth. And the truth is that you like this. That you like me fucking you because I own your pleasure. Face it, you've never been owned like this before. Your body's signals confuse you. It *wants* to be fucked so badly that it's already begging me for mercy. It's time you did the same."

I'm still panting from the pent up arousal, and looking at him and his amusing smile only makes me feel worse than I already did. I hate that I've become so easy and that I've succumbed to my own body's desires. It's like I have no control over what I want. *He* does.

Suddenly, he pulls down his pants to take out his cock.

Just the sight of it makes my mouth water.

It's huge, hard, and when he starts rubbing it, I die a little inside. I'm not prepared for this ... I don't *want* to be turned on, but I have no choice. It just happens. Especially when he notices that I've seen him rub it.

"Like this? I bet you've already thought about what it might feel like if I'd thrust into your pussy right now," he says with a smug smile.

I shake my head, but it only makes him lick his lips and rub faster.

"Lie," he growls. "How many more are you going to tell? I can see right through you."

I close my eyes, but he slaps my cheek. "No, watch me. I didn't give you permission to close your eyes." He directs my chin downwards so I'm forced to watch him jerk off. When I attempt to move away, he slaps my breast harshly. I squeal from the hot streak that travels through my body, and then mutter, "Sorry."

114

The left side of his lip quirks up into a smile. "Good. You're finally learning."

I swallow away the lump in my throat as I reluctantly continue to watch him.

"See how hard you get me?" he muses. "I can't resist much longer, Sky. So it's up to you. Tell me the truth."

"No …"

His eyes narrow, and he steps a little closer so his dick is against my legs. I can feel him rub himself against me, and as much as I want to say that I hate it, it's actually exciting me. I don't know why; maybe it's because he got me so aroused that I'm more focused on coming than fighting him. It was his plan all along to confuse me … and he's succeeding.

He grips my auburn hair and pulls back, forcing me to look him in the eyes while I feel his pre-cum dripping onto my thigh. "Choose, Sky. Pleasure or truth."

"I can't …" I mumble.

"Then I will make the choice for you."

Suddenly, his lips are on mine, claiming me with every last swipe of his tongue. God, his kisses are mind-blowing, so much so that I'm starting to forget why I ever fought him in the first place.

As he takes his lips from mine, he hums. "I'm gonna give you a choice. You can either beg me to make you come, or I'll mark you, and you don't get to choose how. It could be with my belt … or my cum."

A low groan leaves his mouth, which makes goosebumps scatter on my skin. He cups my pussy like it's his. "Come or I will."

"Please ..." I mutter.

"Please what? Make you come? Is that what you choose?"

"Yes ..."

Releasing his cock, he grips my throat. "Say it!"

"Please, make me come," I sputter.

A smile replaces the displeased look on his face. "Good choice."

He doesn't hesitate before immediately fucking me with his fingers again. "Hmm ... just seeing my dick made you so wet," he muses.

It's not a question. We both know it's the truth. He seems to love it while I hate it so much. My body is weak for him, almost as if it listens to him without my command. As if it's completely forgotten the assault from months ago, and it's completely used to the feel of submission. This man ... He's no ordinary man to be able to do this to me.

His hard-on bounces up and down as he flicks my clit so fast my breath is almost taken away. As I look down and try to concentrate on something else, I can see the pre-cum glisten on his tip, drawing my attention. Images flash through my mind of him coming inside me or on me, and I feel dirty for even thinking about it. Especially when the idea sparks my lust even further.

"Yes, Sky. Give in to the pleasure. Give in to me because you have no other choice. Give it to me because you want nothing else. It's inevitable. You are mine, and you will do what I say."

The darkness in his voice brings me to the edge, and my body begins to quiver. His forehead rests on mine, animalistic grunts coming from his parted lips as he fucks me with his fingers. In this cell, there's nothing left but us; a primal desire feeding the intense looks between us.

"Come, Sky. Now," he growls.

And I do. Just like that. His voice and fingers are enough to make me fall apart. There is nothing that can compare to the pleasure I feel as he fucks me raw with just a few fingers, taking every inch of my energy and breath with him.

When the waves subside and his fingers slide out of my wetness, I feel bereft of something unexplainable. Something unnatural. Something so wrong. I hate it. And I need it.

A devious smirk spreads on his face as he touches my sensitive clit again. "One last time. Just for good measure," he muses. "That wasn't so bad, was it?"

"You …" I mutter.

I can't believe this happened.

I can't believe he made me choose, and that I chose *this*.

And worst of all, I can't believe that I actually enjoyed it.

His touch ... his lips ... they all feel so familiar, but I don't know why.

I frown, staring deep into the eyes behind the mask, wondering if I can find out what's hidden underneath. The way they sparkle and narrow as I look at him seems so recognizable.

"Who are you?" I mumble.

The words roll out before I notice I said it, and then the look on his face changes from satisfaction to pure rage.

"You don't get to ask that," he growls.

"Fine, but I gave you what you wanted, now let me go," I pant.

He raises one brow, seemingly pissed off by what I asked. "You think it's that easy? Oh no, I just gave you the choice of punishment. That's all. I'll keep coming back again and again until you tell me what I really want to hear." He leans in closer to my ear, making me shiver. "Every day, it will get worse and worse until you tell me the truth. You know what that is ... and until you do, I'll keep coming back to claim what belongs to me."

With narrowed eyes and a content smile, he leans back and brings his fingers to his mouth. His tongue dips out to lick his fingers, and my eyes widen when he starts to suck on them, moaning out loud.

"So good ..." He hums. "I'll make sure to get a taste every fucking day."

With a half-hard dick, he turns around and walks

toward the door.

"No, wait!" I yell.

He can't leave me hanging like this. He simply can't. I can't take it anymore.

"What? Already missing me that much?" He smiles provocatively.

"Don't leave me here on the wall."

He cocks his head and then pulls his cock back into his pants. "Oh, don't you worry, Sky. I'm not going anywhere. And neither are you. I'll be right back."

And then he leaves.

I'm not sure if I should be happy he's coming back and might take me off the wall, or be afraid that he's coming back in the first place. What is he planning? Is he really going to break me with sex? It makes no sense, and yet it does, considering my past.

I realize I've been stupid because I told him the thing he wanted to know the most. I gave him the key. I showed him where my weakness lies, and now he's using it to crack me open.

Goddammit.

I make fists and bang them on the wall. I can't believe I played right into the palm of his hand. I was so afraid of the pain he might inflict that he took a different route and I just gave him the information on a platter.

However, I won't let it corrupt me. Just because it hurt me in the past doesn't mean it will hurt me now. If I can imagine him as being a lover instead of my captor, I'll be able to do this without completely losing my mind.

It's easy, considering he just made me come.

He didn't even take me for himself. All he did was provide me with pleasure. It's not bad if it feels good, right? I can do this. I can fake my way through these twenty-one days if all he does is make me come.

The only question is ... is that really all he is going to do? I doubt it.

He said so himself, he had more up his sleeve ... Just thinking about it makes a chill run down my spine.

As he re-enters the cell, an unwanted sigh leaves my mouth. But then I notice the bag in his hands. When he drops it on the hard floor, I briefly blink and a shock runs through my body from the noise.

"You pleased me today, Sky," he says. "But you shouldn't have asked that question."

"Don't do this ..." I mutter.

"You know how it goes. Punishment for not saying what I want to hear. Punishment for asking questions you shouldn't be asking."

"No! I'm sorry. Please don't," I murmur.

He ignores my pleas as he walks toward me, and I expect the worst, closing my eyes. But then the bands around my wrists are undone and I'm lifted off the wall like a lifeless puppet hanging in his arms. Confused, I look up at my captor's face hidden behind the mask and contemplate whether I should rip it off, but then I notice the knife in his waistband and realize it would probably mean my end.

He sets me down in his chair and says, "Stay."

I don't know what compels me to listen to him. Maybe fear of an even worse punishment makes me stay. Or maybe because of the way he said it. No one's ever talked to me like that. Or at least not in that way … like he holds a sexual claim on me.

He picks up the bag and takes out a bunch of ropes, the flicking sound making me jolt in my seat. He wraps them around me and the chair, making sure my arms are pinned on the back. I shouldn't have stayed seated. I should've picked up the chair and hit him in the face with it. Why didn't I? Why am I even letting him do this to me instead of fighting him off with what little energy I have left?

When he's done, I can't even move; that's how tight he's made the knots. I'm stuck to this chair, whether I like it or not. As he rummages through the bag again, my eyes widen. He takes out a dildo that looks like a Magic Wand, and I shudder when he brings it to me.

"Remember when I told you to choose?" he says, placing it between my legs. "You chose coming. You didn't choose pain or the truth. You chose this. And now you will get it. All. Day. Long."

He turns on the buzzer, and the intense pleasure it gives me immediately makes me squirm.

However, when he ties it between the ropes, knotting it up until it's stuck between my legs, I realize this isn't meant to be pleasurable. He places the Magic Wand where I have no control over what it does, and I can't move. I'm stuck with a dildo between my legs, but for how long?

The wicked smile on his face makes me shiver. "Comfortable?"

"What now?" I ask.

"Nothing." He shrugs. "You brought this on yourself."

"What?" I pant, getting hot and heavy again just from the buzzing.

He turns around and packs up, making his way to the door again. "Where are you going?" I yell.

"That's none of your business. But, if it makes you feel better, I'll thoroughly enjoy the image of you squirming in that chair, experiencing orgasm after orgasm …" He brings his fingers to his nose and sniffs deeply. "So intoxicating. I'll have plenty of fun with my cock tonight. Too bad you won't get to see any of it."

"Wait! You can't leave me like this!" I writhe against the chair, my pussy thumping from another upcoming release.

"Oh, yes I can," he muses, opening the door. "Watch me."

"But … what do I do now?" I mutter, wondering if he's really going to leave me like this. Tied up. Naked. Forced to orgasm repeatedly until who knows when.

Oh, god.

This isn't going to feel good.

Maybe it will the first time and the second time, but after that, it will get worse and worse until it's so difficult to handle that I'll probably scream out loud.

How much time will pass before he'll come for me again?

I'll probably be begging him when the time comes.

This is going to be hell.

He glances over his shoulder and winks at me. "Survive."

DAY 8

Angel

I didn't want to have to do it, but she gave me no choice.

If she doesn't talk, then I'll have to forcefully drag it out of her.

Whether it's with pain or pleasure, I will do what I must to make sure the job is done.

However, it's getting increasingly difficult to turn my back on her and leave her cell. The more time I spend with her, the longer I think of staying, wanting to see her face. It's selfish, and I know damn well that what I'm doing to her is wrong. Of course, I wish she wasn't in that cell, but the truth is a bitch, and no one can do anything about it.

My father will get his answers, regardless. If I can't do it, then he'll do it himself, and he won't be as gentle.

She thinks this is the worst I can do … she has no fucking clue. I can kill a person with my bare hands. I could squash her windpipe with just a pinch. I could rip her apart.

I could … But I would *never* do that.

I *will* make her talk before the end of these twenty-one days. There's no other way. I won't let her die.

I wonder how she's doing, strapped in that chair with a dildo stuck on her pussy. It must've been so hard … just like my cock has been for the past few hours. The thought of her naked and begging for it to stop has made it almost impossible for me to think of anything else, let alone sleep. I've been awake all night, rubbing my dick, but every time I was about to come, I stopped. I want to save it for her pretty lips, and it'd be a shame if I didn't keep all my cum stored for the best possible orgasm inside her tiny throat.

I admit, I'm a dirty fucker, and I don't give a shit. This is what I was made to do. The only thing I know how. My appetite for pussy will be put to good use when it comes to her. And I think she's starting to realize that.

Yesterday, I ordered the maids to leave her alone for an entire day. I didn't want them interfering, so I got up first thing in the morning to get to my captive. Carrying a bowl of soup, fresh bread, and a couple of crackers, I open the door to her cell and step inside.

The bowl almost tips over when I see her lying with her head on the floor, the chair turned on its side. I manage to tighten my grip and straighten myself before the bowl falls, but I can't take my eyes off the scene in front of me. I'm baffled, so much so that my jaw drops, and I'm left staring at her, wondering what in the hell she was thinking.

She's screaming, moaning, crying—everything at the same time. It's quite amusing but a little worrisome as well. I didn't actually expect her to try to free herself to the point of tumbling over.

"You really are a feisty one, aren't you?" I chuckle a little as I set the bowl, bread, and crackers down and help her up from the ground.

"No!" she squeals. "Let me out of here!"

"Relax. I'm just pulling you up," I say, placing her down in the middle of the cell again.

The antagonizing look on her face makes me smile. "How was it?" I jest.

"Please, take it off!" she mewls.

"Why? I thought you wanted to come?" I muse.

With my finger, I gently tap the dildo, making her squirm in her seat.

"Stop! Please!"

Fuck ... that sound. I love it when she begs.

I bend over and tip her chin up. "First, you tell me ... how many times did you come?"

"I don't know!" she hisses, biting her lip as the

126

buzzing fills her with rage.

I slap her thigh. Not hard, but just to make a point. "Tell me."

She shudders, sucking in a breath, her body completely absorbed in the excruciating nonstop pleasure. "I ... I ..."

"Tell me how many times you came," I growl, grabbing her chin.

"Forty-three."

She lets out an exasperated sigh as I lower the speed on the dildo.

"Hmm ... good ..." I mumble. "And what did you learn?"

"Don't ask questions. You do," she heaves.

"Exactly," I say, circling around her chair. "And what do you give me?"

She shakes her head. "Nothing."

I lean over her chair and stare into her darkened eyes. "Wrong answer."

For good measures, I slap her tit, which jiggles up and down along with her body as she lets out a loud moan.

"Please, don't, it's so ... Ahh!"

I slap her other tit, too. "Painful?"

"I can't take it anymore! Please, turn it off!" she begs.

"Well ... I could do that, but it depends. Will you tell me the truth?"

"I'll do anything you want, just please let me out."

I gaze at her tear-stained cheeks, wondering if she's lying. "Perhaps …"

"Get me out of this chair!" she growls.

I frown at her. "I gave you a choice, remember? You didn't tell me what I wanted to hear, so I had to punish you. You come or I come. You chose this."

"No …" she huffs.

I walk to her front and tilt her chin again. "Actions have consequences. Do you understand?"

"Yes," she says, nodding.

"Good. You will do everything I say. Understood?"

"Yes …" she mumbles.

I grab her hair and pull her up so she'll look at me. "Say it out loud."

"Yes, I'll do anything you say," she says, swallowing.

Just the sight of it makes me smash my lips on hers. I can't help myself; I'm so fucking horny, especially after watching her come without being able to myself. It's time to rectify the situation.

While kissing her, I undo the ropes around the dildo, letting it spring free from its place.

The moment it leaves her sensitive skin, she sucks in a much-needed breath. I don't allow her much time, immediately covering her mouth with mine again. I have to taste her fear, her uncontrollable desire, everything. Sweat drips down her back as I reach for the ropes and loosen them slowly. Her saliva mixes with mine as I tongue her hard, demanding every bit of her submission.

"Give yourself to me," I whisper into her mouth. "Offer yourself."

"Yes …" she mutters.

As the ropes drop to the floor, her hands don't immediately grab my throat, something I suspected she'd do. Instead, she just sits there, accepting my unending desire as I tug her nipples and suck on her lips. She's completely docile, lost in oblivion from the day spent tied to a chair and buzzing between her legs. She must be so tired … but I won't grant her any rest.

Not until she's given me everything she has to offer.

I take my lips off hers and say, "Now … how does it feel?"

She just groans. "Thank you …"

Keeping an eye on her, I grab the bowl of soup, bread, and crackers and bring them over to her. I sit down in front of her, and she looks at me as if I've lost my mind. Her mind must be going crazy, thinking of how she could fight me and escape. Just because I'm sitting on the ground doesn't mean I can't still overpower her. All it takes is a stern eye to subdue her back in her seat.

I lift the bowl and feed her, spooning it into her hungry little mouth. She's eager to gulp it all down along with the bread, not taking the time to chew properly. When she bites on the crackers, she smiles a little, probably delighted at how they taste. Or she's surprised that I brought even more food than last time. She should be. I can give her what she wants, but I can take it away all the same.

I'm the one in control, not her, and with every bite, I can see it become clearer in her eyes … she's finally starting to realize that her life is in my hands now and that she should do everything I say if she wants to live.

Before I give her the final bite, I lean in and say, "What do we say?"

"Thank you …" she mutters.

"Hmm …" I push the final bit of soup-dipped bread into her mouth, letting my finger rest on her tongue. "Suck." My eyes narrow as her tongue wraps around the bread and my finger, and her mouth makes gentle sucking motions. Just the feel of her licking me makes my cock hard.

I think it's time for dessert.

***

SKY

My stomach is full and my energy is back, but my pussy still aches from the buzzing. The moment the Magic Wand left my skin, it felt like all the pain of the past few days was just lifted off me.

I felt happy. Genuinely happy.

I shouldn't be happy, locked in a cell by a man who is only out to hurt me, and yet, in some weird way, I can't help but feel grateful that he removed it. My mind is slowly succumbing to his will, the last fragments of my resistance dripping away. He has me exactly where he wants me.

Vulnerable.

Completely aware of his dominance over me.

Thankful for his mercy.

Almost at the point of begging for it to stop.

At this point, I'd do pretty much anything for more food or kindness, which means I've already lost the fight.

With his index finger and thumb, he tilts my chin and bends over to claim me with his mouth, sucking my very soul out of my body. I'm completely swept away by his assertiveness, the greed in his kisses, and the fierceness in his licks. I've never been owned … but I know without a doubt that this man owns me, whether I want him to or not.

As his lips leave mine, I feel bereft. Like I was finally out of this cell and then I was dropped right back in again. His mouth can do powerful things to me, which scares me a little.

With his index finger alone, he keeps my chin tilted while his other hand cups my breast and kneads it softly. "Now, what will you do?" he murmurs, looking me straight in the eyes.

"Anything you want."

"Oh …" His hand trails down my stomach, and when it touches my pussy, I flinch. "Like finger fucking you again?"

"Please …" I mutter, gazing up into his eyes, practically begging him to stop. "Not that. I can't handle it."

"That sensitive, huh?" He seems amused by my pathetic attempt to sway him, and he keeps his finger pressed on my clit. As if to further establish that I have no control over what he does, he reminds me that the pain could continue, depending on his desire.

As he slides his hand up and down between my legs, I can't help but tighten them.

He frowns, and then a smack to my thigh comes out of nowhere, causing me to squeal. "Don't close your legs for me. Ever. I could do worse things to you."

I know," I say, swallowing away the impending tears.

He grabs my chin and focuses on me. "Don't cry. It doesn't suit your pretty face." The smile that accompanies it confuses me.

"I'm not," I say.

"And you'd better not," he adds, his voice changing to a darker tone.

When he takes his hand off my pussy, I breathe a sigh of relief.

"Tell me what I want to know. Now," he growls.

I think and think, persisting in the notion that I

shouldn't, and yet, without me agreeing, the idea of telling him and letting it all go creeps into the forefront of my mind. In one quick blow, I push it away, realizing the implications of that choice. I can't. I simply can't do that.

Not because I don't want to because believe me, I want to.

Badly.

I would give anything for freedom.

But if I told him the truth, it would turn me into a monster as well.

So I keep my lips slammed together, shaking my head, taking in a sharp breath because I know full well there are repercussions for my denial.

"Fine." He releases my chin, softly stroking my cheek.

He picks up the ropes and starts tying me up again.

"What are you going to do to me?" I ask.

"You'll see …" He hums, a little too excited.

When he's done, my arms are tied to the back of the chair, and he's right in front of me, taking in my naked body like a lollipop he wants to lick.

And then he starts undoing his belt buckle in front of me.

"Time for dessert, Sky," he muses.

My eyes widen as he slips his belt out of his jeans, and when I hear a flick, I flinch. I expect him to hit me with it, but instead, he holds it out like a silent threat. With a demanding posture, he looks upon me as he unzips and his pants drop to the floor.

"Yesterday, you came. Today, it's my turn. Make me come."

His cock his fully erect and I find it hard not to let my eyes zoom in on it.

He licks his lips, biting on the bottom as he says, "Put that mouth of yours to good use. Suck."

I inch forward on the chair, hesitant, knowing that I'm agreeing to something vile. But what other choice do I have? Punishment is always the consequence of not answering him, and I know that. It's just the 'how' that bothers me.

He makes me feel that I have a choice while, in reality, I do not.

The choice is only between three lesser evils … and today I must pick this.

"I have no time and patience for your doubts," he growls. "Wrap your mouth around my cock. Now."

I don't know if this is bad. Compared to the whipping and the nonstop orgasms, this seems like a breeze. I'm really losing my mind.

"C'mere," he growls. "It wasn't a question. If you don't tell me what I want to know, this is what you get. A fucking cock shoved in your mouth. Now open up."

I lick my lips, wetting them properly before opening my mouth, as I think it's better not to go against him. He immediately grips my hair and forces me into his crotch. Directing my mouth over his cock, he pushes it inside, not even giving me time to adjust.

When it touches the back of my throat, I choke a little.

"Yeah, that's it. Make those sounds again," he groans, thrusting his cock in and out of my mouth.

"I can't breathe," I mutter.

"You don't need to," he says with a grin. "All you need to do is take my cock like a good girl. Now open wide."

He shoves it back in before I can protest, making me gag. No one has ever treated me like this—like somebody's fuck toy—but the worst part of it all is that I don't even mind. I did, once, but not anymore. Since I've been stuck in this cell, I've slowly started to fade away, my mind slipping to the point of not caring anymore. Why should I care when it doesn't make a difference? I won't tell them anything, which means I'll die. End of story.

There's no point in fighting it, so I don't. I just sit here and accept whatever he wants to do with me, exactly how he wants. Just like he desires of his little whore.

"Look at me," he says, tilting my head.

I try to look up, but my eyes are watery and my throat is sore, especially when I feel his tip against the back of my tongue.

"Keep your eyes here." He points his index finger and middle finger at his own eyes. "I don't want to see you looking elsewhere, got it?"

I nod, relaxing my throat so it will be easier.

He grips my face and fucks my mouth as if it

belongs to him. One, two, three, and then he pushes in so far that I'm nose-deep against his base, my hands thrashing around on the back of the chair.

I can't move. I can't breathe. I can't do anything except believe in him and his willingness to let me live.

"Take it," he growls, and I can feel him thump in the back of my throat. "Good girl."

When he takes it out again, I heave and gargle, choking on my own saliva. The taste of his salty pre-cum lingers on my tongue; the taste equally as loathsome as it is thrilling. The way he looks at me, as if he's in awe of my ability to cope with his brutality, elates me. Almost as if his approval makes me happy.

He pushes his cock back in and watches me as I take him completely, his eyes glimmering with delight. I don't know why, but I can't stop looking at him. His mouth and the way he bites his lips as he forces himself in and out of my mouth. I'm entranced, feeling connected to him in a way that I can't explain. Like the captor needing the captive, instead of the other way around.

"Fuck. Suck me harder. That's it. Oh, your mouth feels so good," he moans.

For some reason, my pussy thumps from what he says.

I shouldn't feel aroused by what he's doing, but my body has a mind of its own.

Each time his tip reaches the back of my throat, my still-sensitive clit tingles, and I want to touch myself.

It's idiotic, especially after those forty-three orgasms, and yet, it's the truth.

"You like this, don't you?" he says, thrusting even faster. "Do you enjoy it when a man fucks your face?"

I don't answer, but I think he can see it in my eyes. The unwanted longing. The wetness building between my thighs.

"Fuck me … keep looking at me like that. Let me see how much you want my fucking cock," he growls.

Pre-cum drips down my throat, mixing with my saliva and coating his base. I'm feeling out of this world, as he shoves his length into me, forcing me to sit here and accept it. I'm nuts. Completely nuts and drunk on his domination.

"Hungry for more?" he asks. "Eat my fucking cock like a good girl and I'll reward you with my cum."

He seems consumed with lust from the way he talks to me, but I don't even mind; his need to claim me completely enraptures me.

Within a second, he's wrapped the belt he was holding around my neck and is pulling it toward him. I struggle to breathe as he uses it as a leash, keeping my head in place while he fucks me hard. My mind is spinning out of control, wanting to escape, and wanting to beg him to come at the same time.

"Here it comes. I'm gonna blow in your throat," he says gruffly.

He arches his back, holds my head near his base, and then the pulsing begins. Jets of seed spurt into the back of my throat, causing me to gag.

"Swallow," he commands, while he pushes my face deeper into him. "Every last drop."

I push back the thought of coughing it up as it keeps coming and coming, like a never-ending stream of cum. I swallow as much as I can as he keeps going, the salty taste quite good, which I didn't expect.

Five thrusts and his cock turns flaccid, slipping from my mouth. With a content smile on his face, he wipes my lip and pushes his finger into my mouth, making sure I lick up every bit.

Panting, he unfurls the belt from around my neck, allowing me to breathe properly again.

"Such a good girl, finishing your dessert ..." he says, caressing my cheek. "Shame you can't be mine for longer than twenty-one days."

He tucks his cock back into his pants and zips up, clearing his throat.

Then something happens. I spurt out a few words. Words that I already regret. "I could be."

I don't know why I say it.

It's so completely wrong and stupid.

But in the back of my mind, something just clicked when he said that.

And I blurted it out before I could stop myself.

The truth is I would take any life over none, however cruel it may be. If it meant I'd be his forever, I would choose that over death.

He frowns, cocking his head. "You would choose

me? Over death?"

I nod—first slowly, then fast. I wouldn't hesitate to make that decision, which scares me. How far have I gone? Who would choose a man like this over death?

I would.

But I can't guarantee that I would let him live if he did.

I swallow again as he steps back and studies me. He touches his mask, gently sliding his fingers over it as if it's in the way.

"You're lying," he says.

"No," I say quickly.

"Enough!"

His voice is suddenly louder, and it makes me afraid because the belt is still in his hands. He broadens his stance, his lips downward as if he's disgusted with me ... or with himself. Staring at me, he says gruffly, "Don't ever say that again."

"Sorry ..." I mutter, not really sure what else I should say.

He breathes out a sigh. "I'll forget about it, this time, since you've done so well today. For now, I'll let you rest. You'll need it for the next time I come here."

The kindness in his statement is quickly outdone by the threat that follows, and I can't help but wonder if he's actually mad at me for suggesting I could be his for real.

I say the first thing that comes to mind. "Please don't be mad."

"Don't," he says, making a fist.

"I'm only doing it to protect something …" I say.

"Is protecting your secret worth your body? All the pain? The submission? The humiliation? Is it worth your fucking soul?" He's so in my face that I swallow from anxiety. I didn't expect him to be this up-close and personal about it.

"Yes," I say, and the moment I say the word, it feels like a huge burden slides off me. Yes, I would sacrifice anything. Some things in life are more important.

He squints. "It would be so much easier if you'd work with me here."

"No." I frown. "It would be much easier for you to say no to your superior."

His lip twitches. "You assume too much."

"I know you aren't the boss around here. I've deduced that much."

He bites on his lip. "Clever girl. What if I said it was true? It still wouldn't change anything about your situation."

"You don't have to say it's true. I already know it is."

"How?" he growls.

I smile. "Because you don't know what to ask me. You keep asking for the truth, but you don't even know what it's about. You don't know what I can tell you, which tells me your boss won't tell you what you should ask. He doesn't want *you* to know the full truth."

This statement makes him suck in a big breath through his nose, his eyes smoldering with rage.

"Am I right?" I muse.

He grabs my neck, squeezing tight. "You have no idea who you're up against, but you won't know either. You won't get to see the outside of this cell unless you cooperate. You won't even get your fucking life back if you don't tell me the truth."

I turn my head away from him. "I don't care."

"You should fucking care!" he yells.

"Why? Do you? Will your boss fire you if you don't pull the information out of me? Good."

He screams, "I care because I don't want you to die!"

He's breathing out loud, and my breathing has stopped. He said it before, that he doesn't want me to die, but I always assumed it was because it would mean he failed. That he wasn't able to extract the information from me. But from the way he said it now, laced with emotions, I can't help but think that he actually does care more than he tries to let on.

His grip on my neck loosens as we look at each other without really looking. We're both lost in our own minds, the endless tangle of complications and threats that seeped into our lives. Ruled by the shadows ... unable to make our own choices.

He's just as much of a prisoner in this place as I am.

Without saying a word, he gets up and leaves.

He doesn't even pick up the ropes or the dildo. The room is still a mess, and I wonder if he even notices. If he even cares.

Maybe he's too guilt-stricken. Or maybe he knows more than I think he does.

The man behind the mask cares more about me than he should, and in a moment of clarity, I realize that he might be my only way out of here. I have to make him want to drag me out of this cell, so I'm safe. I have to make him believe he has to claim more control over my surroundings and me. This cell isn't it.

And the only way to do that is by alerting his superiors to my insubordination.

Time to put those ropes he left to good use.

DAY 9

ANGEL

Like a possessed man, I hit the boxing bag, quickly switching from one foot to the other, always on the move. I focus on jabbing as quickly and as powerful as I possibly can, blocking out my environment. Other members of the company are training as well, but I ignore them completely. I'm much too obsessed with Sky at the moment, which is why I'm here in the training facility in the first place. I'm trying to take my mind off her, but it's not working one bit.

I hit the bag so hard, it tears open, sand pouring out.

"Fuck!" I growl, punching it once more, so it drops

to the ground.

Others look up at me as I storm out of the training room and into the locker room. I have to get out of this place. My father convinced me a day of training would get my head out of the clouds, but it's only getting worse. I have to get the fuck out of here and back to her.

I quickly shower and dress before storming out of the building and racing off in my car. It's quite a trip from the training facility to the compound where we keep the prisoners. Of course, my father was smart enough not to put the two together or even anywhere near his own home. Disguised as an exclusive dojo that does not take any new members, our training facility is the ideal cover-up for a school that essentially trains killers and assassin. When officials find out the truth, my father bribes them—end of story.

I used to spend a lot of time there, back in the days … when I still had my buddies around me and my teacher hadn't vanished. Those were good times. Unfortunately, it's become impossible for me to step in here without a grudge lately.

Especially, since I should be doing something else. Like fucking with Sky's mind.

When I arrive at the compound, I jump out of my car and make my way to her cell immediately. The closer I get, the heavier my heart feels. I don't know why I care so much. Why she haunts me so. I'm much too invested. I feel too much. It makes me wish I could

144

rip my own heart out. Except, then I'd be dead—and I'd rather not be.

I'm not her. I'm not willing to die for my cause. Hell, I'm not even willing to give up the luxury and privileges that come with being the son of the Don. I'm a son of a bitch, and I know it damn well. But this son of a bitch cares about her, too. I'm not just evil. I don't want her to fucking die, and she knows it.

Fuck, I'm like an open book, waiting to be read.

I knew it. I should've known it the moment I stepped into her cell that she'd feel me. Not just physically, but also mentally … on a different level. I can't explain it. It's as if we're connected in more ways than just as captor and captive. She can see it too … I can see it in her eyes. She feels like she knows me, and yet she doesn't know why. I do, and I fear the day she'll find out.

I thought I could do this. I thought I could break her without revealing myself, but the more time I spend with her, the more I realize that she's going to find out who I am sooner or later. It's only a matter of time.

As I stand in front of her cell, staring at the metal, I think of her and her curves, her sweet lips, those beautiful eyes. I groan, realizing that I can't have my cake and eat it too. I'm torn between getting the information for my father and taking her out of there. I want her—every day more than the day before, and it's eating me up. Touching her brings back memories I should've pushed away, but they keep coming back to the forefront of my mind.

That girl who I spent a week with. The girl of my dreams. The girl I'm now ruining.

I want her, but I can't save her because if I do, my father will probably kill me.

I'm a bastard who can't even choose.

My life or hers.

I can't choose.

I punch the door, roaring out loud.

She'll hate me if I reveal myself now, but I know I must. One day. If I want to save her, she has to trust me, and she's already let me know she won't. But maybe she will if she knows who I am, and maybe she'll finally tell me the truth, too.

But if I do that … she'll never want me the way I want her.

The question is … does it matter?

I'm so consumed by her that I'm not even sure it matters if she agrees or not, which makes it even more disturbing. I'm really fucked up.

I blink, staring down at the floor, wondering what the fuck I'm doing and why. Time is ticking; I can't procrastinate and ponder while she's sitting there in her cell, wasting away.

So I take a deep breath and enter the combination and perform the retinal scan. Then I put on my mask, securing it tightly behind my head. The door opens and I hesitantly step into the cell. I can't see her anywhere.

The chair is still in the middle of the room, but that's all I can see. It's too dark, so I turn around to press a button on the keypad to turn on the light.

That's when something wraps around my head.

It's so quick; I don't even see it coming.

Something sears into my neck, squeezing so tight that I struggle to breathe. My hands instinctively lash onto whatever is gripping me, but the unexpected lack of oxygen has decreased my strength significantly. It tightens to the point that I choke.

I turn around to face my attacker, who's none other than Sky.

Tucked into the top corner of the room like a spider, she weaved a web large enough to keep her above the ground using only the ropes that I'd left yesterday. She jumps me as if I'm the prey, locking onto my back with her legs crossed around my waist, pulling the rope even further toward the ground.

My body isn't prepared for the added weight on top of losing my breath, so it topples over. She quickly makes her way from underneath me and gets up only to tug on the rope so hard, I slide over the floor.

"Gotcha, motherfucker," she yells, as I claw at the rope around my neck.

"Don't. Do. This," I heave, rolling over the floor in an attempt to wriggle off the rope.

"Shut up," she shouts, pulling even harder. "I hope you feel the same pain I did or worse."

I can feel her anger down to my bones, and I know

she won't stop until I'm dead.

There's only one thing left to do.

With trouble, I reach into my pocket, trying to ignore the desire to put my finger between the rope and my neck so I can reach for my emergency beeper. When I push the button, I stop fighting her completely.

I didn't want to do this, but she leaves me no choice.

I already regret it the moment I push the button.

But there is no other way.

***

SKY

When he stops moving, I wait and look at him. He seems to have passed out, but I can't tell for sure. His eyes are closed and he's stopped twitching, so I guess it's safe. There's no way to find out other than just to go for it.

So I drop the rope.

Breathing loudly, I step over his body, making sure he's not getting up to grab me afterward. But he doesn't.

For some reason, the thought of him dying flashes through my mind, and my heart sinks into my shoes. I don't know why it upsets me. It shouldn't bother me in the first place.

There's no time for any feelings or emotions. I have to get out of here, *now*.

The food yesterday gave me enough energy to make a sprint for the door. I was clever enough to attach the rope to loose hooks on the wall, forming a web that could barely hold my body. I waited for him ... minutes ... hours ... maybe longer, I don't recall. All I know is the urge to fight became too strong the moment he told me cared that I could die.

Something about the way he talked sounded too familiar, too intrusive, too close. It snapped me out of my trance as if I was dropped from the clouds. The man in front of me was no longer just my savior; he was also the only one who could get me out of the cell.

I wanted to hurt him.

Badly.

Like he had hurt me, only worse.

I wanted to scrape his soul out of his guts.

So I decided that instead of sucking up to him, I would take it upon myself to get out of here. I realized he had unintentionally left the ropes out of pure frustration, and that I could use them against him.

Just as I pass the door, I feel the air flowing through me. I don't know where it's coming from, but it feels like it's coming from all around me, and I suck it in like no tomorrow.

This is too good to be true.

But I must believe.

My sight feels sharpened and my muscles have renewed energy from the adrenaline coursing through my veins. Completely naked, I run through the big hall, past the kitchen where the ladies are. They're washing the dishes, and the moment they see me, their hands drop everything. Plates and glasses clatter on the floor. Jaw's drop, and that's when I notice the horrible truth. The sole reason they never spoke to me. It wasn't because they didn't want to. It was because they couldn't.

Their tongues are missing.

They scream; the most shrill, violent noise I've heard in a long time.

In a rush, I pass through the hallway to the left, not having a clue where I'm going, but I soak in as many of the details as I can. When, not if, I get out, I need to remember this place so I can describe it accurately. My mind is like a canvas where I paint the pictures that I see, so vividly, that I could tell the police exactly what this place looks like.

Vile.

Like a slaughterhouse, but for humans instead of pigs.

Black paint chips off the rusty walls, the metallic floor underneath my feet clinging as I run.

To the left is a room filled with toys. Adult toys. Whips, chains, crops, paddles, dildos, clamps, cuffs— you name it and I wouldn't be surprised if it's there. He had the tools to use me as he saw fit from this room.

It's both frightening and exhilarating, to finally know where he got it all.

It's as if I'm seeing into the monster's lair, witnessing the full extent of his darkness.

But how far does it reach?

Not soon after, I pass a room that literally makes the hair on my skin stand up.

The sight of it stops me in my tracks.

A chamber filled with racks of weapons, from guns, rifles, and machine guns to all kinds of knives and swords; kitchen knives, axes, butcher's knives, toothed blades, swords, spears, and more. And that's not all.

A range of devices usually found in tool sheds like screwdrivers, clippers, and other cutting tools lie spread out on the table like some sort of exhibition. Medicinal supplies and an assortment of syringes and painful looking tools that you'd find at the dentist or in an OR fill one of the tables. Ropes and ties of all sorts hang on the wall, as well as a shovel, bags, a white suit, and a face mask. In the middle of the room is an electric chair, and in front of that, a table with metallic binds, the ceiling littered with torture devices.

A nightmare come to life.

Holding my breath, I avert my eyes and try to erase the image from my memory. When he said there were worse things he could do, he wasn't joking, that's for sure. Just looking at it makes me feel sick.

I quickly step away from the door and find a robe to cover myself up. After putting it on, I make my way through the next hallway until I arrive at a dead-end. In the middle is a long ladder leading up to an escape hatch.

Could it be …?

I run toward it and climb up the ladder, determined to make it out. I just pray to god that the hatch is unlocked. When I'm there, I use one arm to steady myself while I twist the wheel with the other. Adrenaline rushes through me, pumping me up, pushing me beyond my limits as I put all my strength into opening the hatch. To my amazement, it's working. The metal is actually moving, although slowly.

I don't have much time left. My captor might be passed out, but he'll be back on his feet soon enough, and then he'll be coming straight for me. I have to get away before he's awake.

The final push swings the hatch open. Bright light bursts through the hole, causing me to squint. This is it. This is what I've been waiting for all this time. The moment I could outsmart him, even if it was only for a few minutes. It was enough to escape.

I'm free.

I can see the world, the sky; I can smell the grass, the air.

Freedom is waiting for me. All I need to do is climb up.

As I hoist myself over the hatch and out into the world, my brittle bones graze the metal, and I scream out in pain. A large, gaping wound appears on my stomach. I won't let it stop me from succeeding, though, so I push on and crawl out completely.

On hands and feet, I move away from the compound, breathing in the air that I've missed for so long. It smells so good, I could cry. It's crazy how much a person can miss the smell of fresh grass and the wind blowing through their hair ... How much I've taken it for granted.

Just ten days.

Ten days have passed and I feel completely wrecked.

I take a deep breath and get up on my feet to look at my surroundings and get out of here. I don't know where I should go, but anywhere is better than here.

Right when I'm up on my feet, a hand grips my ankle. I scream as I'm pulled over and land face-first in the grass.

"No!" I scream, my nails digging into the ground, scratching up dirt as someone drags me back toward the hatch. "Let go!"

A growl ensues. "Son of a—"

I look up to see three hooded and suited-up men standing in front of me, guns in their hands.

Fear ripples through me as I look back and see the man in the mask pulling on my leg. No matter how much I twist and turn, he won't let me go.

And then one of the men steps forward and uses the back of his gun to slam me on the head, knocking me out cold.

DAY 10

ANGEL

I pace around in my room, rubbing my chin because I'm fucking annoyed and everything itches like fuck. This always happens when I'm anxious. I'm waiting for my father to finally tell me what he's going to do with Sky.

Yesterday, after she escaped, the men came just in time to get her back into the hatch, but it wasn't without a price. I had to contain her. It's worth it.

Everything is going according to plan.

Damn, my neck still hurts.

When I pass a mirror, I look up at the red mark on my neck that still sears when I touch it. It's a good reminder of her persistence and the stubborn bravery she hid so well. Those ropes fucking hurt. I didn't expect her to actually go for it, though.

I'm a mess because of this. It won't happen again.

I was so weak yesterday. After the attack, I barely managed to follow her. The men who subdued her brought her back to her cell. That's when my father came into the compound, too. He seemed upset, but I didn't care. I just wanted to get the fuck out of there.

So I did. I left her alone in that cell and went back to the mansion to get some assistance from our personal doctor. He did his magic on my neck and told me to take a few hours of rest. My throat felt squished and slammed shut, but according to him, there was no permanent damage.

I'm lucky, he said.

Fuck being lucky, I just want to make it out of this alive.

I sigh, staring at my messed-up bed. My clothes lie scattered on the floor. I didn't even go through the trouble of bringing them to the laundry room. I just threw myself onto my bed and lay there for hours.

I don't know if I slept or not. I can't remember. The only thing I know is that I never feel rested. Not as long as she's in that cell. Alone. Or not.

I don't know what's happening, which is why I'm so restless.

When the door to my room opens, I turn around and hold my breath. It's my father.

"So ... you let her escape."

"Sorry, that wasn't how I had things in mind," I say.

"No, but it did happen." He sighs, stepping inside and closing the door behind him. "Angel, is there something you need to tell me?"

I frown. "No? Why?"

He looks down at his feet. "Well, she seems to have said something about ropes being there ... that you left them."

"Ah god, yeah." I slam my hand against my forehead. "I was so pissed off that I left without taking them with me. It was stupid of me."

"Stupid or not, she used them against you. You could've died."

I cock my head. I could've died, yeah, but this is the first time he brings it up. Why? Something doesn't feel right.

"You don't care if I die," I say.

He shakes his head, frowning at me. "What? That's nonsense. I do care." He smiles at me as if he's said this before, but it's completely new to me. "I always worry that something might happen to you."

I don't believe one word of it. "Yeah, right," I jest, shaking it off.

"Angel ... believe it or not, I am your father, and at this moment, I don't think it's good for you to go back in there."

"What?" My jaw drops.

156

What the fuck?

He holds up his hands as if to soften the blow. "Listen, I know this might not be what you want to hear right now, but I think you should take a day off."

"Nuh-uh. No. No way," I say, stomping through the room to grab my clothes. I'm still only dressed in my pajamas, but I don't give a fuck anymore.

"You really should consider this before blowing me off just like that," he says.

"No!" I say, pointing at him. "You told me I had to do this, now I'm doing it, and all of the sudden you want to take me off the job? That's not what we agreed on."

"I'm not saying I'm taking you off," he says, putting his hands on his side. "I'm just saying you should take a break. Take a day to rethink your strategy."

"And do what?" I shout, feeling more and more powerless.

"I have another job for you, if you want something to do."

"Fuck that ..." I say, putting on my shirt. "*She* is my job."

"And you can continue doing that job tomorrow. Just one day, Angel. That's all I'm saying."

I make a face at him. "I don't have a choice, do I?"

He taps his feet on the floor. "No. I'm making sure she's right back where she belongs while you get some much-needed rest. Plus, the doctor told me you really needed to stay away from her for at least a day. You know, to prevent further damage."

"You think she'd pull that trick twice?" I laugh. "How stupid do you think I am?"

"She seems inventive, and I'd rather not risk another one of these ... problems."

"She is my job. *Mine*."

"And she's my prisoner. You'd best not forget that," he says, clearing his throat. "And you almost let her escape."

"Fine ..." I sit down on my bed, punching the sheets. "But I used the beeper. I could've also just let her run."

"You know what happens if you did that," he says, with a smile that is so creepy, it makes my skin crawl.

"Yeah, I know," I say. I know damn well what he's threatening me.

His love is all a farce. It only exists when he's content; but when he's not, you'd better hide.

"But you did well," he adds. "Now, let my boys handle the rest."

"How long?" I spit.

"As long as needed," he muses.

"No."

"Well, they have her now, and you're not getting anywhere near her for today."

"What are you gonna do to her?" I growl.

"We're taking care of her. Relax."

"She's my job. If they mess it up, she won't talk."

"I know. Just let me handle it, okay?" he says

158

calmly.

I grind my teeth. I thought he'd only keep her busy for a few hours, but not for an entire day. This wasn't part of my plan. How long is he gonna try and keep me away? I can't let him take over.

"I'll do something else. But only for today. I want to finish what I started with her, so tomorrow she's mine again."

"All right. Deal. So long as you take on that other job that I have for you."

I sigh. "What do I need to do?"

He smiles. "I thought you'd never ask."

***

Nine hours later

I'm following my target in a car, trying to be as inconspicuous as possible. I brought my silencer gun with me, and I'm waiting for the best opportunity to attack. I'm not interested in going to jail again, so the best course of action is to wait until they park their car somewhere and come out. I have to follow them to a secluded spot, and I don't care how long I have to tail them for that to happen. So long as I can get this job done, I can go back home and get back to the real work.

Sky.

Just being away from her for a few hours is already killing me. Especially because I don't know what's happening to her right now. It eats me up inside.

All the more reason to get this done quick.

The car I'm following turns left, and so do I. I don't know who is inside. All I know is that there are two people, and my father wants them dead. It isn't even a job for a client of ours; it's my father's wish, so I guess he must know them. All he gave me was a license plate, nothing more. No names. No faces. Nothing. I don't even have a picture, so I don't know what they look like. I find it concerning, but whatever. As long as I get it done, I guess he can't complain.

Suddenly, the car makes a U-turn, swerving in my direction.

Could they have seen me? Impossible, the windows are darkly tinted. But maybe I haven't been careful enough.

I quickly roll down my window and take out my gun, making sure I'm in range before pointing it out.

That's when I notice the person staring back at me through the window as the car passes mine.

It's none other than Phoenix Sullivan and his girlfriend, Vanessa Starr. He's my former companion, an assassin who worked for our company until he got caught and went to jail, just like me. Only, when we came out, he no longer wanted to work for us. He wanted to kill *her* instead.

And yet there she is, in the flesh, alive and well. I

knew he couldn't do it.

He always told me he hated her so much for putting him in jail. I thought he'd actually kill her when I left him to go back to my father.

Maybe he's still thinking about it. Who knows? We haven't spoken in a long time. And now that I see him again, I realize my mistake.

What am I doing here?

Am I really going to kill my partner? The one I used to see as a friend? Someone who made the choice that I couldn't?

"Don't you fucking dare," he shouts through the window.

I sigh and lower my gun.

I can't. I won't. I refuse.

My father wants him dead, but I won't kill him. He's gone too far if he thinks I can kill one of our own. I don't care if Phoenix no longer wants to work with us; he was like me. It feels like I'd kill myself if I'd pull the trigger now.

"Fucking hell," Phoenix growls. "So you're the one who's been tailing us. I should've known."

The disappointment in his voice cuts through me like a blade. "I didn't fucking know it was you, all right."

"Sure, you didn't," he muses. "First, you wanted to kill her, and now, you've come to kill me, too. Great."

"It was a job, and I didn't know it was you. I swear to fucking god." It's the truth. If I'd known my father was putting me up to this, I'd have put a stop to it before it happened.

"Can't you just leave me in peace?" Phoenix yells. "For fuck's sake, Angel. Get a fucking grip. I have."

"Yeah, I can see that," I joke.

He doesn't seem to like it that much, as he pulls out his own gun now.

"Hey, don't do that," I say, holding up my hands. "I wasn't going to shoot you. I can't."

"Of course, not. But I can," he growls.

"Wait! Don't. You don't wanna do that," I say.

"Yeah, I do."

"We used to be friends. I didn't know it was you, I promise. I didn't want to do this in the first place, but it's complicated, okay?"

After a few seconds, he lowers the gun again, and then he growls, "Get the fuck outta here."

I frown and sigh. "I told you I'm fucking sorry, okay? I don't want you dead. If I knew it was you, I never would have followed you."

"Tell that to your fucking pops," he says. "How do I know he won't come after us again?"

"I'll make him stop," I say.

"Yeah, right. Did you forget the part where I owe him for getting me out of jail? He won't let it rest, that's for sure."

"I'll make him stop. You have my word." I nod. "You don't owe him or me anything. And if he hammers on, I'll pay him whatever you owe myself."

162

He frowns. "You'd do that …"

"Yeah. I don't want to see you get in trouble, and I'm done fighting. I don't want to lose whatever friendship we have left."

He just groans and stares out the front window, tapping his dashboard.

"I won't bother you again and neither will the company. You're free. I give you my word."

"Fine …" he growls. "But I don't ever wanna see your fucking face again."

I swallow and nod, realizing the implications of what I've said and done.

Nothing I do will make this right. It's too late. He hates me, and rightfully so.

I once tried to kill his girlfriend because my father made her a target. I thought I could kill her because Phoenix once wanted her dead, too … But, apparently, they got back together. Of course, he didn't take it well. Nobody would.

I understood that I ruined it all.

All those years I spent training with him. Killing targets with him. Evading the law with him.

It'll never be the same ever again.

That's when he revs the engine and races off. I watch his car drive into the distance until it disappears from view.

He's gone. For good this time.

I wonder if I'll ever see him again. And I wonder if I do, whether he'll kill me. He probably would.

DAY 11

ANGEL

It takes me an entire day to get back home.

I even had to sleep in a cheap motel along the side of the road because I couldn't drive any longer without passing out on the steering wheel. The day had been long with all that tailing, and I needed some rest, despite my unwillingness. I didn't stay very long, though, because I had much more important things on my mind—like how the fuck my father decided it was a good idea to kill Phoenix Sullivan, my best fucking friend.

When I'm back at the mansion, I immediately storm up to my father's office. When I find out he isn't even there, I'm livid, but I know exactly where to find him next. He has only one place he'd go. His restaurant. It's my father's cover; a business he uses to mask the real one. This is where he meets his clients and pretends he knows about food, even though his expertise is killing and blood.

He owns many all over the country, and his connections make it impossible to see through the fakery. That's why he hasn't been pinched yet; they haven't been able to prove his connection to anything other than the restaurants. They're a good cover, but stupid nonetheless.

I drive to his biggest restaurant and barge in. He's lounging in the corner with a companion or whoever the fuck. I don't care.

"Why the fuck did you try to have me kill Phoenix?" I yell as I slam open the door.

My father's fork is near his mouth, a juicy steak dripping blood on his plate as he stares at me. He puts down his fork, gently dabs the napkin on his lips, and clears his throat.

"Marcus, I'm afraid I have to step out for a minute."

"All right," Marcus says.

"Excuse me," my father says, and he gets up and walks toward me. "You, come with me," he whispers.

I follow him to the back of the restaurant where the employees take a smoking break.

"Afraid your buddy is going to find out you're a

piece of shit?" I growl at him.

I'm tired of waiting for answers.

"Angel, you know how business works."

"Yeah, I know damn well, unfortunately. You had no fucking right to go after Phoenix." I kick over the ashtray that's on the ground.

"He ignored my requests. Doesn't take orders."

"He quit," I interject. "He doesn't *want* to take jobs from us anymore. It's over."

"Why do you think I put out the order to kill him?" he muses, laughing a bit as if it's one big joke to him.

"He's my fucking friend! You have some balls," I growl. "Enough. I'm done. I don't care what you think, but I'm not letting you kill him."

"He could talk about the business, and we don't want that to happen," my father says, putting a cigar in his mouth and lighting it.

"He won't. I can fucking promise you that. I know Phoenix … I've known him since we were teenagers. He wouldn't do that. He just wants to be left alone."

My father sighs and takes a whiff of his cigar. He offers it to me too, but I pass.

"Leave him alone, Dad. Enough is enough. He's done, and I will be too if you don't let it rest."

"You care that much about him, huh?" he says, looking sideways at me while blowing out the smoke.

I don't answer. It's none of his business.

"Fine," he says after a while. "I'll let him live. But don't think this will be the norm."

"I know. But Phoenix has been a good killer. He deserves his break."

"Right …" My father turns his head and continues smoking.

I can't help but wonder if he sent me because he knew we were friends and that it was all a test. If it was, I failed, but I don't give a shit.

"I'm glad you showed a little backbone, Angel," my father mutters. "It's become a rare trait in this world."

I frown. "What do you mean?"

He looks at me with a grin. "Well, not a lot of people dare to stand up to me."

I shrug and take the cigar from him when he offers it again, taking a whiff to calm myself down.

"I failed the job. If you need to punish me, so be it. I don't give a fuck," I say, blowing out the smoke and handing the cigar back to him.

"No need. You've already been punished."

"How?" I look him in the eyes. I don't get what he means, but I don't like the sound of it either.

He just smiles awkwardly at me. And that's when I realize what he means.

"Fuck, no …" I turn around.

"Where are you going?" my father yells as I run back into the restaurant.

I don't reply. He already knows anyway. That motherfucker. He's toying with me. Playing with my mind because he wants me to be something more than just his son. More than just a killer. A soulless, cold-hearted creature with a heart of stone.

Enough is enough.

He can ruin my fucking life, but he can't ruin hers.

Sky.

It's all about her. It's always been about her.

That's why he wanted me out of the building in the first place. That job to kill Phoenix wasn't just another job. It was a distraction so my father could work on her instead.

My father walks out of the restaurant right when I pull up my car. He yells something, which I can't and don't want to hear as I hit the gas and race off. I ignore all stop signs and drive so fast, I could risk the cops pulling me over, but it doesn't matter. Nothing matters except getting to her. Now.

When I finally arrive at the compound, I jump out of my car and rush toward the hatch. I jump halfway down the ladder and run through the hallways. That's when I spot the men. Hooded, still carrying whips and knives. Blood drips from their blades.

Fury coursing through my veins causes me to lash out, grabbing the nearest one standing in the torture room and hitting him in the back so hard he breaks his back. As he falls to the ground, I grab his head and twist until I hear it crack.

Roaring out loud, I charge at the next one, who doesn't even see it coming before it's too late. I grab the knife he's holding and jam it into his chest, muffling his screams with my hand.

"Shut the fuck up!" I scream. "You don't get to fucking make a sound! You fucking hurt her, didn't you? You fucking touched her!"

"Angel!"

I hear my father's voice behind me, and I turn my head while still sitting on top of my victim. He followed me all the way here from the restaurant, despite his conversations with one of his partners. I guess some things are more important, but fuck, I wish he hadn't come after me.

"Get the fuck off my men," he growls.

"They fucking hurt her!" I scream, getting up on my feet. "With fucking torture devices."

"Yes," he says.

I make a face. "You fucking knew? You knew they were going to do this?"

"You were on a break. I still need the information, you know."

"You fucking put them up to this, didn't you?" I growl, picking up the nearest piece of equipment I can find and throwing it against the wall. "You fucking let them hurt her!"

"Calm down, Angel."

"I will not fucking calm down! She's mine. *Mine.*"

"I understand you might have … feelings for her … but—"

"No, you don't get to decide what I think or feel. It's over. It's done. I'm in charge now," I scream in his face. "I don't give a damn if you want me off this case, she is mine and mine alone."

"I still require her information," he says calmly.

"I don't care. I will get it out of her, don't you fucking worry about that. I'll do whatever the fuck it takes to get her to talk, but I will not let anyone near her again. No one except me. Got that?"

He shrugs. "All right. If you insist."

"I am not taking a break again. You will leave me in peace, with her, and you will let me do my job. I will decide how I go about that," I say, breathing out loud.

"As long as you give me what I want."

"I will give you what you need, but don't you dare fucking lay a finger on her." I'm so close to his face, I could bite off his nose.

I would if he was some ordinary guy.

If he weren't my father, I would've impaled him on that goddamn rack of weapons already.

"She's mine," I repeat.

"All right ..." he says, stepping back a little. "But did you really have to kill my men?"

"That's what you get for trying to mess with my job. I don't give a shit about them or their lives. I told you I wanted to deal with her *my* way. You know how I am and *you* gave me this job, so it's your fucking responsibility. End of story."

I push past my father, still furious as hell. I walk straight to her cell, do the retinal scan and press the numbers to open the door, not even caring to put on my mask.

What I find is a broken girl.

Lifeless.

Her body lies on the floor like a wet rag.

Buckets of water thrown on the floor near her.

A chair in the middle painted red from blood. Her blood.

Red welts and puncture wounds mark her body. Welts and wounds that aren't mine.

How fucking dare they.

She's *mine*.

As I step into her cell, I take a second to wipe my bloody hands on my shirt. No matter how hard I try, it won't disappear completely, and for some reason that makes me feel bad. I look at her small, frail body and wonder how in the hell I'm going to fix this. They've beaten her to the point she's lost her will to live. I never thought he would go this far ... that he would ruin her to a point of no return. This shouldn't have happened ... and it's all my fucking fault.

Going on one knee, I gently pick her up and hold her in my arms as I get back up. She's cold, and she isn't even shivering. Holding her close to my body in the hopes that it'll make her a bit warmer, I walk out of the cell and into the light. Right now, the only thing on my mind is her safety, and nothing's gonna stand in my way of securing it.

My father stands in the middle of the big hall, watching me, along with the three women who've been working in the kitchen all day. Their silent looks tell me enough, but nothing will stop me. Rage has taken me beyond what I thought I was willing to sacrifice. I feel invincible, capable of destroying the world if that's what it takes to keep her with me.

"Don't," my father says. "You're making a mistake."

"No, you did, the moment you took me away from her! Don't fucking dare to interfere again."

"Angel …"

"You might be my father, but I'm the best you have. You know damn well no one in this company can win against me, so don't even try to take her away from me. You'd better not get in my way."

"I can't let you take her out of this place," he says.

"Watch me," I growl, walking toward him.

"Angel, you know this place is specifically designed to contain our prisoners. If you take her out, who knows what will happen. She might escape, and this time for real. You don't want that to happen. You know what the consequences are."

"She won't," I spit.

"You don't know that."

"I'll make sure of it."

He blocks my way, standing in front of me, so I stop next to him. He doesn't attempt to grab my arm, even though I suspected he would. He's smarter than I thought.

"So you're just gonna leave? You do realize this will never end well?" he says.

172

I glance at him. "I will give you your information. But I will do it *my way*. Where I want. How I want. My terms."

"You know it will fail."

"We'll see about that," I growl, gripping her body tight. "Now leave me the hell alone."

I walk past him, blowing out a deep breath as he lets me pass. He doesn't attempt to stop me like before. Probably because he's seen my determination and realizes it has its strength. Or maybe because he fears it.

With Sky's life hanging by a thread, I wrap my hands around her body and let her head rest on my shoulder. For a second, as I walk through the hallway, I glance over my shoulder. An unfamiliar feeling rushes through me the moment I see my father's stupefied face. Amusement, maybe. But it feels more like pride.

"Where are you going?" he yells after me.

With a confident sneer, I answer, "Home."

DAY 12

SKY

I wake up on a warm, fluffy surface with bones that feel like they've been sawed in half. But it smells oddly good here … like freshly plucked flowers. Like I've been bathed in soap without my knowledge.

My eyes are barely able to open, but I force them to show me where I am.

Yesterday, I passed out in my cell after being cut too many times. I still remember each slice of the blade as it pierced my flesh. The memory alone makes me sit up straight in bed, screaming my lungs out.

Only then do I realize that I'm actually in a completely different room. A real bedroom … with curtains, a soft bed, light. Simple things, but they make me so happy I could cry.

Where am I? And how did I get here?

When I touch my own skin, it feels weirdly soft, like silk. As I lean in I can definitely tell someone has washed me. I wonder if it was *him*.

Right at that moment, the door slightly opens and a foot steps in.

When the mask appears, I crawl back to the headboard, holding my legs, yelling, "Stay away!"

It's him. The guy who tormented me for so long.

How long, I don't know exactly.

Days turned into nights without so much as a sliver of sunlight passing by to show me the time. How many days has it been? How much time do I still have before they kill me?

I pull back, prepared to draw my claws, as the man steps further into the room. But when I notice the tray of food he's holding, I succumb to the saliva building in my mouth.

"It's okay," he says. "I'm not here to hurt you."

"I don't believe you," I say, but my voice is barely there, only a raspy sound coming from my throat.

God, I'm in really bad shape.

"Where am I?" I ask with quivering lips.

"In the guest room." He cocks his head, gazing at me.

When he comes closer, I hold my legs tight, but then a sharp pain in my stomach makes me loosen my grip. I peek under the sheets and notice the bandages covering my belly, legs, and arms.

"You were wounded quite badly," he says, setting the tray down on the nightstand. "I had no other choice but to bring you here."

He makes it seem as if that's a negative thing, but this room is a huge upgrade for me. Not that it makes me any less of a captive.

I watch him with hawk-like eyes as he sits down on the bed and just looks at me. The gentle smile on his face eases me a little, but not enough to trust him, even though I think that's exactly what he wants. As if I'm gonna fall for that trap now.

"You ..." I mutter, unable to come to terms with what happened to me.

"Shhh ..." he says, lifting a finger to his lips.

I frown at him, unsure of what to do. When he picks up a biscuit and puts a little jam on top, I almost die inside. Just the smell of it gets my stomach growling.

He brings it to my lips slowly; as if he's afraid I might jump up and make a run for it.

I probably would, if he wasn't waving food in my face.

"Eat," he murmurs, his lips parting in a way that makes me open my mouth, too.

The food that slides in tastes heavenly, better than anything I've ever eaten before. Probably because I haven't eaten anything like this since ... I don't know how long. When I've lived off bread, water, and a bit of soup for so long, something like strawberry jam can actually make me cry.

I suppress the upcoming tears and allow him to stuff another bit into my eager mouth. He seems quite enamored with feeding me like this, watching me bite for bite. When it's finished, I'm still hungry for more, and I glance over his shoulder to see if there's anything left.

He licks his lips and smiles. "Patience, Sky. You need to take it easy," he says.

"Like you care," I say. I sigh and dip back under the blanket.

He squints. "Just because you don't believe it, doesn't mean it's not true."

"You're the one who kept me in that cell. Who used and abused me. And for what?"

"I'm also the guy who took you out of that hellhole and brought you to this room. So be thankful." He leans forward. "Let me take a look at you."

He doesn't wait for my permission before peeking under the blanket and checking out my bandages. "How does it feel?" he asks, touching them.

I hiss a little when he grazes a wound. "Painful. But better than yesterday."

He sighs of relief. "Lucky I could get a doctor in here quick enough before you bled to death."

I nod, but there's an uncomfortable silence between us. I feel like I'm supposed to be grateful, and it's weird because it almost feels as if he's glad that I'm still alive.

What's also weird is that he doesn't even seem remotely angry with me for choking him with the ropes.

He grabs a glass of milk and puts it against my lips. "Drink."

It's not as if I have a choice, so I open my mouth and drink up. It's so good that I actually chug back the entire glass before he can take it away again. He sets everything back down on the tray and returns his attention to me.

"Can you tell me what you remember about yesterday?"

Yesterday.

Just the thought makes me shiver and choke up.

"Pain," I mutter. I don't want to think about it.

"What did they do to you?" he asks.

I make a face. "Why would you ask *me* that? You're the one who did this to me!"

He frowns, gazing down at the sheets and sighs out loud, visibly distressed.

And that's when it hits me.

"You didn't know?" I mutter.

His silence tells me enough.

I swallow away the lump in my throat. "They … hit me. Harder than you ever did. I wasn't even asked a question. All they did was torture me. They tied a cloth around my head and poured water over me. It felt like I was drowning." I take in a couple of shallow breaths, trying to compose myself. "And, of course, the knife … God, I can still feel it push through my skin."

He slides further onto my bed, and I flinch, but his hands aren't threatening in any way. Instead, he grabs my arm and pulls me toward him. I let him drag me into his body, giving in to his warmth and his gentle touch as he wraps his arms around me, his hands gripping my hair is if I'm his prized possession. I don't know what drives him to be this kind to me, or why he's taken me out of that cell. All I know is that, for the first time in days, I feel safe.

Safe … in his arms.

I'm truly going insane.

"Why …" I mutter. "Why are you doing this?"

"I can't answer your questions, Sky. But trust me when I say I want to answer them more than anything in the world."

"But why are you so nice all of the sudden? I tried to kill you."

"I'm not nice … but I do take care of what belongs to me."

His statement makes me shudder, although I'm not sure if it's in a good or bad way. I gaze up into his dark, sultry eyes, and for some reason, they feel so familiar. I just don't know why.

"Do I … do I know you? It feels like I do."

He stops breathing for a second, his lips parting but then closing again.

He shakes his head and tips up my chin. The way

he looks at me makes me feel like he desperately wants to tell me, as if it could roll off his lips with a slip of the tongue.

But then he presses his lips onto mine.

His kisses are sweet and gentle, not demanding like before. Still, they claim me as nothing else can, his lips melding with mine in an attempt to soothe the pain and extinguish the doubt.

But all it does is instill a certainty within my heart.

I know this man … this kiss … this person.

With difficulty, I take my lips off his. They feel numb and raw and badly want to cling to his, but I have to speak up.

"Tell me who you are …"

He grips my arms and leans his forehead against mine, staring deep into my eyes. "I'm the guy who killed for you."

"What do you mean?"

"They hurt you." He cups my face and caresses my cheek. "They hurt my Sky … so I killed them."

A chill runs down my spine.

"You're mine. He tried to take me away from you, thinking I couldn't handle you because you escaped. But he doesn't know that I helped you."

"I don't understand …" My breathing comes in short gasps as he holds my face. "Who is *he*? And what did you do?" The 'he' must be the man controlling him. The one who's really after me.

But then he says something that shakes me up

180

completely.

"I left those ropes on purpose. Did you think it was your idea?" He smiles. "I wanted you to use them to tie me up. Although, I didn't think you'd actually choke me."

He laughs as if it's funny to him, but it's not. I'm sitting here, terrified, nailed to the bed, wondering who in the hell he is and what he's doing to me. "I wanted you to escape so you'd see there were worse things that could happen to you than me. Although I didn't think they'd treat you this badly … I wouldn't have done it if I knew beforehand they'd be that rough on you."

My lip quivers and I back away slowly. "No …"

"Yes, Sky. I put the ropes there because I wanted you to see the truth. You think I'm bad, but now you've seen the worst. I am the only one who goes easy on you. Who even remotely cares about you. I'm your only choice. Your only means to get out. To save yourself."

"Stop …" I say, shaking my head.

He holds the back of my head so I can't move away from him, gripping my face to keep me close.

"Listen to me, Sky. It will never end. Not until you tell me what I need to know. Not until you give up."

"To you? After what you just told me? How dare you …" I hiss.

How could I even believe for one second I could escape? Of course, he planted the ropes there. I should've known he would mess with my mind. To make me believe I could flee, while in fact, it was only a way for him to show me that he is the only one I can rely on.

This monster is the only one who wants me to live.

And he shows me by taking away his pain and replacing it with a pain that is much, much worse.

I can't even begin to describe how much is wrong here.

He practically handed me over to the devil.

"I hate you …" I mutter under a heavy breath.

"Good … you should because I'm unredeemable. I will *not* stop until you tell me the truth."

"Is it worth it?" I growl. "Is it worth the hurt, the anger, the pain you're seeing? Is it worth it to save your own goddamn fucking worthless life?"

"It's worth it to save yours."

With just a few words, he always manages to take my breath away.

Just like that. As if it comes naturally to him.

"Sky …" he murmurs, pulling my lips toward his.

I have no choice, nor do I want to resist. I want his kisses to drown me in a lie. To tell me something different from the words that roll off his lips. I want to believe in something else than what he's trying to make me believe.

His grip on my face is so tight, so fierce, that I start believing in his need to protect me more than the fear he instills in my heart. It's gullible and totally wrong, but my mind has been lost and alone for so long that I desperately want to latch on to someone I can trust.

I hate him, and yet I want nothing more than for him to numb the pain.

After everything he did to me, it baffles me that I can accept his touch.

He let me believe I could escape so I would see that he was the lesser evil of the two. That there are worse people out there who are trying to hurt me, and that he's the only one I can trust.

Why is it that I find it easy to believe?

And worst of all, why am I falling for it so goddamn hard?

It's as if I have no choice. As if my heart has already succumbed to his desire to make me trust him. He wants me so much that it's becoming impossible to separate the real from the fake, the truth from the lies … good from evil.

He is both sin and virtue.

A monster and a saint.

Someone who strangles my heart in order to claim it for himself.

And I just let him because I know that I have no other choice.

His kisses hypnotize me to the point of letting him push me back into the pillow as he crawls on top of me. My body might hurt, but my heart bleeds. It needs reassurance, guidance, and hope. Even if what he is offering is just a trickle of love, it's enough to have me hooked.

When he takes his lips from mine for a second, he murmurs, "If only you knew ..."

"Knew what ..." I mutter, sucking in a much-needed breath.

"How much I want to tell you. Everything. I need you," he whispers, pressing another kiss on my heated lips.

"Tell me," I say. "I can tell you more, too."

He keeps kissing me sporadically as if he wants nothing more than to fuck me right here, but we both know my wounds are too fresh, both inside and out. So we're stuck in the middle of a disconnected embrace, desiring more than the other is willing to give. But I can't stop. I can't let it rest.

"Just give me something," I murmur. "So I can trust you."

Trust isn't something I give away easily, but I'm willing to try if it means I'll have a chance at freedom again.

"You don't want to ... trust me," he says. "You don't want to know ... it would kill you."

I shake my head and he nods, all while our lips keep grazing in an attempt to stay connected. But I know it's futile. One way or another, someone is going to find out the truth. And it'll be ugly as hell.

Something tells me that his truth wouldn't just kill me.

He would kill me.

"Fuck me ... why are you so irresistible," he

184

murmurs into my ear, pressing a kiss to my neck. "Only you can do this to me. Only you can make my heart beat ... My Sky. My azure night."

Azure night.

My eyes flash open, my heart skipping a beat the moment I hear him say this.

I never thought I'd hear that nickname again.

Azure ... the color of my eyes ... and the night's sky ... all those nights of pleasure.

In one quick motion, I hook my fingers under his mask and pull it apart, causing the mask to fall off his face.

It's him.

"Angel ..." I mutter under a heavy breath.

I can't believe it. It can't be true, and yet it's the only explanation.

The man after me for all this time.

It makes no sense and yet it does. The complete and utter horrifying truth.

In one split second, I make the call.

A thrusting knee in the balls is all it takes to make him curl up in a ball, dropping next to me on the bed while I jump up. Sharp pain envelops me as I press a hand to my stomach and run to the door, but it won't stop me. Adrenaline is the only thing keeping me together right now as I jerk the handle and set myself free.

But what I see doesn't liberate me.

It entraps me.

Consumes me.

I spent days and nights in this house with a man I thought was worth every second of my life, until the time came when I had to leave.

I never knew I'd be back here, in chains, stripped from all that makes me *me*.

The hallway with its red carpet and wooden wall panels looks exactly as I remember it, with his bedroom only a few steps away. All the memories come flooding back in, crashing into me like a wave.

Angel, the man of my dreams … the man from my nightmares.

He is my captor. My lover. My tormenter.

He ruined me. My heart once belonged to him and now he's come to claim it forever.

I thought I could handle the truth.

I was wrong.

DAY 13

SKY

1 year ago

It's during one of my sparse nights out that I first meet him.

It feels like a fluke because I normally never go out. I'm too busy studying, but occasionally, I do have the time to go out to have some fun with my friends.

However, I never expected to run into a guy like him.

Quite literally, we bump into each other while I'm holding a beer, and I spill it all over him.

"Sorry," I exclaim.

It's dripping down his shirt and mine, but my eyes can't help wandering to his face. He's beautiful. Slick, black hair combed backward, demanding, pitch-black eyes, and thick lips. A square, scruffy jaw and broad shoulders ... god, he's broad everywhere. Like, physically fit as can be. In his dark suede shirt, he looks like a dark, fallen angel.

Imagine my surprise when he tells me his name.

My smile must seem like one of those smiles a giddy schoolgirl gets when her crush talks to her. I feel silly, like a bumbling idiot, which isn't me. But something about him turns me completely inside out.

"So ... are you going to tell me your name?" he asks.

"Sorry, it's Sky," I say, blushing.

His smile makes my heart thump in my throat. "Beautiful."

It feels like he just fucked me. With just one word, he manages to leave me speechless.

It seems as if the attraction is mutual because his body leans in, almost as if an invisible force pulls us together. I don't know him, and he doesn't know me, but I feel as if I should.

Like I was meant to meet him.

It's ridiculous and completely unrealistic.

Nobody meets like this. Nobody falls in love like this.

It doesn't exist.

At least ... that's what I've always told myself.

What people keep saying when they think of love at first sight.

And yet … I can't help but want to be closer to him.

He holds out his hand, biting his lip so seductively that I almost forget about the fact that I came here with friends. But one dance won't hurt, will it? They're already chatting with a few boys near the bar while I always drink on my own a bit. I've always kept more to myself. Sky, the girl who floats through life without living it. I've always felt a little numb, as if my friends were living the life while I was wasting away, not knowing what to do about it. I often feel lost in this world, wondering when my time will be.

But then this happens.

An angel knocks me off my feet. He calls to me in a way no other man has. As if he commands the very space he walks, including me.

Without thinking, I set my beer down and grab his hand.

The connection feels instant. I feel like I'm floating as his warm hand grips mine and he walks me to the center of the dance floor. I'm letting him guide me, and the more I stare into his striking eyes, the more I realize I'm not going anywhere. He has me under his spell.

I tuck my hair behind my ear, not knowing how to act in front of him as he grabs my hand and dances with me. His sultry look has something dangerous about it, but I can't exactly tell what. Something untouchable, far beyond my reach, hides inside his armored shell, but something about him makes me want to find out.

He pulls me closer and wraps his arms around me as if I'm a lover and we've done this a million times before. The strange thing is that I feel exactly that. This is insane, and yet, I don't want anything else but this. It's as if he's taken over my mind.

"Do I know you?" I ask, looking up at him from under my lashes.

"No … but you could," he muses, tipping my chin up.

He hovers closer, tentatively waiting for me to move away. But I don't … I'm crazy … I should move, I should stop, but I can't. I'm frozen in his grasp, wondering what will happen if I just let him.

So I do … I let him kiss me.

When his mouth is on mine, everything inside me feels like it bursts into flames.

Like his lips set me on fire, burning brighter than a thousand suns.

My heart practically explodes out of my chest just from touching him and having his lips on mine. It's indescribable, like something I've never experienced before. Something I want, more than anything, right now. His kisses fuel a fire inside me that I didn't know I had, and now I'm ready for more.

"Wow …" he murmurs into my mouth, our lips

desperate to latch on to each other again.

"I know ..." I can hardly believe it either.

Could it be fate? I'd call someone a fool who'd say this to me, but now I'm starting to believe it's true.

We meet in a dream, two lovers connecting as if they've known each other years and years before. It's too good to pass up on. Too heavenly to ignore.

If it makes me a sinner for wanting someone—no, needing someone—before I even know who they are, then so be it. I've only known him for minutes and I already feel closer to him than anyone I've ever talked to before.

Just the way he stares at me is enough to confirm our mysterious bond.

It doesn't take long before we're back to kissing, with nothing but our clothes in the way. Hours pass before I say good-bye to my friends and leave the club with him. It's stupid and completely risky, but nothing will keep me away from him, not even the voice in the back of my head telling me this is wrong.

I'm about to break all the rules.

When we arrive at his house, I'm baffled at the enormity of it. A mansion of epic proportions, but I don't get the time to explore it all, as he immediately takes me back to his lavishly decorated room. My head is still spinning from all those kisses and as the door closes, I realize too late that I've stepped into a room with a beast. I might not make it out alive.

"Don't worry, Sky," he murmurs. "I won't hurt you

… much."

The devious grin on his face makes me shiver as I step back and almost fall down on his bed.

The moment I try to open my mouth, he places a finger on my lips and says, "Shh … I'm going to take good care of you. Forget about everything. Turn off your thoughts and let me give you what you need. What we both want."

And I do.

I let him take me over completely.

Not just physically but mentally, too.

I'm lost to him. To his touch, his kisses, his licks, his forceful grip as he pushes me onto the bed and ties me up with two ties from his closet. I've lost my mind, but I don't regret a thing. For once in my life, I feel like I'm truly alive. Living. Breathing.

Him.

Everything. He encompasses everything I've been missing for all these years.

The missing piece of the puzzle that makes me *me*.

That turns me from an insecure girl into a self-aware, grown woman.

His hands are all over me, touching me in places I didn't know existed. He's skilled with his tongue, his mouth, as he laps me up and then some. I writhe underneath him, desperate for more, as I let him control my body and bend it to his wish. Pain turns into pleasure as spankings and belts push me beyond my limit. I've completely given in to lust; my mind only focused on him. Us. Love.

Unconditional love for one night.

He calls me his Azure Sky. A sky so blue and infinite he says he can lose himself in me.

And I feel good. Genuinely good … happy even.

Meeting him was the best thing that ever happened to me.

But also the worst thing that ever happened to me.

The next morning, I can't leave.

No matter how many times I try, I don't want to lose what we have, and it feels like I would if I take one step out. So I stay and eat breakfast, enjoying the sunlight while wearing his thin, white shirt.

But it isn't just this one day or night that has me hooked on him.

Neither is it two nights. Or three. Before I know it, it's become seven.

One entire week of kissing, love, sex, hugging, talking, fucking, and connecting on a level I thought was impossible to achieve. We were both looking for someone to share our wants without being constrained. A relationship or not, this experience is one I won't forget anytime soon.

Especially when the day comes that I have to leave.

My mamma is the one who pulls me aside and asks me what I'm doing. She tells me that I should leave immediately.

I didn't know she worked here, but it all makes sense the moment I see her fearful eyes. She infiltrated this house as an agent, working as a maid, and I just had the most wonderful week of my life with someone who lives here, in this house ...

I'm in danger. The longer I stay here, the more my life is at risk.

So I do what any sane person does. I grab my stuff and go.

It isn't without regret and a stabbing pain in my heart, but I have to do what's right. I have to trust my mamma and save myself because she wouldn't tell me this otherwise. If I have to choose between staying with him and living, I choose to live.

However, the choice isn't simple.

It's anything but simple.

Because the moment my mamma and I leave that house, my life would never be the same again.

***

ANGEL

Present

She saw me.

Not just the guy, but the monster beneath the mask.

A devil disguised as an angel.

And to think that I was stupid enough to believe I could hide from her.

She knows who I am now.

The moment she tried to leave my room was the second I realized I had to stop her and tie her up again, even though it was far from what I had planned.

I wanted her to trust me. To need me in such a way that she wouldn't be able to say no anymore. That she'd speak up and tell me what I needed to know so that I could save her life.

Instead, I was forced to grab her and pull her back into the guest room, locking her inside, with me … the beast.

It was just as I remember … like those nights we spent, with her standing in the middle of the room, trying to protect herself, while I stalked toward her, determined to get her on my bed. Only this time she wasn't as willing and clawed at me until I tied her ankles and wrists to the bed.

I haven't been back in the guestroom since yesterday.

I couldn't face her wrath, her anger, the sadness in her eyes when she looked at me. I know she hates me now and rightfully so. Still, that doesn't make it any easier to deal with.

I've let some of our most trusted maids feed her and tuck her in as much as possible of course, seeing as she's tied up and all. But I can't continue like this. I have to get back in there and face the truth.

And so I do.

When I open the door, I blow out a big breath before entering the room. Seeing her look at me with fear-laced eyes makes me want to punch the walls, but I contain my anger by focusing on my job; I have to make her speak. It's the only way for her to live, and I fucking *want* her to live.

"You ..." she hisses. "What are you doing here?"

Her snappy voice hurts me to the point of wanting to rip my own heart out.

"You know why I'm here," I say. I'm here because I have to be here.

"You're here to make me talk? Not a chance." She laughs as if I'm pathetic. Maybe I am, but I won't stop trying.

"You did this to me," she snarls. "It was you from the beginning, wasn't it?"

"Yes, it was me. It was always me." I close the door behind me and walk toward her. She doesn't tremble, doesn't even flinch, as if her courage has mastered the fear brewing inside her.

"No wonder I recognized you," she spits.

"You always knew ..." I say, squinting. "You didn't need to see me without the mask. You've known it was me since I first kissed you," I say. "You just didn't want to know."

I sit down beside her on the bed, and she immediately jerks away.

"Don't come closer."

"Why?" I ask.

"You used and abused me!"

I lean in and hold my hand above her leg.

"Don't you fucking touch me!" she screams.

"Do you think you have any choice?" I muse. "You're bound. You have nowhere to go."

"I escaped once. I can do it again."

"With my help." I glare at her. "I won't be giving you a second chance."

A grumbly noise comes from her throat and she turns her head away from me. "Leave me alone. I'd rather die than spend one more second with you."

"You don't mean that," I say, grabbing her face and cupping it so she'll look at me. "You only say that because you're confused about your feelings."

"You're the reason I'm stuck here. Why I got hurt. Why I'm physically and now even mentally broken. I'm not confused. I'm fucking angry." She jerks the ropes that are around her wrists. It won't free her; I tied them securely.

"The more you wriggle, the tighter they'll get."

"Fuck you," she hisses, trying to bite me.

"Sky …"

"Don't you say my name! You don't deserve to say it."

"I did once …" I say, looking down at the sheets. "My Azure Sky."

"Stop it …"

"Why?" I look her deep in the eyes. "Because you

can't handle the fact that, after all this, it still does something to you?"

"It does nothing to me."

"You only say that because you're mad. I know you still think about those days, deep down in your heart." I press a hand on her chest where her heart is. Feeling it thump loudly makes me smile. She might hate my guts, but at least she still lives. It's better than nothing.

She makes a face. "Just go away. I'm not going to say anything, so don't even think about asking. I'm done. I'm just done. Just let me die."

I shake my head. "Why would you say that? Is your life that invaluable to you?"

"I've been hurt enough ..." she says, closing her eyes for a second before continuing. "And you ... you're ..."

I grab her chin and tilt it, demanding her full attention. "Just because it's me doesn't mean I suddenly stopped caring. I am still the same man, the same guy who was behind the mask."

"And that's the problem ... it's you ..." She shakes her head, blinking away the tears. "Why did it have to be you?"

I sigh, caressing her cheek. "I asked myself the same question over and over again."

"Then why don't you stop? Those days we had ... they were better than anything I've ever experienced, and I thought it was the same for you."

"It is, but I can't stop, even if I wanted to."

"Why? Tell me why?"

I get up from the bed, reluctantly unbuttoning my shirt. I didn't want her to know, but I realize that, if I want to push this any further, she has to see the truth. She has to know who I really am in order to move forward.

As I remove my shirt, her eyes start to widen and her pupils dilate, her jaw dropping.

"That's …"

I step closer so she can witness the extent of my involvement.

"The dragon tattoo," she murmurs, her eyes gliding up and down my torso. I only got this tattoo after I escaped from prison. To show my father how dedicated I was I got the family tattoo. Now I regret it more than anything I've ever done.

"Why do you have that?" she asks with tears in her eyes. "Please don't tell me it's true …"

"The man you were talking about before, who took you in that alley with his men … he is my father."

She gasps, a tear rolling down her cheek, and then she turns away.

I quickly cover up again in an attempt to calm her. "So you see now why I can't stop."

"Your father … he's the one behind this all. He's the one who wanted me tortured."

"Yes."

"And you're helping him." She chokes on a ridiculous laugh. "I can't believe this. I think I finally meet a guy worth it all, and then here he is again, telling me he's the son of the man who ruined my life."

"I can't say anything that will make it okay," I say, grabbing her leg.

"You can, but you won't. That's the problem."

"I can't because he'd kill me if I didn't get the information out of you."

She winces, trying to move her leg, but I won't stop touching her. "So you care more about your own life then."

I lean in so my forehead rests on hers. "I'm trying to save both our lives."

She frowns, blinking a couple of times, but she keeps her mouth shut. Maybe she's given up trying to fight me, although I'm not sure that's a good thing. There's a lot that's still left unsaid.

"You stole something from him. He wants it back, and he's not letting you go until you tell me what and where it is."

"He's *your* father. Why don't you try to figure it out?" she says. "Ask him. Not me."

I frown at her, grinding my teeth.

"Oh, right, I forgot … he doesn't *want* to tell you. Say … doesn't that mean he's actually hiding something from *you*?"

I grip her leg tighter, my nails digging into her skin. "Watch it, Sky. Don't test my patience."

"You know I'm right. And yet you still work for him, even though he can't even tell you what he wants from me. If only you knew …"

Anger gets the best of me, and I grip her neck. "Don't. Play. Games. I'm not my father, but I *will* finish this job. He didn't tell me because he knew I recognized you, and he realized I was personally involved."

"You think he's trying to save you from getting hurt? Too late … you're already in deep," she says, gurgling because my grip is so tight, my hand cuts off her air.

My nose twitches. She's right, but I won't let it get to me. "Hate me. Despise me. But I will save your life, whether you like it or not," I growl.

The look on her face softens and she stops struggling, her eyes slowly closing. I let go of her and she gasps for air.

"Now tell me what you stole from him or I'm going to keep ravishing you in ways you can only imagine."

"I don't care," she says.

I cock my head. "Oh, really? Now that you know who I am … I dare to say that you can't resist me." I let my hand travel up her thigh until I reach the highest point and then stop, right before her body begins to arch. I knew it. Even after everything that happened, her body still craves me.

"I know your body better than any man who's ever stepped into your life."

"Use me all you want, but I won't talk."

"I'm not just going to use you, Sky … I'm going to

claim your heart," I growl, grabbing her hair and pulling her head back so I can smash my lips on hers.

They're salty from the tears she wept in her sleep, and I lick them up like a lion licks its wounds. I adore all tastes and every part of her equally. I'm greedy, and I don't give a fuck. It's time she realized I will do anything, even the most gruesome, loathsome acts, to save both her and my life.

"Answer me now, Sky, and I'll stop," I growl into her mouth.

"No ..." she murmurs, her lips still latching onto mine.

"No to the answer or no to me stopping?" I muse, grinning as I see her arch toward me to kiss me again.

She sighs and frowns, groaning from frustration.

I lick my lips and get up from the bed.

"Where are you going?" she asks.

I don't answer because she'll find out soon enough. Plus, it's none of her business. She seems to think that it matters whether she knows or not, but she has no say in what happens to her.

I come back with a bucket of ice and set it down on the nightstand.

"What are you going to do?" she asks, peeking over my shoulder at the bucket.

"I'm going to make you talk," I muse, grabbing one of the ice cubes.

Reaching for the blanket, I slowly drag it downwards and watch her face as she realizes I'm exposing her body for play. When I place the cube on top of her nipple, she jerks her bonds, hissing as the ice instantly puckers her nipple. I pick up another one and rub it on the other nipple, making sure both are equally hard.

"I know you say you hate me ..." I muse. "But it doesn't matter because you belong to me now."

I place the next ice cube on her stomach, which jolts up and down when it touches her skin.

"So sensitive ..." I say, licking my lip at the sight of the water rolling down her tits.

"It's freezing," she says.

"Hmm ... this must feel good on your wounds," I muse, lifting her bandage and slipping an ice cube underneath it. She hisses and groans out loud. I look up at her desperate eyes, which are practically begging me to take her. "Does it hurt?"

She nods, but I can see the truth in her eyes. I pick up the ice on her nipple and roll it around. "Don't lie to me, Sky. I know you enjoy it when I make your body feel things you never felt with any other man. Just because you're my captive now doesn't mean you're suddenly not attracted to me."

She growls when I place another ice cube on top of her pussy. When she jerks her leg, I say, "Don't move." I grab her leg and push it down. "Or I will make you stay put."

She blows out a breath but then moans when I slide the ice cube over her clit.

"See? You like this ... the sting of cold against your heated body ... it makes me want to lick you off."

My dick is already getting hard at the sight of her barely covered body, and I want nothing more than to lick the goddamn juices off her skin. The ice makes her skin glisten and glow like a raw fucking diamond ready to be cut. I'm anxious to plunge into her and feel the depths of her arousal, but I'm more interested in pushing her beyond her limits. Making her beg is my goal, and I'll do anything in my power to reach it.

I pick up a few more cubes and place them all over her body, covering her with them like she's a fucking glass and I'm about to throw a martini on top.

She hisses when I press the cube down near her clit. "Feel that?" I muse. "That's your body telling you it wants me."

"No ..." she groans, her tongue swiftly dipping out to lick her lip as she struggles to suppress her desires.

"Keep denying yourself the pleasure and I'll continue serving it to you."

"Why are you so ... cruel?" she mutters as I pick up an ice cube with my mouth and slather it all over her body. Her moans make me grin as I hold the cube between my teeth and drag it up her body and toward her mouth. As I dip it into her mouth, I kiss her, licking the top of her lips, and then I lean back and watch her expect my mouth. It's sweet as sin to see her crave me and yet deny herself the very thing that makes her thrive.

"Am I cruel for showing you your true nature?" I murmur against her lips. "That you're turned on by my dominance isn't a crime, Sky."

She spits out the cube and looks at me with half-mast eyes, not speaking a word. But we both know what she's thinking.

I lean over her and take a knife from the drawer in the nightstand. "If you hold still, I'll cut your ankles loose."

She nods softly, not speaking a word as I bring the knife to her feet and cut them loose. She doesn't move, but her eyes watch me like a hawk. I put the knife back into the drawer and hover over her to plant soft kisses on her chest, which makes her body arch up.

I pick up a few more ice cubes and scatter them on her body, listening to her delectable moans. Her eyes open and close in a desperate attempt to escape yet watch me do my thing. I know she can't take her eyes off me, even though she tells herself she should. Our inseparable connection and past tie us together and force her to face her demons. And I'll be with her every step of the way.

I bend over and lick the water off her body, causing her to squirm underneath me. Her muscles tense and relax as I play with the cubes and her nipples, letting my tongue travel down her belly. She arches her back the moment I reach her pussy and push past the cube to lick her sensitive clit. Her moans and gasps rile me up like nothing else, and my cock tents in my pants as I struggle to contain myself.

With an ice cube in my mouth, I kiss her pussy until the frostiness has dissolved in my mouth and a tingly numbness stimulates both our senses. I lick and kiss her until she's practically undulating against my mouth.

"Yes, Sky, give it to me. Give me your fucking heart and soul."

"I can't …" she keeps muttering.

I grip her ass cheeks tight and lick her so hard she mewls. "Let go of your fear and fucking come," I growl. "I'm not going anywhere until you do."

"No," she whispers.

"Say no again and I will make it hurt," I growl. I plunge my tongue into her sweet pussy and suck up all her juices, making her moan out loud.

"No …"

"Fuck." That's it.

I grab a bunch of ice cubes from the bucket and spread her legs, watching her big, scared eyes glow as I hold them in front of her pussy.

"Please …" she moans.

"Beg me," I say, and then I push one of the cubes inside.

She gasps and sucks in a breath, but slams her lips together.

"Beg me to make you come!"

I shove in two more ice cubes until her lips part without her permission and let out a noise that's like music to my ears. "Please, fuck me!"

206

I grin like a devil. "Well, fuck me. I'll take it."

"Oh, god …" she moans. "It's so cold, and it's dripping out of me."

I grin. "Hmm … I love the sound of that."

My cock just bounced in my fucking pants. Goddammit, why does she have to be so fucking sexy when she's tied up and begging for it? I can't help myself. I'm a dirty motherfucker, but she's always known this and she's always liked it, too. She doesn't need to tell me … I know because of the way she reacts to my every move. She and I both know she likes me to ravish her … and I fucking love to do it.

I lower myself on top of her and suck on her pussy until the water drips from her, and then lick that up, too. I let nothing drip onto the bed as I suck up all her juices and then some.

"Fuck, you're so fucking wet," I groan as I taste her sweetness.

Her body rises to meet my mouth as I latch onto her clit, nibbling softly as she moans. My licks have made her clit red and swollen, and the moment I lick it, a loud moan escapes her mouth.

"Fuck …" she mutters.

"Yes, come all over my face." I groan, licking her until she starts to quiver.

She shudders so badly that I have to hold her down with my hands, her body literally shaking with need. I can feel her pussy thump against my tongue as she comes undone, and fuck me, is it hot.

Her breathing comes in short gasps; her body covered in goosebumps from the frigid ice melting on her skin. I crawl on top of her and kiss her on the lips, the raw, salty taste of her lust a fucking turn-on.

"See how good you taste?" I murmur. "How much you really want me?"

"Fuck ... you ..." she says with a shallow breath.

I smile against her lips and cup her pussy. "*Mine.*"

I spot a tiny smile on her lips before I lift myself off her and grab a few more ice cubes to spread on her body as if she's a work of art. I stand up on the bed and unbutton my shirt, looking her straight in the eyes as I slowly undress. I love how she looks at me with those hungry eyes, pretending she's not interested when all her signals indicate differently. She wants me, and I'm going to give it to her right now.

I throw off my shirt and zip down my pants, taking my hard-on in my hand. Her eyes immediately zoom in on me and my cock bounces from excitement.

"Stay still. Don't fucking drop an ice cube or I'll spank you."

"No ..." she growls.

I squint. "Don't fucking tempt me," I say, licking my lips at the thought.

I admit there is nothing more that I want to do than mark her with my hand and belt, but her body isn't ready for that yet. Maybe tomorrow ... if she begs hard enough.

I start rubbing my dick, making sure her eyes are on

it at all times as my eyes swipe over her body. She's a sight to admire, a girl with the face of a doll and a body that makes me want to commit sins.

I jerk myself off to her, feeding on the lust that flows between us as I watch her with the full intent of blowing my load all over her. I love how she knows, how she blinks and bites her lip, preparing for what's to come. It fills me with excitement, drives me insane, to the point of climaxing.

"Fuck ..." I growl, as I unload my cum on her.

It squirts onto her tits and face, her lips parting in surprise, which makes me aim for her mouth. I want her to taste my desire, my authority, my demands, as I mark her with my seed. The drips fall on the ice cubes and coat her body as it mixes with the droplets of water. She shines with glistening cum, like a sparkling nymph come to seduce me. Such a sight to behold.

With ragged breaths, I fall to my knees between her legs, watching her from afar.

"You are ... perfect," I say, admiring her beauty.

She shuts her mouth, her tongue quickly dipping out to lick her lips, before she averts her eyes.

"Hey. Look at me," I say, leaning over her. "Don't you dare look away."

"I hate this ..."

I grab her face and force her to look at me. "Look at me and tell me what you see."

Tears stain her eyes. "Lust and rage."

"Exactly, and why do you think that is? Tell me."

"Because you want me, but you hate that you have to punish me," she says, swallowing.

I narrow my eyes. "I knew you could read me like a book." A smile spreads on my face as I pet her hair and let my thumb run across her lips. "You knew me before we even met."

"This isn't okay …" she mutters. "I shouldn't want this. I shouldn't want you."

"It's okay," I say. "I know it's hard, but there's no denying it. We need each other. We crave each other."

"I shouldn't feel this hot when I'm icy cold." She shivers.

I silence her with a finger. "Shh … don't talk. It will only make it more difficult."

I pick up an ice cube and drag it through my cum. "Unless, of course, you want to tell me exactly what you're hiding. I could stop this right now. No more confusion. No more pain. No more pleasure. Nothing. Unless you'd want it, of course, because I'm always willing to take you if you'd beg."

"No …" she mutters. "I can't tell you. It's not that I don't want to, but it would put more than just me at risk," she says.

"Who else would it put at risk? Who are you talking about? Your friends? Your father?" I frown. "You don't have to worry about your father."

"What? Why?" She leans up as far as she can with her hands still tied. "What do you know about my papà?"

"Enough not to tell you," I say, and I hold the ice cube above her lips. "Open your mouth."

"No. Tell me what you know about my papà."

I slap her thigh, which makes her squeal. "Open your mouth. I won't say it again."

She does what I say reluctantly, and I slide the cube onto her tongue. "Suck this until it melts. I want you to taste my cum so you know who owns you."

She makes a face. "And then what?"

I give her a devilish smile. "And then you finish them all."

Her eyes widen as I jump out of bed. "What?" she exclaims.

I quickly stand next to her and slap her other thigh for good measures. "Keep sucking or else."

"My mouth will be numb by the time I finish them all!"

"Exactly," I say with a wink as I tuck my cock back into my pants and zip up. "I hope it numbs a bit of the pain." I lean in and tuck her hair behind her ear, watching her pouty lips as she sucks on each ice cube. With a devious grin, I say, "You'd best start sucking hard, because you're completely covered in my cum, and I'm not going anywhere until you're completely clean."

DAY 14

SKY

I'm in deeper shit than I could ever imagine.

The guy who I thought was one of a kind turns out to be my captor. The guy who I spent nights in a room with, knowing nothing but his name and how much pleasure he could give me. *That guy.*

And then on top of that, his father is the guy who took me without permission one year ago.

I should be pissed. Viciously angry, the murderous kind.

Except, all I feel in my heart is pain. Like a knife has been jammed between my ribs and has split open my soul.

I feel beyond sad, and I don't know why. Or maybe I don't want to recognize the reason behind it … as if I'm regretful that I even know it's him.

His tattoo proves he is connected, so he's not lying, which makes me even more depressed. I should hate him just for being the monster's son. But I can't. I simply can't be mad at him for the sole reason of being of the same blood. It's not in my nature to blame people when it's not their fault.

But it is. He *is* the one to blame for putting me in here.

And still, my heart beats for him.

Each time he enters my room, each time he opens his mouth, each time he touches me, each time he makes me come. My mind won't admit it, but my heart is already sold.

Our undeniable connection is what pulls us together and breaks us apart.

I thought I could fight him for as long as he hid behind the mask, but now that his true identity is revealed, the past and present have started to fuse, making it impossible for me to ignore the growing attraction I feel toward him.

How can I want a man like him? How can I live with myself?

And yet, it seems like he can, simply by surrendering.

Maybe he's right. Maybe I should just give in to my wants and needs instead of telling myself it's wrong. It would be the easy way out.

Still, I won't talk. Not with him hinting of information about my papà, and then not spilling what he knows. Something tells me he knows more than I do ... a dark revelation that I might not want to know and yet I desperately do.

I'm still waiting ... waiting for his return so I can question him about it.

Yesterday, he got me tested for diseases and showed me his papers too. I'm glad we're both clean. I don't know why he cares. Maybe because he thinks it will make it easier for me to give in to what he does. To succumb to his demands to pleasure him. And maybe he's right. The idea that at least my body will remain safe makes me feel more at ease, which is strange considering I might die in a matter of days.

The brain works in strange ways.

After minutes, maybe hours, he finally returns to the guest room.

I've been preparing for this moment, but the second I spot his demanding eyes, I'm at a loss for words. The way he looks at me is so utterly captivating ... I don't even know how to react.

"How do you feel?" he asks as he steps inside.

"Better ..." I mutter. "If I wasn't tied up." I look at the wraps around my wrists.

He cocks his head and smiles. "Sky, you know that's only for your own protection." His eyes narrow as he walks toward the bed. "Who knows ... if you

214

weren't tied up and started running, I'd be forced to chase you in a not-so-pleasant way. In fact, I'm sure I would probably pin you to the ground and have you begging for mercy ... after I plunged into your tight pussy."

Wow.

I'm baffled.

Completely blown away by his scandalous words.

And completely turned on.

Dammit.

"Or maybe that *is* what you want me to do." He smirks, sitting down on the bed beside me.

I swallow away the lump in my throat. "I promise I won't run."

"Promises, promises ... you've already run twice, so who's to say you won't try it thrice? Although, that one time was my fault."

"I know what the consequences are. I won't try."

"Really? You fear the pain and pleasure more than you'd want to escape?"

"I don't fear you. But I won't run either. As long as you tell me what you know about my papà."

He frowns. "And what makes you think I would tell you?"

This is it. This is what he wants. Don't back down now. "Because I'd let you do anything to me. Anywhere you want."

For a second, I think I spot a faint smile on his face, but he hides it well. "Sky ... you do realize that I can already do whatever I want, wherever I want, to you?"

"But not with my approval."

He smiles, shaking his head. "You're a smart girl."

"I could be your smart girl," I say. "What I told you before hasn't changed. If you give me what I want, I'll give you what you want."

He leans in, hovering dangerously close to my lips. "You think I need your permission to take what I want?"

"No ... but you want it. You want me to say yes. I know you do."

"Hmm ..." He licks his lips as if he's thinking. "You tempt me so much ... I'd almost take you up on your offer."

"What's stopping you?" I ask.

"You," he says. "You'd get hurt. Trust me on this."

"I can take it."

"I don't think you can." He sighs.

"You don't know that until you've given me a chance."

"All right." He grabs my wrist and pins me down on the bed. "I will tell you. But you will do anything I tell you to. No buts. No ifs. Even if what I tell you tears your heart out, makes you fall on your knees and burst into tears ... you'll still suck my cock, take my cum, and thank me for it, just because I tell you to."

My lips part and I suck in a breath as he waits for my answer. I feel like I'm making a deal with the devil

… or an angel disguised as a beast. Nowadays, I can't tell the two apart anymore.

"Yes," I say after taking a deep breath.

"No matter what truths spill out or what you learn, you will obey me. You will be mine. Understood?"

I nod.

"I won't take anything less than you, completely and utterly mine. I do hope you understand what that means," he says with a grin.

I bite on my lip, unsure if I should even ask. "I'm yours."

"Even past these twenty-one days. In fact, for the rest of your life. You're mine. Forever," he growls.

His mouth connects with mine, sucking eagerly on my lip as he takes me to be his.

I don't fight him. I don't bite or resist. I kiss him back, giving him my all. Because, after all, I promised it to him and I don't break promises. Ever.

His kiss isn't as rough as before, and his lips rest on mine for a moment before they unlatch, almost as if he's savoring the moment.

"I love kissing you, especially when you're still oblivious to the darkness all around you."

"What do you mean?" I ask.

He rummages in his pocket and takes out a knife. When he brings the blade to my wrists, I flinch.

"Hold still," he says.

The knife cuts through the bonds like butter as he frees both my wrists and ankles. When I'm released, I reach for the painful spots that remain and rub them. He stops me by taking my hand with his and starts rubbing my wrist himself.

"Thank you ..." I mutter, unsure of what to say.

He's being so gentle, caressing and massaging my hand as if he really cares. Maybe he does. Maybe he's been speaking the truth all this time and I've just been blatantly ignoring it to soothe my inner virtue. As if that would save me. But trusting him blindly would be like handing over my life to sin itself.

Could I?

Would I?

What if the answer was yes? What then?

His cough interrupts my flow of thought.

"You're free now. You could run. You could leave this house. You know where the exit is."

"But then you'd chase me and I'd be pinned to the ground," I say.

"Right. The question is ... what do *you* want?"

I look up at him with parted lips, but I don't know what to say. I'm not even sure what I want anymore.

"I think you want both ... freedom and me," he muses. "What if I told you there was a way to do just that?" He grins when he sees me gasp. "All you have to do is tell me what I need to know."

"Hmpf, not a chance. Your father would kill me if he knew the truth."

"But he'd kill you anyway if he doesn't."

My eyes widen at this blatant admittance. "So I *am*

going to die."

"That depends on your reluctance. Or rather, willingness to play along."

"Play ... along?" Is he suggesting that I lie?

"All I want is that you tell me what he wants to know. You know the answers ... I don't."

"Right ... so you don't know what your father wants. I was right all along." I shake my head. "And you kept denying it."

"Just because we both know doesn't mean I will show you my only weakness."

"There's more weakness in you than you're willing to admit," I say, staring straight into his eyes.

He knows exactly what I mean. What I'm talking about. His heart ... with my image locked inside.

Suddenly, he lets go of my hand and gets up from the bed. "I will tell you what you want to know about your father."

Oh, wow. I didn't expect him to come with this so quickly.

"How do you know my papà? Have you seen him? Is he okay?" I ask in a hurry. It's as if the questions never end, but I have to ask them now before he changes his mind.

He turns his back away from me, his arms folded, almost as if he's afraid to face me. Is it that bad?

"I wasn't part of the group that took you fourteen days ago, but I do know your father."

"How?"

"The men who took you told me." He sighs out loud, rubbing his fingers over his forehead. "I didn't want to be the one to tell you this, but … your father, he basically sold your life for his."

"What?" I make a face.

He turns around again, a concerned look on his face. "I can't explain it very well … but maybe you should ask him yourself."

My mind spins in circles as I listen to his words, my palms sweating and my heart racing.

"He's in the building," Angel says.

"Where?"

"The same place you were kept."

The same place … the dark, damp cell that ate away my soul.

"He's there? Right now?" I ask, my voice quaking.

"Yes."

Just that one word makes me jump out of bed and sprint toward the door. Angel doesn't even stop me when I run out the door and sprint through the familiar hallway and down the gigantic staircase. When I notice the guards standing near the door, I run into the nearest room and rummage through the drawers, picking up the first sharp object I can find. A letter opener. It's not much, but it'll have to do. I grab a long sleeve shirt along the way and put it on to cover up a bit of my nudity so I won't get cold. Because I know that it's going to be cold where I'm going.

I storm out of the room and charge at the men

when they least expect it. They look surprised as I jab them in the stomach and the other one in the arm, screaming with pain as I push open the doors and rush past them. Adrenaline is fueling my body, making me go to the extreme, beyond what I thought I was capable of, as I run out into the garden. There's a stone path leading into the woods, which seems to be the only route not surrounded by fences, so I take it.

Maybe I will find my father here in the woods that remind me of the trees I saw when I first escaped. Or maybe I won't. But I won't stop looking until I do.

"Come back here!"

When I look behind me, I realize it's Angel.

"Sky!"

"No! I have to see him!" I yell, running for my life.

Tears wet my eyes, blurring my vision as I run past the trees, the branches scratching me until I bleed. The pain won't stop me from seeking my papà. Now that I know he's here, in that exact same place I was dying in, I have to get to him. I can't leave him in there, alone, to die.

"You can't!" Angel yells at me.

His voice seems closer, and when I glance over my shoulder, I see him catching up to me.

"Papà, I'm coming for you," I mutter, not daring to look back again.

He's on my heels and he's not slowing down.

But I am.

My muscles grow weaker and my oxygen intake

diminishes with every step I take. By the time I'm lost in a sea of trees, one slip of the toes, and I fall to the ground. Huffing into the sand and leaves, I pick myself up.

But not before Angel has his hand wrapped firmly around my ankle.

"Got you …"

The darkness in his voice makes me turn around and squeal.

He crawls on top of me and pushes me to the ground, placing a hand over my mouth so I can't scream. "Shh … it's no use. Nobody can hear you but me."

"Let me go!" I murmur through his hand, and then I bite as hard as I can.

"Fuck!" His hand drops from my mouth as he looks at his wound and then growls at me. "You had to go and do that."

"I have to see him," I say, trying to push him away so I can get up, but he just won't get off me.

He grabs my wrists and pins me to the ground again, my hair mixing with the leaves and the dirt, tears staining my face.

"You want to see your father? Fine, I'll take you to him. But don't say I didn't fucking warn you. You think you want this, but you're wrong. Too bad you won't believe me."

"I just want to know if he's okay …" I whisper, forcing the tears back.

"Take her inside."

The voice I hear is a new one, and yet I recognize it immediately.

With widened eyes, I gaze over Angel's shoulder to meet the devil himself.

"You ..." I whisper, my voice crackling with fear.

"I didn't want to have to do this, but you gave me no choice," Angel says.

He lifts me up and puts me over his shoulder like a stuffed doll, carrying me toward the man ... the man I have feared since long before I was taken.

"Hello, bambina."

His eerie smile alone shakes me to my core.

It's *him*.

The owner of the beast.

The real monster behind the pet.

My screams aren't loud enough to overwhelm his poisonous words. "You want to see your papà? Sure, you can talk to him ... and afterward, I'll give you his head."

DAY 15

SKY

When I open my eyes, I'm in a dining room sitting at a table that smells of food. My eyes drift to the clock hanging on the wall in front of me. The noise it makes booms in my ears. Tick. Tock. No matter how much I focus on the arrows, they still look wobbly and move incredibly slow. My vision is blurry, but I can make out a couple of figures sitting close to me at the very same table.

"Oh … she's awake," I hear someone say.

Where am I? How did I get here? I dig through my clouded mind, sifting through the foggy memories until

I find what I'm looking for. Yesterday, someone held me, and then stuck a needle in the back of my neck. That's when I started feeling drowsy.

They drugged me.

When I try to move my hands, I can't. As if glued to the very chair where I sit.

As I blink and look around, my vision becomes clearer by the minute, and I can finally keep my head up while looking around. That's when I see him. The man I've feared for over a year. The scum of the earth that took me that night in the alley with his accomplices. I will never forget that day and the promise I made to myself.

I will stab him in the eye the first chance I get.

"Hello, bambina," he says with a rotten smile on his face.

"You …" I mutter with difficulty.

"Are you feeling all right? You look a little tired."

"What did you do to me?" I growl.

"You took a little nap for a day. You seemed so tired from all that running and fighting."

"Where am I …"

He leans forward. "You're sitting at my table now. Hungry? Today's lasagna day."

"I'll kill you," I murmur.

He laughs, first without parting his lips, but then a full maniacal laugh bellows out of him. "Sure, you will. Oh, right, where are my manners? Let me introduce myself. My name is Joseph DeLuca. Some people call me Joe. Others call me Boss. Whatever you like. And that is my son, Angel DeLuca, but you're acquainted with him already."

Suddenly, I feel someone grab my hand. I turn my head and notice Angel sitting right beside me.

"You, too?"

"I'm sorry, but you asked for this yourself," he says.

"My son told me you wanted to see your papà. Well, here he is."

From the corner of the room, a maid pushes a wheelchair toward us. The man is swollen, bruised, and bleeding, and his arms and legs are strapped to the wheelchair. It's my papà, and the moment I see him, tears form in my eyes.

"Papà ..." Words cannot describe how I feel right now.

He gargles up blood in response.

I try to move, but still my body feels stuck, and when I gaze down, I notice ropes bind me from head to toe.

"Sky ..." my papà murmurs.

"Shh. Don't try to talk," I say.

I wish he didn't have to see me like this. I wish we could've met again under different circumstances. But at least we're both still alive. As we gaze into each other's eyes with regret, sorrow, and guilt, I feel more connected to him than I have for the past year.

"Don't talk?" Joseph jests. "On the contrary, I think you're eager to hear what he has to say."

"Shut up!" I yell, thrashing in my seat.

Renewed energy fills my veins and fuels the desire to break free and kill them all.

"Calm her down, will you," he says to Angel, and Angel grabs my shoulders and presses down enough for me to be unable to move the chair.

"Relax, bambina. You wanted to see your papà, so here he is. Now, let's all enjoy a bite of lasagna, shall we?"

Angel scoops up a bit of the lasagna from the plate in front of me and brings it to my mouth, but I knock it away with my face, not giving a shit if I'm covered in tomato sauce.

"I don't take food from monsters like you!"

"Oh, you hurt my feelings," Joseph says, placing his hand over his heart. "I cooked this myself. For our special guests."

"I don't give a damn what you did. Release us. Now!"

He cocks his head and frowns. "Bambina ..." He sighs. "You know that's not how it goes. What happens is ... you tell me what I want to know and maybe I'll release you."

Angel leans in to whisper in my ear, "Don't believe him."

I squint at him, but his father clears his throat. "Angel. Let me handle this."

Angel raises his brow and lets out a big breath. "You know this isn't going to end well."

"Of course not," his father says, laughing as if it's one big joke. "But she *will* tell me what I want to know."

"Over my dead body," I say.

"Really? You prefer dying over telling me the truth?" he says with raised brows.

"She means it," Angel says.

"Stay out of this," his father growls. "You told me she would talk if I brought her father from his cell."

"Papà, are you okay?" I ask, ignoring the men.

"Hey," Joseph flicks his fingers at me. "Focus."

"Papà, don't let them get to you," I say.

"Sky, it's gonna be okay …" he murmurs.

He's so strong in the face of danger. I admire him.

"Oh, shut up." His father suddenly punches my papà in the face.

"No!" I scream.

"Stop your whining," Joseph says.

"Don't hurt him!"

"Why?" he asks, grabbing a hold of my papà's head as if he's a doll. "You care for this man? You think you should, but you have no fucking clue what he's done, have you?"

"What are you talking about?" I say, gazing at Angel too. "What is he talking about?"

Angel just frowns and stares at his plate, unmoving.

"Do something!" I scream at Angel, but he ignores me.

"He's not going to help you, bambina," his father

228

jests. "And you don't want him to. You can't trust anyone, you know. He is *my* son after all."

"What is he talking about?" I ask Angel, but Angel merely frowns.

"What I'm talking about is my son being part of your misery," Joseph says with a smile. "Do you remember the day your mother died? You were the one who went to the police and showed them a picture of a license plate. That license plate belonged to my son."

My lips part, but no sound comes out, not even in despair.

I can't believe what I'm hearing.

"You killed … my mamma?" The words manage to slip out on their own, almost as if I'm not in control over my own voice.

In a long breath, Angel says, "Yes."

When he gazes at me, I can feel my heart shattering into a million bits.

"You …"

"I'm sorry, Sky. I didn't know it was your mother I had to kill until it was too late."

"You killed her!" I scream, almost lunging out of my chair if it wasn't for these ties.

Joseph laughs out loud. "Look at that bambina … so feisty!"

"It was a job and I wouldn't have taken it if I'd known it was your mother." Angel throws an angry look at his father.

"See? I told you?" Joseph says to me. "We're all

bastards."

"I don't give a shit what you have to say. Release my papà and me. Now."

He places both his hands on the table. "Not until you tell me everything I want to know."

"I'm not telling you shit," I spit. "And you ... I can't believe I almost trusted you."

Angel just looks away, defeated.

"It doesn't matter who you trust or don't, bambina. You're in my house now, and we play by my rules. I will show you there's no hope, and that your own papà can't even be trusted."

"I don't want to hear it!" I yell.

"But you must," Joseph says. "Your deadbeat papà was the one who led me to you, bambina," he says, grinning like a devil. "You think you know who he is, but you've been lied to."

"What?" I gasp, my breath faltering.

"He gave you up."

Joseph grabs my papà's head by his hair and slams him on the table.

I scream in shock; the realization of what he says and what's happening sinking in like a brick tied to my ankle while I sink to the bottom of the ocean.

"Your papà is a rat. A scumbag who couldn't keep his daughter under control."

"Don't listen to him, Sky," my papà mumbles.

"Shut your mouth." Joseph stuffs my papà's mouth with a napkin. "Now, as I was saying ... your papà was supposed to keep you from going to the police after your madre died. But we all know how that turned out."

He shortly glances at his son.

I don't know what to say; I'm too shocked to even consider replying.

"Which is why I came for retribution. I came and took you. Guess who told me where exactly you were that day you went to pick up your papà's medicine ..."

I look at my papà with tear-stained eyes. "Please ..."

"Yes, Sky, look at him and realize he is the one who led me straight to you."

My papà shakes his head, not even having the will to look me straight in the eye.

"Papà? Please tell me it isn't true."

He can't speak with the napkin in his mouth, but I know he can hear me, and he can spit it out if he wants. Instead, he lets Joseph do the talking for him.

Angel's father starts playing with a knife. "When it turned out you had something of mine, your papà begged me to give you some time. And you know? Being the kind man that I am, I gave you time. In fact, I told him that I'd wait until your birthday. But it turns out neither of you learned from your mistakes. Never double-cross me."

He rams the knife into the table, causing me to jolt in my seat. "You tried to flee. You tried to steal from me. And now you pay the price."

"No ..." I mutter, shaking my head.

I can't believe it.

This isn't true.

My very own papa ... betrayed me?

"It is because of him that you've been captured," Joseph continues. "I wouldn't have known your location if it wasn't for him. Your papà told me where you were when I promised him to return you after twenty-one days. It was a bargaining chip ... however, I never said how you'd return. If it's up to me, he will get you back in pieces."

My lips quiver and a tear rolls down my cheek.

This can't be happening.

"No," I say. "I don't believe it."

"What? Do you think I'm lying?" Joseph says, making a face. "Do you think I'm capable of that? That I even fucking care?"

He takes another knife, a bigger, sharper one, and holds it in front of my papà's neck. "Do you really believe this scumbag is worthy of anything but death? You think you love him, you think you want to talk to him, but what he has to say will make you wish you were already dead."

"No ..." I shake my head.

"Yes, Sky. Your papà is a coward. When I came for you and you weren't there, he fucking begged for his life. Like some cockroach not worthy of life." He spits in my papà's face. "He fucking gave you up to save his own miserable life."

232

I look at my papa, whose tears have also started running. "Tell me it isn't true," I mutter.

His face shows defeat as he spits out the napkin and says, "I'm sorry, Sky. I'm so sorry."

"See what a pain in the ass he is? Why do you think I dragged him back here?" He looks at my papà with a stupid grin on his face. "Hey, you only asked me to let you live. You didn't specify how."

"You … you gave me up? While I was hiding at my friend's house, you just told them where I was to save your own life? And you're the reason I was attacked in that alley? When I went out to get *your* medicine, you betrayed me? Tell me it isn't true, Papà. Tell me!"

"I don't deserve you," is the last thing he says.

Because with one quick flick, Joseph uses the knife to cut his throat and end his life.

DAY 16

ANGEL

Yesterday

"No!" Her scream is louder than anything I've heard before.

I immediately pick up her chair and turn her around. "Fucking hell!"

I can't believe he just fucking killed her father right in front of her.

Fuck. "Are you insane?" I scream at my father.

Her sobs and screams cut through me like a knife. She's wrestling me in the chair, probably desperate to turn around and run to her dad, to hug him, to bring him back to life, even though it won't help. That's why I keep her in place as I cut the ties that bind her and pick her up from the chair.

"Let me go!" she screams, trying to look at her father over my shoulder. "Papà!"

"Where are you going?" my father asks.

"I'm taking her back to her room. End of story."

"Why? She wanted to talk to her papà. Now she has," he says with a laugh as if it's some sort of cruel joke.

I turn around, viciously sneering, "I didn't say you could kill him!"

"He was a rat. He deserved to die."

"He was her father!"

He shrugs. "So?"

"We'll talk about this later," I growl, and I turn around and stomp away from the scene.

I don't want her to witness any of this. It's too sadistic, too barbaric to make her watch this for one more second. Hell, it probably scarred her for life now … and it's all because I told my father she wanted to see her father before she'd talk.

Goddammit.

She pounds on my back with her fists, screaming in my ear, "Let me go!"

"Don't look," I tell her, grabbing her legs tightly as I walk up the stairs with her.

She fights me all the way to her room, but it doesn't matter to me. All that matters to me is that she's safe, that she forgets this, and that I finish this once and for all.

"Put me down!" she says, as I close the door behind us.

The moment I place her feet on the floor, she runs for the exit, but I have the key tucked away where she won't dare to look.

"You're not going back there." I grab her arm and pull her away, standing in front of the door myself just to make a point.

"Let me through!" She pushes me, but I'm not moving anywhere. "Get away!"

"It won't help," I say.

She starts punching me in the gut and the arms, but my muscles are made of steel when confronted with her weak body. She's not nearly strong enough, but that's okay. I'll be her punching bag. I know that's what she needs most right now.

"You piece of shit, get out of my way! You fucking killed my mamma, and now my father's dead, too."

She keeps slapping me—kicking, scratching, anything to get past me—but it's futile. The more she fights, the more she seems to realize this, as the energy she puts into it diminishes with every blow.

"I hate you! I fucking hate you!"

"You have every right to hate me, Sky," I say, looking down at her with remorseful eyes.

I wish I could change the cold, hard truth, but I can't. All I can do is stand here and accept her rage.

"You killed her! You don't deserve to live!" she yells, punching me until her knuckles start to bleed, and my stomach begins to ache.

Soon, her attacks turn into sobs as the tears flow down her face. She mumbles, "Mama ... Papà ..."

When her fingers stop forming fists and her nails dig into my skin, her head falls to my chest and the noise stops. All that remains are the cold, painful tears that seep into my heart.

"Papà ... You can't ...die too," she mutters.

"Shh ..." I place my hand on the back of her head and soothe her.

Her body collapses on top of me, her muscles losing the will to fight, and I sink to the floor with her, holding her close to me. My body will shield her from harm, and my warmth will comfort her in the darkness.

It's the least I can do.

After all ... not only did her mother die by my hand, but I'm also responsible for killing her father now too.

***

Present

I grab a strand of her hair and tuck it behind her ear. She looks beautiful when she's asleep. Like a real angel fallen from the sky. My Azure Sky.

She hates me.

She despises me and rightfully so.

I destroyed everything that's good about her. And for what?

The more I think about it, the less I want to give my father what he needs, but I know that if I stop now, he'll not only kill her but also me, too. The fact that he cut her father's neck in front of her means he's getting impatient and angry, and that's bad news. It means he could explode at any moment and might just decide to kill her out of the blue, for no reason, and without any answers.

Then everything would've been for nothing.

I can't let that happen.

Suddenly, a little yawn leaves her mouth, and I smile as I see her eyes open.

She's lying in my arms as I sit on the floor. We spent the night sleeping on the floor. I held her close in my arms and watched her fall into slumber out of pure grief. She fought the sleep as long as she could, but she seemed so tired that I kept her here until she did.

I didn't want to move and risk waking her, so I stayed down here with her instead.

Except, the moment she spots my face hovering above hers, her pupils dilate and her lips quiver.

She stumbles away, falling to the floor, crawling backward like a terrified lamb. "What happened?"

"You fell asleep. Calm down," I say, holding up my hands.

"Get away from me!"

I go after her. Knowing full well there's nowhere she can go, I take it easy on her. "I'm not going to hurt you." I know she doesn't believe me, but it doesn't hurt to try. I have to gain her trust again. Whatever it takes. It's the only way to make her talk.

"You killed my mamma! And my father's dead too now, thanks to you! Of course, you're going to hurt me." She reaches for the nightstand and throws out whatever she can find. Taking a hold of a pen, she waves it like some sort of weapon.

I smile and gently walk toward her, trying not to scare her. "Stop. This isn't helping you."

"You aren't helping me either."

"I know you hate me—"

"Damn right, I do," she growls.

"I promise … I'm not going to hurt you." I hold out my hand. "What happened was out of my control."

"You were the one who killed her! You could've decided against it."

"And then I'd be dead," I say. "Now give me the pen."

"No!"

I take it from her, whether she wants me to or not. She fights me over it, jerking my hand and pushing me away. I throw the pen into the far corner of the room and wrap my arms around her as she struggles to let go of her fear. "Sky, calm down."

"My parents … I need to avenge them. You're a

murderer."

"And you will, but not now." I tighten my grip on her. "I'm still that same man you once knew. The one you couldn't stop spending time with, the one you went home with. I haven't changed."

"I didn't know you were a hired killer!"

"No, but it doesn't change the fact that I still care about you. More than I have ever cared for anyone else." I spin her around in my arms. "Stop fighting me. I'm not going to let you kill either of us, even though I deserve it."

"Yeah, you do," she growls.

"I think you and I both know who you want to kill first," I say, looking down at her. "And it isn't me."

"But you're partly responsible."

"I know … and I'm sorry for causing you so much pain. I wouldn't have done it if I knew this would happen. I didn't know it was your mother, nor did I know he'd kill your father. I never would've gone through with it had I known."

"But you did … and now they're dead." Tears well up in her eyes again. "I can't believe they're really dead."

I tip her chin up. "And I'll repent that every day for the rest of my life. I hate to see you break down, Sky. I hate that I'm the one who caused it. Why do you think I brought you back up here?"

She frowns, not answering me, so I lean in to rest my forehead on hers.

"I didn't want you to have to see that. I wish …" I caress her cheek. "I wish I could take the memory away. All of it."

"Even yourself?"

"If I have to. If it means you'll live," I say, closing my eyes.

It's quiet for some time. All I feel is her heartbeat against my chest as I hold her tight, afraid that if I let go, then she might try to run again.

After a deep breath, she says, "I'll never forgive you."

"I know you won't, and I don't expect you to."

"You say you want me to live, but all I want is for you to die."

"You don't mean that," I say.

"How do you know?" she says.

"Because you're holding on to me, too."

She looks up at me with red cheeks, and that's when I know she's realized it too. Her fingers have instinctively grabbed hold of my shirt and pulled me closer to her, in an attempt to soothe her aching heart.

"I know you hate me, but you need me, too. And I need you, too," I say, grabbing her face with both hands.

She doesn't flinch or try to run, so I take the opportunity to kiss her on the lips, knowing it could very well be the last time. Except, she doesn't fight me, she lets me take her mouth with mine, as I attempt to kiss away the pain.

"Forget what you saw," I murmur against her lips. "Let the memories fade away. It's only you and me. Just you and me."

"You're no angel," she says, as I lick her lips. "You're the devil himself."

I smirk as she arches toward my mouth when my lips unlatch. "I'm here to make you sin."

"It's wrong," she whispers.

"It's so wrong, it becomes right," I say, kissing her even harder.

"Don't ..." she mutters. "It isn't right."

"It's right if we want it to be, Sky."

"But my papà ..."

"Your papà was right. He doesn't deserve you," I say. "And I don't either, but I *will* fight for you, with every fucking breath I take. He didn't fight for you, Sky, but I will. I promise you."

She licks her lips. "Did he really ... betray me?"

"I didn't want to tell you because I knew it would break your heart," I say, sighing.

She looks down at the floor. "But I know now ... I guess that's better than not knowing."

"As they say, ignorance is bliss," I say, but I know it won't help her.

"He was supposed to be someone I could look up to. My papa. Someone who'd protect me and who'd come and rescue me."

"But he didn't. He chose himself over you."

She huffs, nodding into my chest, breathing out a

difficult breath.

"But I'm here now, and I'm not letting you go." I look down at her and grab her chin. "Do you hear me? I'm not giving up on you, and I won't let you give up on you either."

Tentatively, I press my lips on hers again, wanting to suck out every bit of negativity until she feels nothing but happiness again. I don't care what it takes, but I will take her out of the darkness and back into the light. Even if it means taking her body, mind, and soul ... I will make her push the memories away and make a place for new ones. With me. Only me.

"Only think of me," I murmur, kissing her deeply. "Just me and what you feel for me. Nothing else."

"I don't know what I feel ..." she says.

"Feel me," I say, kissing her so long she loses her breath.

I pick her up from the floor and place her on the bed, devouring her mouth. I'm not letting go of her and I won't stop kissing her, no matter how many times she begs me ... because I know it's only lies. Her brain is telling her that she needs to fight, but this battle has already been lost. All she can do now is accept what I'm about to give her.

***

SKY

244

I try to push him off me, but he's just too strong and my muscles are weak from fighting all the time. I'm tired of fighting, tired of battling my inner demons. But I can't allow myself to give up just like that. It wouldn't be right.

"Let go of your inhibitions, Sky," Angel murmurs against my lips, crawling on top of me.

"I can't … you're so wrong for me," I say between kisses.

Words that come from my mouth don't ring true in my heart, but I must resist.

"Wrong can be right as long as you believe it."

"I don't—"

"Then I'll make you believe," he growls. He grabs my hands and pins them above my head. "I don't care what happens. You're mine, and I won't have it any other way."

Holding me down with one hand, he reaches into the nightstand with the other and takes out a set of cuffs, hooking them onto my wrists and the top side of the bed. I should be terrified; angry with him for chaining me up again, but for some reason my heart feels at ease. With his mouth on my neck and my hands tied up, I feel powerless, left at his mercy … something that I desperately need right now.

I hate to admit it, but it's true. His kisses calm me; his claim makes me forget. Even if just for a moment, it still is what I crave the most—to lose control. To feel nothing but pleasure while stuck in the abyss. He's my light in the darkness, my source of energy when I'm at my weakest, most vulnerable state.

And he knows this far too well.

I need his love more than anything right now, and he's using it to his advantage.

He's using *me*.

And I don't even care.

I let him kiss me all over, not kicking or even flinching as he licks his way down my chest. The shirt that I was wearing as a sort of dress barely covers my nipples as they harden from arousal.

His fingers creep underneath my shirt, checking the wounds that seemed to have healed overnight. "How does it feel?" he asks.

"Okay."

"Good enough to fuck?"

The bluntness in his voice makes me blush.

I nod, unsure if I can even say no.

With one quick, relentless tug, the buttons pop, flying all around the room as he rips my shirt apart and throws it away with a grunt. "God, I fucking want you so much right now," he growls, not taking another second before ravishing me completely.

My back instinctively arches toward him, even though I keep telling myself I shouldn't. I shouldn't allow him to take me like this, bound to a bed that isn't mine, strapped up while my father just died a horrible death. What am I doing? What am I thinking in going along with it? And yet, I can't stop. No matter how many times my mouth tries to tell him to stop, I find it harder and harder to believe in it myself.

"You want this, too, don't you?" he murmurs, grasping my breast and sucking my nipple hard.

I moan, hissing when he nibbles. "No …"

He looks up at me with a smirk, my nipple popping out of his mouth. "Yes, you do."

His hand travels down my body and I'm helpless against his demanding touch as he spreads my legs and lets his hand slide down my pussy. "Hmm … so wet."

He slides it up and down, careful to pay only minimal attention to my clit, teasing me to the limit. Then, out of nowhere, he plunges his finger into my pussy. My legs immediately pull together, feeling him swivel around inside.

With one hand, he smacks my inner thigh. "Open."

I do what he says, relaxing my legs as he inserts another finger and plays with me, watching my every huff and puff. After toying with me, he licks his lips and leaves me with a thumping pussy.

"You taste so fucking good," he says, his fingers hovering above my face. "Taste yourself, Sky."

He pushes his fingers into my mouth, and my tongue wraps around his fingers as if it's desperate for cock. I'm stupid, like a little girl swooning over a much older, more dangerous guy, but I'm so lost in the moment. My mind is spinning with desire at the sight of his hungry gaze.

When he takes his fingers from my mouth, he starts tugging my nipple so hard, it hurts.

"Does it hurt?" he asks.

"Yes …"

"Good," he says, licking his lip in such a seductive way that it makes me shiver.

The more I start to hiss, the harder he tugs, pulling until I feel his hard-on press against me.

"I like it when I see the pain in your eyes …" he murmurs. "I don't know why, but it's so fucking arousing."

"I thought it was punishment," I say. "For running away again and not telling you what you want to know. Even after—"

"This isn't punishment. Oh no, this is pure pleasure. For me." He winks. "And for you."

"But … why?" I moan, as he releases my tender nipple, which still buzzes and sears.

"Because this is what we both need right now. End of story," he growls.

It's as if he doesn't even want to know the answer himself.

Maybe we're both so lost in each other that we've discarded all rhyme and reason.

Questions and answers aren't there, only pain and lust. And I'm fully okay with that.

"Do you know what I'm going to do?" he asks, leaning up so I can take a good look at him while he unbuttons his shirt.

I shake my head.

"First," he says, taking off his shirt and throwing it into a corner. "I'm going to fuck your tight little pussy." He squints, watching my reaction, as his muscles flex with every sentence that comes from his mouth. "And then I'm going to fuck your asshole."

"What?" I say, my eyes widening. "No!"

He pounces down on me, causing me to shut my eyes as I worried he might fall on top of me, but he manages to catch himself just in time, hovering dangerously close to my face. "Or maybe I should fuck that pretty little mouth of yours instead since you seem so intent on defying me still."

"No, no," I mutter. "I'm sorry."

"Don't say you're sorry, Sky," he says, twirling my hair around his finger. "But I do want you to do everything I say. When I say it. Wherever. Just like you promised me."

"I didn't ..." I gasp, interrupting myself because I'm starting to remember.

"Oh, yes, you did. You promised to give yourself to me if I gave you your dad, and that's exactly what I did." His tongue dips out to lick my skin, goosebumps scattering all across because I know what I've done.

I promised him that I would do anything he says.

I gave my soul to the devil, knowing full well what it meant, just so I could talk to my papà one final time.

And now I pay the price.

The funny thing is that I don't even know if I should be upset or delighted. Angel has this effect on me that turns me into a delirious girl filled with lust and desires she didn't know she had. It only happens when I'm around him. He's always done this to me … swoop me off my feet and tie me up until I'm left begging for mercy. It's mind boggling that I would want someone like him, but I do. I really do, no matter how much I try to deny it; my heart made its choice long ago.

"Now …" The darkness in his voice is a drug to my ears. "Spread your legs and let me fuck that pussy of mine."

He pushes himself to his feet, undoes the button, and pulls his zipper, dropping his pants and boxer shorts in one go. When his cock pops out in its fully erect state, I'm so flustered that my lips actually part. Salty pre-cum drips down the tip, drawing my attention and making me want to stick out my tongue. I don't know what's wrong with me, but I can't stop thinking these dirty thoughts either. He makes it impossible for me to hate him and so easy to adore him.

"Getting a little excited now?" he muses, playing with his cock as if he finds it amusing to watch me stammer.

"No, no …" I lie.

He smirks, biting his lip. "Don't worry … I'll make sure you'll feel me deep inside you."

He pounces back down on top of me, spreading my legs and pushing the tip of his hard-on against my entrance. I hold my breath when he enters, slow and steady, almost as if to torture me by not giving it to me.

"Look at me," he says, staring at me with those black eyes.

The moment I do, he plunges in, causing me to gasp and moan out loud. Oh god, he's huge, and I can feel him everywhere.

"Oh … fuck me, so tight," he groans, thrusting in and out.

His entire body works me, grinding me from top to bottom, putting ample pressure on my core as his chest rubs my nipples, teasing my senses. He covers my mouth with mine as I struggle to breathe, moaning into his mouth when he kisses me deeply. I've never been so overcome with lust that I'd want to beg him to fuck me, but damn, I'm so close now.

He thrusts carefully, avoiding contact with my wounds as he slides in and out with ease. His rugged hand cups my face as he licks me like some lion, marking me as his. His other hand grabs my breast and kneads it, toying with my nipple and pushing me to the brink.

"Oh, god …" I mutter when his mouth leaves mine to allow me a second to breathe.

"I'm not gonna stop until you come all over my cock," he growls, sucking my neck to the point of leaving a warm spot. My muscles tighten around his length, desperate to open and close at the same time. I want to come so badly it hurts, mentally, knowing that

I'm this far gone.

"Tell me how much you want it," he says.

I shake my head.

He slaps my breast, making me cry out. "Yes! Yes, I want it."

"Every time you deny it, I'll punish you for it," he growls.

"Please ..." I mutter.

"Please what?" he asks.

When I don't answer, another slap follows, this time on my other breast.

"Please fuck me!" I blurt out.

"That's more like it," he says with a grin.

His thrusts grow in intensity, and I hold on to the headboard as he ravishes me. He hits all the right spots at the exact right time. He was right; once he fucked me, I'd be lost to him forever. I tried to forget what he could do to me, but now I know it's in vain. He's the only one who knows how I really am, what I like, what I feel inside. I love being whisked away and taken, and now he's managed to use it against me.

"Why does it feel so wrong ..." I mutter when he takes my earlobe in his mouth and gently nibbles.

"Don't think. Feel me with your body, not your mind," he muses, kissing my neck, plunging in again.

The deeper he goes, the more intense my pulses become, and my legs instinctively wrap themselves around his body, wanting him even closer. I'm so close to ecstasy I can feel myself hinging on the edge.

But then he takes his cock out.

Just like that, he leaves me feeling bereft.

"What?" I stammer, looking up as he slides his hard-on across my pussy, teasing me to the max.

"Beg me for it," he says, his tongue darting out as he looks down at my swollen lips. "Do you want to come, Sky? Beg me."

I sigh, dropping my head to the pillow, looking up at the ceiling.

He smacks my inner thigh, which makes me squeal.

"Answer me. Now."

"Please, make me come," I say in one breath.

My thumping pussy has clearly taken over control.

The smile on his face makes me shiver. "Good girl."

When he pushes back in, it feels heavenly, too good to be true, and too wrong to feel right. But my body is insane and so am I, as I let him take me again, willingly, begging for him to make me come with his cock alone.

"Can you feel that, Sky? Your slickness covering my cock? That's your body telling you it wants me."

"I'm gonna …"

"Yes, come for me. Let me see that pretty face as you milk me," he growls.

His dirty words send me over the edge. I quake beneath him, pleasure rolling through me, complete bliss ensuing. I can feel him pulsing inside me, a warm explosion filling me up the brim.

He grunts. "Fuck!" Cum jets into me, intensifying

the euphoria. For a few seconds, I'm in heaven before I come crashing right down again as his flaccid cock spills from me and he whispers into my ear.

"You didn't scream my name, which means I'll keep fucking you until you do. Every hour of this entire day and tomorrow as well. And when you finally do scream my name, I'll fuck your asshole, too."

He gets off the bed and rummages through the nightstand until he finds what he's looking for. Something that both scares and excites the shit out of me.

A butt plug.

Biting his lip as he grabs the lube, he says, "Now turn around and pucker up."

DAY 17

ANGEL

I wasn't lying when I said I'd fuck her asshole.

That tight little ring was begging me to claim it as well.

She panicked at first; knowing the size of my cock would probably hurt her more than my spankings would. But she had no choice in the matter, considering she gave herself to me, willingly. And now I want from her what I've been craving for so long.

God, her ass has been on my mind for a long time now. Good thing she finally screamed my name after fucking her five times. We went at it the entire night. Her pussy must feel really sore right now ... or really good. I can't tell because she can't even talk straight anymore. I love it when her eyes roll to the back of her sockets as if she's practically losing herself when I fuck her. It keeps making me blow my load, that face of hers. Maybe I should mark it again. It's too pretty not to.

As she's lying on the bed, completely drained, I lick her skin, the salty taste a turn-on. "Ready for more?" I ask.

She shakes her head, her body shivering when I twirl my tongue around her nipple.

"Wrong answer ..." I murmur, twisting her other nipple until she screams out loud.

"Yes!" she mewls.

I reach for her hips and pull her up from the bed, twisting her on her belly.

"What are you doing?" She jerks the cuffs that bind her to the headboard because her hands are now crossed.

"I told you what I was gonna do if you didn't tell me what I want to know ..."

I rub her little red ass and take out the plug I put in earlier. She bites the pillow as it plops out, which makes me grin. She put up quite a fight when I first pushed in a finger. After a while, I attempted to put in the plug, and I had to spank her a few times until she understood there was no denying me this pleasure. No one has that privilege. I take what I want, end of story, and now I *want* her ass.

Spreading the lube all over her hole, I muse, "How does it feel?"

"Empty …" she says.

"It won't be for long," I taunt.

"Please …" she mutters, her breath hitching when I plunge in a finger.

"Yes, Sky, I'll give you what you want."

I throw the tube on the bed, grip her hips, and push my cock against her tight little entrance. Pushing in, she squeals, her muscles tightening around me, providing ample pressure as I bury myself in her ass.

"Fuck me …" I grunt, unable to explain to her how good it fucking feels to finally fucking claim all her holes.

"It hurts," she growls.

I slap her ass cheek, making her squeal. "And it'll hurt even more if you resist. Now spread your legs and let me claim this tight ass of yours."

I start thrusting, slowly at first, but then faster as she adjusts to my length. When I really start plunging into her, her tired body starts to move along with me, still desiring more. Pure need drives me, my energy having run out long ago, but sleep won't hold me back from taking what belongs to me.

As I ravish her ass, I growl, "Take it!"

Her face is buried in the pillow, unable to hold itself up, so I help her by grabbing her hair, twisting it, and pulling it tight, causing her to buck.

"That's it. Take my cock like a good fucking girl."

Lust has completely consumed me, feeling her tight ass squeeze my cock until it begs me to come. Or maybe I will make her beg instead. "Fucking beg me to come in your ass and maybe I will."

"Yes, come in my ass, please," she says with a ragged breath.

Her tits bounce as I fuck her hard, my fingers digging into her skin while I hold her tight, spanking her between each thrust.

"You want it?" I growl.

"Yes, please!" she begs.

Her cries push me over the edge yet again, causing my seed to burst out of me. I moan out loud as my cum squirts into her tight ass and I finally feel released of my needs.

Fucking the entire night has taken its toll on the both of us. When my cock slides out of her, I don't even have the energy to breathe.

I slap her one final time, which makes her fall down onto the bed, panting out loud, just like me.

I quickly tuck away the lube and toy, deciding that I'll clean them later. I grab my pants and quickly put them on again, fetching a blanket to cover her. When I return, she's still lying motionless on the bed, her face buried in the pillow like before. I reach for the key and uncuff her. Still, she doesn't move.

I would've expected her to run.

Hell, I even thought she might attack me.

Instead, it's as if she's lost her will.

Did I go too far this time?

Did I break her, even when it wasn't my purpose anymore?

I lie down beside her and turn her body around. That's when I see the tears lining her eyes. She blinks them away and tries to turn her head away from me, but I cup her chin and make her look at me.

"Tell me where it hurts," I say, folding the blanket over her body.

She holds her hands above her stomach. "I ..."

"Was I too hard on your ass?" I frown. "Because I swear I could hear you moan."

Her cheeks redden even more. "That's not it. I did like it ... even though I shouldn't have ... but I ..."

"Say it."

She looks up at me with those doe-like eyes of hers. "You didn't use protection. I don't want ... I don't want it to happen again."

"What? You mean ..." I grab her arm tightly. "Again? What are you talking about?"

Her lips part and then she shuts her mouth again, her brows drawing together as she shakes her head.

"You have to tell me," I say.

"If I do, it'll all be for nothing."

"It means we're one step closer to saving your life, and I am not going to let you die." I crawl in front of her, grab both of her arms, and make her look at me. "Do you hear me? I will *not* give up on you. You are mine and I protect what's mine, got it? *Nothing* will stand in my way, so you *will* tell me. *Now.*"

"It happened before," she mutters. "I'm not on the pill. I …"

"What are you trying to tell me? You were …"

"I was pregnant."

Shock ripples through me, and I find it hard to control myself right now. A part of me is about to explode, risking tearing everything in my vicinity to shreds, including her. My hands grip her too tight, so I release her and get up from the bed, standing by her side, not knowing what to do to contain the situation.

"You were fucking pregnant?"

She nods, softly, as if she's scared of the consequences.

I don't blame her.

I would be scared of myself too now if I looked in the mirror.

"You were pregnant and you never told me?"

"I couldn't …" She sniffs. "If I did, you would've killed me."

"Why? No, of course not." I rub my head. "Fuck. Seriously. You're not joking now, are you? You really were pregnant?"

"It's the truth … for once …" she says, her eyes drifting off into nothingness as if her heart has already broken just by admitting it.

"But … Oh, Jesus fucking Christ." I rub my whole face with my hands, breathing in and out as slow as I can while I feel like a motherfucking bull on the inside.

"I fucking fucked you. Day in and out. I tortured you." Every word I speak adds to the weight of my burden. My crime.

She's right. I'm fucking evil.

"You were fucking pregnant ..."

In an instant, I grab the chair in the corner and fling it against the other wall. She crawls into a little corner, her body shaking as I throw around the table, too. I'm livid. Not at her, but at myself. How could I be such a piece of shit? How could I not see this? Just looking at her now, I can already see the stretch marks on her belly. I didn't think anything of it, but now it all makes sense. That's why she feared my touch and me so much. Why she chose pain over pleasure.

Overtaken by fury, I roar out loud and reach for the lamp, throwing it against the wall as well, the light bulb shattering into a million bits. Her squeal is deafening, and it immediately makes me stop in my tracks. My animalistic instincts tell me that I should protect my woman. It's all I ever wanted, her. And yet it's me who's been ruining her all this time.

"Stop ..." she mutters.

"You were fucking pregnant!" I scream. "How long ago?"

"A year ago ..."

"FUCK!"

"Please, stop," she says, a tear running down her cheek. "You're frightening me."

"I can't believe you never told me. Fuck. I mean, I

fucking hurt you. And you're ... you're a mother?" The dread in my own voice scares me to the point of wanting to sag down on the bed.

The way she shakes her head softly makes me wait and squint.

"What?"

"I'm not ... I'm not a mamma." Her voice trembles as she speaks. As if she doesn't want to say it. Not even in her head.

"What do you mean?"

"They took it out."

"You aborted it?"

She nods silently, which makes me sigh out loud.

"Goddammit ..."

She makes a face. "Please don't be mad. I didn't want to tell you because it means I'm no longer useful to you. It means you'd have a free pass."

"At what? Killing you? Why on earth would I fucking kill you?"

"Because this is what your father is after. Why you had to capture me. Why I couldn't tell you the truth ... if he found out there is no baby, I'd die."

At first, all I can do is stare, blinking rapidly. But then it hits me.

"One year ago ..." I mutter.

It can't be.

No.

This can't fucking be it.

"Tell me you're fucking lying. Tell me it wasn't a

year ago," I growl.

"I'm not lying, I swear," she says.

"Tell me I'm wrong. Tell me my father isn't looking for his fucking baby you aborted."

Her silent sobs and wistful looks tell me enough.

A rumbling howl pierces the walls of this mansion, signaling the entire household that shit's about to go down, as I rip open the door so hard it breaks off the handle. "That's it. I'm gonna fucking kill him."

DAY 18

SKY

On the day I realized I was pregnant, my life as I knew it was over.

I can still see the stripes on the test I was holding in my shaky hands. I can still feel the dread washing over me as I came face to face with the truth.

Everything clicked together.

The nausea I'd been feeling for weeks. The cravings, the emotional outbursts, the undying need for love and affection.

It all made sense. And yet this revelation would crumble my world.

The first few days I cried, wasting away on my bed,

not wanting to eat or sleep. I didn't want my papà or life itself. I just wanted to die. I didn't know what to do. I wanted nothing else than for this baby to go away. This spawn that was given to me without my consent.

I couldn't tell my papà. He almost died when he saw me hurt from the assault, his heart almost giving in that very day. I had to call an ambulance and get him to the emergency clinic. If I'd tell him what happened in the aftermath … well, let's just say I don't think the ambulance would make it in time.

I knew I would have to tell him someday, but I kept making excuses, kept pushing it forward.

In bed, I pondered what to do. I could go to the police and become a victim in their database. But this was only a fleeting thought because I knew they were corrupt and would never help me catch the guys who did this to me. I doubted they would even help me with this baby.

Nobody would help me. It was a lost cause.

My second thought was suicide. I honestly wanted to kill myself. I never thought I'd become one of those girls who'd throw their lives away just like that, but I was on the edge. After what happened, I was shattered, and I didn't think I could go on living feeling the way I felt. The men who'd hurt me, who'd haunted my every living thought, would come after me if they found out that I was pregnant. Of course, they'd want the baby. There would be no way I'd be able to escape. I'd be doomed forever.

Which meant it was a choice between being a prisoner to my own body and ending it all. Right here, right now.

I was so close; I could literally feel the blade cut into my flesh.

But right then, at that very moment when I held the knife over my wrist, I felt a bump against my belly. At first, I thought I imagined it, but as I pressed the knife deeper into my skin, another bump followed.

The knife dropped from my hand, and for the first time, I felt life inside me.

I didn't know what it was that I felt. It was still too early for kicks, but it didn't matter to me. What I felt was real. It forced me to get up from my knees and clean my wrists in the sink, washing away the sentence I was about to give myself.

I couldn't die. Not as long as something inside me lived.

I couldn't die ... so the only choice left was aborting the life that was silently growing inside me.

Twenty-one weeks had passed before I made the decision. I knew it was late, but I was still on time. It was just such a difficult decision ... no one would be able to make it on a whim.

I swore to myself I wouldn't tell my papà until it was done. After it was over, he would hear my story.

As I walked to the clinic with a heavy burden on my shoulders, I wondered ... would it hurt? Would the baby feel anything?

Regardless, I had to push on. I knew that once it was done, I'd be in grave danger. After all ... if they discovered I had aborted it, they'd kill me. But if I didn't, they'd come after me all the same, only with a baby instead of without one.

I was exchanging one evil for the other. And I knew then that—no matter what I did—the scars that covered my body and soul would never disappear.

I guess it was for the best.

Now that I've told Angel, it feels like a burden dropped off my chest ... and my body is flung into a deep, dark hole.

I shouldn't have told him, but what else could I do? I'm terrified that it will happen again. He didn't use protection, which means I could become pregnant. I don't want another mistake. It's the only thing I feared when I came here ...

And now it might become real.

***

ANGEL

Speeding like a motherfucker, I drive to my father's restaurant, thoughts spinning through my mind about how I'm going to kill him. I don't want him to just die. I want it to be a slow and painful death. I don't care about the consequences or that the whole company may come after me. Nobody does this to *my* girl.

No one.

As I drive up the parking lot, I make a mental memory note of the fact that I did, in fact, lock Sky's door. I don't want anyone else coming anywhere near her right now, so she's safest in that room. There is only one key, and that's currently in my fucking pocket.

They'll have to pry it from my dead hands if they want her.

Fuck me, I'm livid.

Sky tried to stop me from going; she said it would get me killed. We discussed it for an entire day, but in the end, I realized that only my father's imminent death could solve this situation. Nobody will stop me from having my revenge, not even Sky.

My father did what no man ever should, and now he'll pay the price.

With a rifle, I storm inside the restaurant, loading the barrel as I walk. The second I open the hallway door, a man is in my face. Marcus, one of my father's contacts.

"Get out of my fucking way!" I scream at him.

He smiles and says, "Wow, hey now …"

"Move," I growl.

He holds up his hands. "Don't shoot. I come in peace." He laughs. "Are you sure you want to do that?"

"I'm gonna fucking kill him," I say. "Where is he?"

"I just had a chat with him about his business. Do

you know who I am?"

I frown, holding the gun up to his chest. "Do I look like I give a shit?"

He smiles, and it's one of the calmest, most gentle smiles I've seen in a long while. It creeps me the fuck out. "No, but I do believe you should hear me out. Your father deserves your anger, but know that you won't come out of this unharmed."

"What do you know?" I say, grabbing his collar.

"I know more than you think." He shrugs. "Let's just say your father and I go a long way back. Not in terms of old friends ... but more like a mutual agreement kind of thing."

I don't know what in the hell he wants from me, but he's starting to piss me off. "Tell you what ... why don't you just get out of my way so I can shoot the motherfucker and then there will be no more 'agreement' you need to worry about. Sounds good?"

"Hmm ..." He nods. "You do whatever you need to do. I just wanted you to know you're not alone." He winks. "You're quite something, you know that? I see a great future ahead of you."

Flabbergasted, I stare at him as he tips his hat and then walks past me out the door. What the actual fuck was that about? My father's business partners are straight up insane, just like him.

Must be part of the business.

You gain infinite wealth, but you lose an equally infinite amount of sanity with it.

Determined to end the charades, I push through the hallway door and find my father drinking wine at the table.

"You fucking son of a bitch," I growl, lifting the gun to shoot the very glass he's holding.

Nobody is gonna get fucking wasted on expensive wine while my girl has been treated like the scum of the earth. "You're gonna pay for what you did."

"Angel? What the fuck is the meaning of this?"

"I'll tell you what the fuck is up. You fucking got her pregnant!" I scream, stampeding toward him.

"Why are you aiming that gun at me? I'm your father, Angel. Is this how you treat your father, huh?"

"Don't call yourself my fucking father when you've done nothing to prove it to me, you lying sack of shit!"

"Hey now, hold up. I haven't lied to you," he says, patting his shirt with a napkin.

Angry, I hold the gun up to his face. "Oh, no? First, you didn't tell me that you'd taken her with your buddies, and then, you didn't tell me that she was fucking pregnant with your baby?"

"I didn't tell you because you didn't need to know. It's not lying if I didn't even give you an answer."

"You knew exactly what would happen! This," I growl, pushing the rifle into his forehead. "Give me one good reason why I shouldn't just shoot you in the fucking head right now."

"Because I'm your father. I raised you. You need me."

"Fuck, no."

He looks at me, and I get the sense that it's the calm before the storm. "You can't kill me yet, Angel. Trust me on this."

"No, I think I should torture you instead. Give you the same treatment that you gave my girl. Would you like that, huh? Being locked away and beaten all day? Maybe you'd like to be the victim for once!"

"You won't do that. You're not me. You don't have it in you," he says.

Fuck him for taunting me. "The fuck I do."

"Okay, so I didn't tell you why I wanted you to torture her? Can you blame me? I wanted the answer to my question, and I'm wondering now if you have it."

"Why did you put me on her case? Why?" I yell. "You knew I loved her. You fucking knew."

"Yes, I did. I've seen you prance around in my house with that bambina. I knew how much you fancied her ... and how much she destroyed your life by sending you to prison."

"I don't fucking blame her for it! I killed her mother ... but you ... you fucking took her without her permission and you let me do your dirty work. You fucking piece of shit."

"Now, now, calm down," he says. "You're my son, Angel, and I care about you, so I took care of her. Of course, I didn't expect that side effect would happen. Which is why I let you do the talking with her. I knew she wouldn't tell me, but she would tell you. And now you can tell me."

I want to rip the smug smile off his face. "Why the fuck do you think I would tell you?"

He pushes aside the barrel of the gun as if it's his god given right to do so. "Because your little bambina will die if you don't."

"Bullshit. You were still looking for the answer when I came here. You couldn't have known what I was about to tell you."

"Have you never noticed those cameras hanging on the wall in my house?" he muses. "You seem to think you're in control, but I've been keeping tabs on you all along."

"Motherfucker ..." I growl.

"The moment she spilled the truth and you left that room, I made the call. I'm guessing they're already out there getting their hands on her right now."

"I have her locked away where no one can get to her."

He smirks. "Who needs a key to break into a room when you have all sorts of tools lying around the house? Considering what we do ... did you forget?"

Agony fills me in an instant, my veins turning icy cold.

"Tsk, tsk ... shouldn't have left her alone now. That was your first mistake," he muses, his finger hovering in the air like some teacher schooling a child. "She'll be safe, as long as you tell me what I want to know. Now."

"You're fucking lying," I growl.

"Wanna bet on it?" he says, holding out his hand.

Anger makes me roar out loud as I kick a chair into oblivion. "Tell me where she fucking is or I swear I'll fucking kill you."

"If you kill me, you'll never see her face again. They're taking her away as we speak. I'm the only one who can stop it."

"Fuck. Tell me you're fucking lying or I swear I'll blow your fucking head off right now," I scream.

He picks up a cigar from the table as if the gun in his face doesn't even faze him. "You played the game well, Angel. You were quite useful to me."

The sharp sound the lighter makes as he snaps it shut makes the sweat drip down my back. "But now the show's coming to an end. You outlived your purpose. Well done."

"Purpose? Don't fucking talk to me about purpose."

"You were only a peon, Angel. A peon in my game. And good peons sacrifice themselves for the benefit of their king. You did well, but enough is enough. Now tell me … what happened to the baby? Where is it?"

"It's dead."

He frowns, making a face. "Excuse me? Don't be messing around with me now."

"I'm being fucking serious. It's dead. She aborted it because she couldn't stomach the thought of living another second with your cells inside her body, you dirty pig," I spit.

He takes a deep breath, gazing out the window. "Well, I guess that makes sense." He takes a whiff of his cigar.

"What? You're not even fazed?" I say.

"Well, I would've liked a different answer, but oh well. Case closed, I guess."

Something's not right. He's far too calm, too calculated about the way he speaks. He's playing me.

"You're ... you're still going to kill her, aren't you?"

He looks sheepishly at me, blowing smoke out in my face. "Well, now that I know the truth, she isn't of much use anymore, now is she?"

Fuck. I knew it.

The bastard was planning this all along.

For a second, I contemplate shooting him— whacking him with my gun, and then dragging him back to the same cell he put her in just so I can torture him—but then I realize what's at stake here. What happens if I kill him.

"Sky." It takes me exactly one second to spin on my heels and run toward the door.

She's in danger, and she's all I have left.

My father means nothing to me. Nothing.

The only person worth living for is about to slip through my fingers. I won't let it happen.

The last thing I heard before my father's rumbling laugh after he's taken another whiff, are the words, "Game ... Set ... Match."

DAY 19

SKY

Yesterday

The banging on the door wakes me in my sleep.

The thuds become louder and louder until they're no longer just thuds and the door breaks right through the middle. Men with guns ram the wood until it cracks enough that they can worm their way through.

I scream, jumping off the bed to hide in the corner of the room and grab the nearest weapon I can find. I make do with the lamp from the bedside table and hold it out in front of me like a goddamn sword.

"Don't come any closer!" I say to my attackers.

Their faces are smug and their smiles make me shiver.

"Oh, hello. Has he left you all alone in here, huh? Do you need some company?"

"Stay the fuck away from me!" I yell, smacking one of their hands with the lamp.

"Aww, look at that. She's still naked. The dirty fucker sure had his way with her," one of them says with a laugh.

I grab the bedsheets and wrap them around my cold body, fearing the worst.

Are they here to take me back to the cell again?

Or will they do even worse things to me?

One of them manages to snatch the lamp away from me and picks me up from the ground. I squeal as he throws me over his shoulder, slapping my butt in the process.

"Shut up or I'll make you," he growls.

"Put me down!" I scream in his ear, bashing his back.

"If you don't stop, I'm gonna take your pussy right here, right now," he says, pointing at one of the other guys who's already licking his lips like a hungry wolf. "And maybe he will, too."

Oh, god.

I can't let them take me away.

Terror takes over as I reach for the knife in his waistband and ram it into his stomach. He howls, his body collapsing underneath my weight. I fall to the ground but manage to catch myself and quickly get back up. I rush to the guy in the doorway, who seems surprised by my tenacity, and make use of the opportunity by jamming my knee in his crotch. Rushing past the two, I run out the door, still holding the bed sheets as if they could provide me any protection.

Then I notice the men all running toward me.

It's as if all the dogs have been taken off the leash.

I run into the opposite direction and take the stairs down, but even there they are waiting for me.

Why is this happening? Does Joseph know the truth?

It has to be it. There's no other explanation … which means I'm done for.

I shouldn't have talked. I already regretted it the moment it blurted out. Now it's too late.

I've sealed my own fate.

I try to evade them as much as possible, but the more I run, the more I stagger, and these men are fast. The moment I reach the front door, they've surrounded me.

I fight them off as best as I can—pushing, shoving, biting, clawing—using everything I have against them. But it's no use. Soon they overwhelm me, and when one grabs me and covers my mouth with his hand, I know I've lost.

"Gotcha …" he growls in my ear.

I want to cry. I want to beg. I want to do anything

to make it stop.

Why isn't Angel here when he promised me he'd protect me? When he said I would live?

I wanted to trust him—I desperately did—to the point of me actually believing in the hope he gave me.

But now, all of that is shattered in the blink of an eye.

In a moment of panic, I scream.

That's when the front door bursts open.

Tears stain my eyes, but I can clearly see Angel storming inside.

Everything feels like slow motion as I watch the scene in front of me unfold.

Angel pushes one of the men so hard that he rams his head into the wood, crushing his skull. Then his rifle fires. One, two, three times. Bang. They all go down like flies, one after the other.

Except, the more he shoots, the more turn up from rooms behind us and even outside. Even Angel is surrounded, and despite the fact that he's much stronger than anyone else I've ever met, he's no match for this amount of people.

The more he shoots, the less he can catch up with them.

One of them hits him in the back of the head, causing him to buck and fall to his knees.

"Angel!" I scream.

That's when the man who's holding me drags me backward across the floor. I resist, jamming my foot into the ground, but I can't seem to stop him.

"RELEASE HER!" Angel's thundering voice is the only spark that gives me hope.

With my eyes, I beg him to save me. I beg him to take me back.

I'll be his. Forever.

Only his.

I bite the man's hand. "Don't let them take me away!" I scream.

"Argh, you little bitch!" he says.

But then the unthinkable happens.

Angel's gun is stolen out of his hand and used against him. One hard punch with the cold metal to the back of his head is all it takes to get him facedown on the ground.

A sharp pain in my neck follows. My vision grows blurry; my muscles stop working, and then everything fades to black.

***

Present

When I wake up, I feel dizzy, and my head hurts. I felt the same way on the first day when I was drugged. The sharp pain I felt in my neck must've been another needle they used to contain me and drag me back to …

A cell.

The moment I can open my eyes and witness the unending darkness again, I scream.

The fear that I felt in this place still overwhelms me, and it makes me think I've lost my mind.

I can't take being in here again. Anywhere but here. Why did they have to bring me back?

My muscles ache, but I force myself to get up. I feel drowsy, completely wasted, but I know it's from the drugs. As long as I keep that in mind, I know I can do this. I have to move. I have to show I'm not weak. That I'll fight until the very end if I have to.

But nothing prepared me for a return to this darkness.

The absence of light makes me feel like I've gone blind.

I stumble around the cell, touching my way to the side until I reach a wall, which is when I'm finally able to lift myself up on two feet. My body is weak, but the wall supports me as I drag myself along it, grabbing a hold of anything that feels like the door. If I can find it, I could do what I did before ... surprise my captor and take him out. Only this time for good.

Pure will drives me, pushing me to continue searching until my feet quake. The moment I feel the door is when I gasp for air.

That's when I hear a throat clearing.

My heart beats in my throat as I turn around toward the sound.

"Going somewhere?"

It's him.

Joseph "Joe" DeLuca.

"What did you do to me?" I say.

"What had to be done in order to get you here," he says.

Suddenly the light turns on, and I cover my eyes as they get used to the light. Only then do I notice he's sitting in the very chair I'd been bound to for so long.

My first instinct is to attack him.

But as I jump him, he pulls out a knife and shoves it in my stomach.

I heave; the pain is so intense that I sink to the ground, coughing up blood.

"Oh, you are a feisty one indeed."

"Let. Me. Go," I growl.

I know he won't, but I can threaten him at the very least. I won't go down easily. He might have a knife, but if I get a chance, I will take it from him and use it.

"I suggest you stay down if you don't want me to slice you open."

The cruelness in his words makes me crawl back a few inches.

"You might be wondering why I brought you here. But, instead, ask yourself this … why are you still alive?" he muses, throwing the knife in his hand as if it's a toy.

"Because I fought the men, and I'll fight you. I'm not going to give up," I say.

He smiles at me. "Don't you think you would already be dead if it weren't for me?"

I don't answer him because I'm not going to feed his already too large ego.

He gets up from the chair and starts pacing around the cell. "You know, I would've pegged you for a smart bambina, but you keep making the same mistake."

"Likewise …" I say, holding my stomach to stop the bleeding.

Suddenly, he grabs me by my hair and pulls me up from the ground, the pain making me squeeze my eyes. "Never fight the boss. You will end up bleeding to death," he growls, and then he releases me from his grip again.

I curl up so I can stop the bleeding in my belly, but the pain is almost too much for me to handle. There are already plenty of scars on my body and they haven't completely healed yet. My body isn't ready to take another beating … I don't think I will survive.

But I have to.

I must.

There's no other choice.

"How long have I been here?"

"One day …" he says.

"Where's Angel?"

"You don't need to worry about him." He steps closer to me, and I cower, fearful that he's going to attack me again. I'm not ready to strike back yet. "The only thing you need to worry about is keeping yourself alive."

"You'd better not hurt him," I growl.

"Who, Angel?" He laughs. "He's my son …" For a moment there, I think he might actually care, until he says, "I can do with him whatever the fuck I want."

"You're a monster. You would hurt your own son?"

"I don't care what he wants! I gave him plenty of opportunities to learn from his mistakes. But he couldn't get his head straight. Something about you …" he huffs. "You make him weak, and I don't like that."

"You can't do this to him. He's your own flesh and blood."

"What I do to him is my business," he growls, grabbing my chin. "But you … you have far too much control over his heart."

He holds out the knife, and I shiver as he draws a line across my cheek. "Is it your beauty? Your intelligence? Or something else?"

I jerk until my face is freed from his grip, but I pay the price with blood. He's managed to slice into my skin with just the tip of the knife. I can't imagine how sharp it must be.

"Careful, bambina. Don't anger me."

"Or what? I'm already dead."

"Maybe … or maybe not."

I frown, my eyes widening as I hear what he says.

He starts twirling the blade between his fingers

again. "You see, I believe you haven't been completely honest with him or me. I get the sense that you're still hiding a few things. You've done it before, so I think you can imagine my distrust of you."

Distrust? He is the only one who can't be trusted. What a snake.

As he paces around the cell, he says, "I should kill you for not coming directly to me and telling me in the first place."

"Do it."

There's a hint of a sparkle in his eyes. "But ... I could let you live. If you speak the truth."

"What are you talking about?" I ask.

"Tell me," he says, pointing the knife at me again. "Is the baby still alive?"

I shake my head, my breath hitching when he puts the knife to my throat. "Say it to my face. I don't believe one word that comes from your mouth."

"It's not a lie, I swear. I aborted it. How could I not?"

"Really now?" he hisses.

"Yes, why would I keep a baby ... from you? I'd rather die than go through that."

Smack.

My head ends up on the cold, harsh floor with a red mark across my face. I lie there, unmoving, blinking away the tears that come with the pain.

"Figa!"

I don't recognize the word, which sounds like

swearing, but it probably isn't something I'd want to remember.

"You think you can outsmart me, bambina? Think you are something, huh?"

"No," I whisper into the stones, closing my eyes as he holds the knife against the back of my neck.

"You're just a whore. A filthy whore who's caused nothing but trouble for my family and me. You know, if you told me my baby lived, I could've let you keep your life. I could've let you be a part of this family. But now, I'm afraid I'll have to kill you."

"Kill me then," I mutter, feeling the energy slowly slip away with each drop of blood spilling from my body.

"Oh … you think it's that easy?" He laughs. "You should've made my son do it because at least he was merciful. He would've gone easy on you. Me? I raise hell."

I'm smacked so hard against the head that everything turns dark and then I'm gone.

DAY 20

ANGEL

The moment I wake up, I feel sick.

I don't know what happened to me, but my head fucking hurts, and when I try to move, I can't. My arms feel unnatural, as if they're no longer there. When try to I lift my leg, which also feels bound, I notice I'm not even on the floor.

Blinking rapidly, I force myself to come to my senses and look up at the ceiling. My arms have a big chain wrapped around them as I hang above the ground like a slab of meat ready for slaughter.

I jerk around in the chains, but to no avail; they're wrapped so tight around my wrists that it fucking hurts.

Blood drips down my skin, my wrists barely able to hold my own weight as I try to remain still. Swinging too much could dislocate my shoulder, and that's the last thing I want to happen.

Looking around, I notice I'm in one of the cells used to contain prisoners. My prisoners. And now I am the victim.

Goddammit.

They fucking got me.

I should've paid more attention to who was behind me, but rage blinded me so much that I couldn't stop for a second and look around. I had to get to her. They were hurting her as they took her away from me.

And now I still don't have her with me.

Fuck!

Why did I let her slip through my fingers? I'm such a fucking failure.

They caught me, and I didn't even manage to rescue her from their grasp. And why the fuck am I here anyway? Did they bring me here to torture me? My father must've finally had enough of my rebellion.

Well, fuck him. He shouldn't have gone after my girl then.

When the door to my cell opens, I growl, "Where the fuck is she?"

The man is one of our own. Our butcher; the one who takes care of the victims after the interrogator is done with them … if they're still alive at that point.

He's one of the family's best torturers. Knows

exactly where to hit and slice in order to make you bleed without killing you.

And now he's got it in for me.

Well, I don't give a shit as long as I don't know where she is.

"Answer me!" I growl.

He just smiles and prepares his tools, laying them all out on the table for me to see. He wants me to experience the fear. That's standard procedure here, but I'm no standard victim. Nothing scares me … except when they break her.

Fuck me … I hope she still lives.

"Tell me where she is!" I yell.

"Relax …" the guy mumbles, bringing a syringe, and flicking it in front of my face. "Don't move."

"Get that thing away from me," I scream as he brings it to my neck.

"It's only a precaution. You know … to make sure you don't accidentally break free." He grins. "I know your power." He pushes the needle into my skin. "There. All done," he says, turning around.

"Come here then and fucking meet my fist, you son of a bitch," I spit.

"Save your energy," he says. "You'll need it."

"Where is she? Tell me if she's safe."

"Why do you care so much about that girl?" he asks.

"Because she's *mine*," I hiss.

He cocks his head and grips the chains that hold

me. "Correction … she *was* yours." He swings the chains back and forth, causing intense agony in my arms.

"Fuck …" I growl, trying to suppress the pain.

"Well, you're in luck," he says. "She's just about to arrive."

"What?"

My eyes grow wide when he puts on gloves and a mask. "Time for some fun."

"No," I say as the door opens and in rolls a wheelchair carrying her limp body. "Sky!"

Men I once considered family place her in the middle and hoist her up using the same chains, hooking her to the ceiling as well.

"Sky, wake up!" I scream, but she doesn't respond. "What did you do to her?"

"Just a little sedative," he muses.

"I swear to fucking god, if you touch her, I'll kill you," I say, as the men drive the wheelchair out and leave us alone again.

"Hmm … yeah, I don't think so." He points at my chains. "You're outta luck."

"Fuck you! Take me down right now." I try to kick him, but the chains around my feet limit my movement. "Don't you fucking know who I am?"

"Not important enough, it seems," he says, holding out a knife against my belly. "You think you're something special just because you're the boss's son? Wrong. He *wanted* you here. Tortured. Dead."

He cuts through my skin, carving a line from left to right across my abdomen.

Grinding my teeth, I stare him straight in the eyes. He seems to find it very amusing.

"You'll fucking pay for this …" I growl.

"I doubt it." He shrugs. "By the time I'm done with you two, you'll both be as good as dead."

Right when he says that, I hear a little groan coming from Sky's mouth.

Now his eyes are on her.

Fuck. Shit. Fuck!

Why did she have to make that sound?

"Wakey, wakey!" He slaps her face, abruptly pulling her into the world.

"What? Where am I? Who are you? What are you doing to me?" she blurts out. Then she starts kicking and swinging the chains. "Let me down!"

"Oh, wow … I like this," he muses, and then he slaps her again, this time so hard she bounces back, her head almost spinning.

"Don't fucking touch her!" I scream.

"Shut up," he says. "I've had about enough of you."

"That's right. C'mere then. I can take you," I say, as he steps toward me.

"Angel?" Sky says. "It's you … you're alive."

"Not for long," I say.

The fucker stabs me with the knife, right in the arm.

Goddammit, I didn't need more pain there.

"I told you to fucking shut up."

"Don't hurt him!" Sky yells.

"Oh, what? You too now?" he says, laughing. "Boy, you two really have it in for each other, don't you? What kind of fucked-up relationship is this?"

He grabs her chin, holding the knife to her throat.

"Please ... don't," Sky begs.

"Don't! Focus on me," I growl. "Cut me instead of her. I'm the one you want. Not her."

"Well ... she is pretty, you know. So fucking pretty ... I think I should slice that pretty face up," he jests, sliding the blade across her cheek. "Tell me, where should I start? Your eyes? Your mouth? Or a little lower ...?"

"No, please ... have mercy," she says, tears running down her face.

"Kill me, take me instead of her. Please ..." I say. I've never begged. Not one fucking second in my life have I ever thought of begging, but for her ... I'll do anything to stop her from having to feel the pain.

The guy returns his attention to me. "Please just let her go in peace. No pain. No nothing. Do it all to me. Anything you wanna do."

He squints. "You want me to do all the things that I wanted to do to her ... to you? Are you insane?"

I swallow. I've never been much of a receiver of pain, mostly just the giver. But if there's no other way, then I'll do it. For her.

I nod.

He shakes his head, making a face. "I don't understand you. You'd give up your life, experience excruciating pain, just so I let this one off the hook?"

"Yes. Please … honor the code. The family code. We're from the same blood, the same family, the same company. You must honor my dying wishes. I want her death to be painless."

He licks his lips, his eyes going from one place to another as if he's thinking about it. "Well … I might … if you beg me again." The smug smile on his face makes me want to bash his head in.

Instead, I sigh and take a deep breath. "Please, I beg you … torture me instead of her."

"No!" Sky yells. "Angel, don't!"

"Too late," the guy muses, laughing maniacally, before slicing me again. "Deal."

"No! Don't touch him! Let him go, please!" Sky begs.

It's too late. I've already offered him my body, and he's accepted my plea.

I exchange my life for hers.

I surrender my pain to his whim.

We're both trapped in the most horrifying nightmare before death, but if I can spare her the pain, I will.

I've served my purpose.

At least she'll have a peaceful death.

It's the least I could do.

***

SKY

My vocal cords are hoarse from the amount of screaming that I've done today.

For hours, I watch Angel getting tortured.

At first, I tried to look away, but the man forced me to look by turning my body toward Angel. Seeing him tied up and at the mercy of some monster makes my insides churn.

I'm dying. Not physically, but mentally … dying at the sight of Angel losing his will to live.

With every drop of his blood, more of his energy spills out along with his reason, his sole motivator to fight.

It was me.

All along, it was me.

He wanted me to live, and in his effort to save me, he sacrificed his own life.

I wish I could turn back time and tell him not to. That I could stop him from even coming into the house and attempting to rescue me, just so I could spare him this pain.

I don't want to see him hurt. I don't want to see him bleed to death.

I love him.

It's not hard to admit when I witness the man carve a hole into his body right on top of his heart … the heart that belongs to me.

I am his and he is mine.

And now we're set to die.

I can't let him do this. I can't go down knowing he suffered so I could die in peace. I'm not going to just hang here and let this monster work him like some pig.

I have to do something.

"Angel, please! Fight it!" I yell, crying.

Salty tears have ran and dried up on my cheeks over and over again because I can't take watching someone butcher Angel's body. Cuts cover his body, blood seeping out of every hole, puncture wounds scattered across his skin.

It's a bloody fucking mess.

And it's all for me.

I can't look, so I close my eyes for as long as I can before the man forces me to open them again.

Suddenly, the cell door opens, and the person entering the cell draws both of our gazes.

It's Joseph DeLuca and the smug look on his face gives me renewed energy to the point of wanting to claw my way out of these chains that hold me back to attack his face.

"You …" I growl.

"Bambina, you're still alive?" he says, stepping into the cell.

For a second, Angel glances up to see his father, but then his head drops down again, too tired to even respond.

"You. Out," Joseph tells the man who was torturing Angel, and he immediately leaves the cell. Joseph slams the door shut behind him. "Wow."

Joseph circles us, and I cough when he spits on my face. "You dirty whore. You managed to escape death yet again?"

"You'll pay for this," I say.

"Oh, I doubt it," he muses. "But I am enjoying the sight of you two."

"How could you do this to your own son?"

"Simple. He betrayed me." He shrugs as if it means nothing. Then he steps over to his son and grabs his cheeks with his index finger and thumb, forcing his head up. "You disappoint me, Angel. So much so that I felt obligated to do this. I hope you realize that I hate this as much as you do. However, when you went against me, you crossed a line."

"How could you say that? Just because he wanted to save my life doesn't mean he needs to die!" I yell, thrashing around. "Angel, wake up! Do something!"

"Hmm ..." Joseph smiles. "He seems quite out of it."

Angel's eyes can't even stay open as Joseph slaps his cheeks. "Wake up, boy. Let me see that agony."

"Stop," I say. "You've hurt him enough."

"Me?" He raises his brows at me. "Hurt *him*?

Bambina, you don't even know what you're talking about."

"He is your son. Your flesh and blood. And you would rather have him killed than forgive him? I don't care what he's done to you. You are no father. Not to anyone. You're a monster," I hiss.

He cocks his head at me, seemingly amused. "Well, well. Finally, you see … there is no rescuing us." He grabs Angel's face and holds it up as if to show him to me. "See this? This is the face of defeat. This isn't a man. He's a worthless peon, and he didn't even do his job. You think he's worth the life he's been given? Wrong. In case you forgot, he's the one who ruined you."

"No, you did, the moment you gave him the order," I say. "You're the venom that poisons his veins. You're everything that's wrong with this corrupt world, but I can promise you now that your empire will end. One day. I don't care if I live to see it … but you will die whether it's by my hand or someone else's … you'll feel the pain you caused. I guarantee it."

He just watches my mouth as I speak. "Interesting. What a speech. I'm amazed." He claps slowly, mocking me.

"Why are you even here?" I ask, ignoring his taunt.

"Oh, I just wanted to see the looks on your faces before you died."

The depravity in his voice sends a shiver down my spine.

296

"But I've seen enough," he says, disgustingly looking at his son before wiping his hands on his pants. "Good-bye."

"Don't you dare fucking leave," I growl.

"Who's going to stop me? You?" He laughs as he walks toward the door.

"I'll see you in hell, asshole," I say.

And then the door shuts behind him, leaving us alone again.

The silence is overwhelming, but not as much as the soundless breaths Angel takes. He's at his limit. Almost over the edge. It won't be long now before he's really gone. His body can't take any more pain. He's far beyond what a human should be capable of surviving … I don't even know if he's still alive.

I can't see him breathe.

His limbs hang lifelessly from the chains, blood streaming down his body.

This can't go on any longer.

He has to wake up. He has to find the strength to fight this.

"Angel," I whisper. "Please, don't give up."

I know he won't respond. In the past few hours, he told me he'd given up for me. That he wouldn't fight the pain so he could assure my painless death. He still thinks I accept that.

But I won't.

I won't let him go through with this.

"Don't give up. Do you hear me?" I say. "You have

to stay here. Not for me. For you."

A small nudge of his head tells me he's saying no.

"Dammit, Angel! Fight this! I know you can. You're stronger than anyone I've ever known, stronger than any of those men out there ... you can beat these chains!" I thrash around in mine, attempting to reach him, but to no avail.

"It's no use ..." His voice is soft, so soft. I feel like he's already broken.

"You can't give up now. Not when ..."

I realize nothing in this world will make him move because he already made the promise to himself that he would die for me. His love goes beyond what I thought anyone would ever do for me, and for that alone, tears spring to my eyes.

However, he's wrong when he says there's no use.

"You still have a purpose," I say. "Don't give up your life."

He shakes his head again.

That's when the butcher comes back inside.

Shit. I've wasted my last and only chance.

As he walks to the table with a slight waggle and a happy smile, he picks up a surgeon's scalpel and then looks at me. "Well ... I think it's about time I started on you."

"What?" I gasp. "But you said ..."

He laughs. "Did you really think I was going to keep my word? Do I look gullible to you?"

"Don't ... touch ... her," Angel mumbles, every

word costing him so much trouble I wish he wouldn't speak.

"You thought you could exchange your life for hers?" the guy says. "Your father just wants you to pay, but he never told me to actually kill you. Now, he *did* tell me to kill her ..." he muses.

"No ..." I say, shaking my head.

I can't believe it.

After everything Angel went through to save me the pain, we're still being fooled, and he had to pay the price.

"No!" I scream, but it's too late.

The scalpel has already cut into my skin.

It hurts. It hurts so fucking badly, and the next one is even worse.

The sizzling, sharp pain doesn't stop, not even when my own blood covers me.

"Leave. Her. Alone," Angel huffs with his last breaths.

The pain has made it impossible for me to look up as my attacker walks toward the door. "Be right back. I'm getting a more interesting tool that's much more fun to use."

My feet dangle below me, blood dripping down onto the floor as I stare at the tiles, my vision getting blurry. I look sideways at Angel, who's hanging just as defeated as me. Blood has crusted on his feet, painting a picture of sacrifice. But as I look more closely, I can't help but notice the dark spot on his ankle, which isn't blood but a birthmark. I can't believe I'm looking at it, but I realize there is only one thing left that I can do to save us as I focus on it.

"Angel …" I say, coughing as his eyes find mine. "Fight for her."

Just those few words are enough to make him turn his head. "What?"

I check the walls to see if there are cameras, but there don't seem to be any.

"I lied," I hiss, looking at the door to make sure the man hasn't come back yet. "She's alive." Swallowing away the lump in my throat, I take a deep breath and tell him the truth for the first time. "My baby is alive, and she needs a mother."

DAY 21

SKY

Yesterday

I knew it the day I stood in front of the clinic that I couldn't kill this baby.

It wasn't because of religion or faith or someone telling me not to. On the contrary ... My life would've been less at risk if I just went ahead and did it, so I could run away and never come back. It had always been Plan A: To get rid of the baby and run away with my dad.

Except ... it changed the moment I felt the baby kick. I changed.

That feeling of life growing inside me made me question everything I ever thought. Everything I knew about myself.

This baby wasn't just a baby. Hatred and pain didn't make her.

I made her. From my cells, she grew, from my body, she nurtured, and from my protection, she flourished.

My love was what made this baby whole.

I have no explanation for the choice I made that day when I decided to turn around, walk away, and never come back to that clinic. The only thing I felt was that I needed to do this. This baby was mine and I would rather die than kill it. What I felt was insane, but it was real. It was as if the baby's voice itself spoke to me and begged me to let it live. So I made the choice to keep it. It was the best decision I ever made.

After weeks, when my belly grew too big to hide it under a thick vest, my papa asked me if I was pregnant. I didn't have to tell him; he could see it in my eyes and feel it for himself when I placed his hand on my stomach. The smile on his face when he felt a kick quickly vanished the moment he looked me in the eye.

He knew as well as I did that this would mean I'd have to keep running. It wouldn't take long before the men would find out. News traveled fast. I'd have to go into labor someday, and the hospital nurses talked with the police. Gossip alone would alert the family that I was delivering … and then they'd come for the baby.

After all … a baby from the Don would be raised by the Don, no matter what. I knew this from what my mother had told me about those women she rescued and the babies they had. Now it was happening to me.

I didn't want to risk it, so I decided I'd go into hiding instead.

My best friend, Jamie, agreed to let me stay at her place. I had told her everything that happened to me, and she still welcomed me with open arms. We tried to make the best of it, but we both knew that I was a ticking time bomb and that once the baby was delivered, they'd come looking for it. But no matter the cost, they would not get my baby.

They say there is nothing stronger than a mother's love for her baby. I didn't know the meaning of the saying until I came face to face with my own image … a baby girl who looked exactly like me. I loved her the minute she showed me that perfect little smile. Her existence forever carved into my heart.

My love for her was what made me understand what my mother had meant all those years ago … when she'd said she named me after the sky. I was her world … just as this baby was now my world.

I knew then that I would fight until the very end to protect this baby of mine. I would lay down my life if it meant she would survive.

Because that was what mothers did.

However, mothers will fight until the very end, so that their babies don't have to grow up as orphans.

And now Angel knows why I didn't tell him the truth.

***

ANGEL

Her words ignite a spark inside my chest, which burns up the desire to move.

The baby ... is alive, and she needs her mother.

I can't let her die.

Renewed energy fills my veins, fueling me with a need I didn't know I had. I *want* to make this right. I want Sky to be free and live her life. For once in my life, I have to mean something for someone ... I have to save a life instead of destroying it.

I gather all my strength, breathing in and out through my mouth to push through the pain.

Blood pours from my arms and legs, but I won't let it stop me from breaking through these chains.

It's as if an invisible force has taken control over my body, urging me to pull away from this nightmare and fight. Fight for this life. Fight for love. Fight for the right taken away from us both ... the right to live and be happy.

I don't care if it's my father's baby. Sky needs her and she needs Sky.

I need them both.

Hanging here, knowing I would die so she wouldn't feel the pain, has made me weak. It has made me blind to the truth, but Sky's words woke a part of me I didn't know existed. This baby means more to Sky than her own goddamn life. Every single day here, she has fought to keep her baby safe, regardless of her own health. This is what she wants most of all, and I will honor her wish.

Groaning, I swing the chains, careful not to break an arm. It hurts so goddamn bad, but I bite through the pain. I have to … for her …

I didn't want to admit it at first, but I know in my heart that it's true; I will fight for her with my very last breath if it means she'll see her baby again.

So I keep swinging through the pain, pushing my body beyond its limit, gazing up at the ceiling as hope drives me forward. The hinges that keep the chains secured are starting to come undone, squeaking with every swing, until finally the plate breaks off and I crash down onto the floor.

With an aching body, I crawl up and rip away the chains around my wrists and feet, roaring out loud.

That's when the guy comes back inside. The moment he sees me, he yelps with terror-filled eyes, and I run toward him and throw him to the ground. With one big blow, I punch his face against the tiles, ramming his head so hard it splatters on impact.

I quickly turn around and witness my girl hanging

lifelessly from the chains, her body painted in her own blood.

Grabbing a large bolt cutter lying on the table, I cut through her chains and catch her falling body in my arms. I cut away the chains that bind her feet and throw away the bolt cutter, making my way to the door. The guy's head has kept the door opened up for us, and I step over his body and into the hallway of the oh so familiar compound. This time not as a peon, but as a fighter finally on the right side of justice.

The alarm sounds, as one of the women in the kitchen has pushed a button, and when I look her way, she cowers in fear. They aren't worthy of my time. The men storming into the building, however, are.

I walk toward them with pride, putting Sky over my shoulder as I ready myself for a fight with one hand only. My body may be weak, but my mindset more than makes up for that. If I was invincible before, I'm a god now.

There is nothing on this motherfucking planet, in this goddamn universe, to stop me from walking out of here with *my* girl.

When one of them aims his knife at me, I block him and snatch it from his hand, jamming it into his skull. Another one runs at me with a fucking hatchet, but I manage to trip him and then with my feet slam his body into the wall. The next uses a gun, but I hide behind a pillar until he tries to reload, at which point I run straight toward him, knocking him to the ground.

As I walk past him, a few more come from the exit, so I pick up one of the guns from the guy's hand and shoot them point blank. Making my way toward the hatch, I run past all the doors, holding Sky's naked body close to my heart. The alarm rings in my ears, but it won't stop me from climbing up the ladder, making sure I don't drop Sky.

As I reach the top, I use the last bit of my strength to open the hatch and push Sky out first. The light of day is a welcome sight, one I didn't think I'd see again. As I crawl out of the compound and breathe in the fresh air, I feel more alive than ever.

Until something jabs me in the back.

I trip over, and a foot in my back stomps me to the ground.

"Son of a bitch ..." my father growls.

I turn around and twist his leg, so he drops to the ground, too. One second is all it takes to confirm that Sky is lying still in the grass, but it's enough for me to know that it's not too late. I can still protect her. If I can beat all those men, even after already going over the edge, then I can fucking win this fight, too.

"Don't you fucking stand in my way," I say, crawling on top of him so I can punch his head into the dirt. "I'll fucking kill you!"

A struggle ensues. We punch each other, wrestling on the floor, changing positions as much as exchanging hits. Clothes are torn and his pockets empty, spilling out into the grass. It's like an all-out brawl.

Too late do I notice him reaching for something in his back pocket. "Angel ..." her faint groan distracts me.

A sharp pain cuts into me, and I fall on my side, holding my stomach. The fucker stabbed me with a knife, and he's getting up on two feet while I'm down on the ground.

"Did you forget who taught you the dirty tricks, Angel? I am your father and the head of this family. You think you could get away with the things you did?"

"I don't give a shit what you are, but you're not taking her away from me. I'll fucking fight you with everything I have if it means she gets to live."

He punches me in the face and jams the knife between my ribs again, making me howl.

"Even if it means your death?" he growls.

"No ..." Sky mumbles, her hand inching toward me.

Even when she's down, facing imminent danger, she still cares too much to let me die.

"Why, Sky? Just let me go. Run. Save yourself!" I yell, as my father punches me again and again.

"No!" Her muscles collapse beneath her as she tries to get up, but she won't stop. Even when the blood pours from her wounds, she continues to fight until she's up on her hands and knees, gasping for air. At first, I think she's lost her vision, her hands erratically sliding through the grass, but when she grabs ahold of my father's ankle, I realize she's trying to save me instead.

"Let go," my father says, kicking her.

I take the opportunity to pull the knife from my stomach, a stabbing pain replacing the empty space, as I jam it in his leg as hard as I can.

Screaming out loud, he drops to his knees, and I take out the knife and push it into his chest.

"Hurts like a bitch, doesn't it?" I say, as I crawl away from him and get up on my feet.

He doesn't respond, his body sinking to the ground as mine stands up. I don't know how I do it, but my legs start moving on their own. I don't have any energy or strength left to walk, and yet I do. Pure will drives me to Sky, and as I pick her up from the ground, she spits up blood.

"It's okay … we made it out," I say, brushing the hair out of her face. "You're alive."

"Thanks to you …" she says, her hand reaching for my face. "You're a hero."

I shake my head, tears staining my eyes. She doesn't realize she's the one who saved me.

Without her words, I would be nothing.

A vapid memory of a man who could once love.

Her refusal to give up pushed me to move, and her desire to live gave me strength beyond what I felt I could ever achieve. Her love for her child and her will to live gives me pure energy.

She is what saved us both.

With her in my arms, I walk away from the scene of

the crime, my father's bloody body curling up on the ground. He groans. "Don't you fucking walk away from me!"

I ignore his pleas. He's not worth my time. "You can't control me anymore."

As I stumble through the forest with Sky in my bloody hands, I hear a rattling, metallic sound. A barrel of a gun. When I turn around, my father is aiming at me … his finger resting on the trigger.

"See you in hell," he says.

But before he can pull the trigger, something flies in his direction so fast I don't even see it. It jams into his eye, causing him to cry out in pain, and then heave over to puke. Afterward, he starts rolling around on the ground, wailing, completely drowning in his own pain.

I don't know what it was, but I turn around and keep walking. I don't look back. Only after a while do I realize what it was.

Sky had been searching the ground, but it wasn't just to grasp my father's ankle. She found a small knife that had fallen from his pocket and used it to puncture his eye.

The thought perks up my lip. My Azure Sky saved us both once again.

I look back a final time to see my father lying in the grass, facedown.

I force my legs to take a step forward, each one heavier than the previous, but I keep going. I won't stop, not until we hit a road. I keep walking until a truck passes us and I manage to stop it, which is when I collapse, holding Sky high up so her head won't hit the ground. We both lie there, on the asphalt, our bodies bleeding out on the ground.

"Oh, my god," I hear a lady say, and a truck door is slammed shut. "I'll call 911."

"No … call … Phoenix Sullivan …ask him to help … tell him … it's Angel." I mumble the number that I remember, hoping it's the right one, but with each syllable, I fade away.

I hope she calls him. I fucking hope she won't call 911 because if she does, it'll all be over. The company's ties with law enforcement are too strong … they'd find out we'd be in the hospital … and then we'd die.

So I beg her with my last breath to do as I ask.

I don't know if we'll make it out alive. If Sky will ever see her baby again.

But I know this … we made it out of that hellhole. We saved ourselves instead of succumbing to death by someone else's hand. We saw freedom again, for the last time.

It has to be worth something.

***

SKY

Present

The light that fills my eyes as I come back from what feels like an eternal slumber fills me up with hope. I breathe in completely, feeling the pain in my lungs and the excitement in my heart flow through me at the same time. I don't know where I am or how I got here, but I made it. I'm alive.

My veins fill me with hope, causing me to open my eyes and look around.

"Hey …"

His familiar voice creates a beaming smile on my face as I realize it's none other than Angel sitting by my bedside. He grabs my hand and squeezes tight as I look at him and wonder how in the world we made it out alive.

"I'm here," he says.

Bandages cover his body. He literally looks mummified with the exception of his hands and face. It's quite a funny sight, and when I start to giggle a bit, he says, "Hey now, that's rude. I know I don't look pretty, but at least you could lie to me."

"Sorry," I say, coughing.

"Take it easy," he says. "You lost a lot of blood."

"So did you."

He smiles. "But we're alive, and I'd rather not see you kill yourself with laughter in the end."

"At least I'll go down happy," I say.

He rolls his eyes. "I'm glad you can make jokes

about this serious matter."

I smile, looking around the room. I don't recognize this place one bit, but it looks like a hotel or motel to me.

"Where are we?" I ask.

"Motel room. Funny thing, actually. Do you remember what happened after you threw that knife at my father?"

"Yeah … I think so. You walked us out of the woods and onto a road where we collapsed."

"Exactly … I managed to stop a truck, and the lady did call for help."

"Oh, thank god," I say.

"Well, the funny thing is, I asked her to call Phoenix Sullivan, an old buddy of mine, instead of 911. I guess it worked out because he was the one to take us to a doctor he knows personally. Someone who won't rat us out."

I frown. "Who's Phoenix?"

"Someone I owe a lot to," he says, smiling at me. "I'll tell you about it some other time."

I don't know what he means, but I'm glad someone came along to pick up two stranded bodies on the road. We would've never made it out alive if it wasn't for him.

"Well, thank him for me, will you," I say.

"You can do that yourself once you get out of this bed." He winks at me. "It might be a while before you can move, but we have some time. Phoenix drove us all the way to some secluded town where no one will find us. At least, not for a long time."

"Oh ... What about your father? Is he ...?"

"Dead?" He frowns and sighs. "Probably. When I looked back for the last time, he wasn't moving. But I don't want to spend one more second thinking about that bastard." He makes a fist with his hand. "He's ruined my life long enough."

"I'm glad you've finally broken free of his rule," I say, smiling at him.

He smiles back, and for some reason, I have to blush.

He scoots closer and caresses my cheek. "I'm really glad you're okay. I wouldn't have been able to live with myself if you hadn't made it out."

I place my hand over his, tears staining my eyes. "Thank you. Thank you for fighting."

"Shh ..." He leans in and tentatively pecks me on my lips, waiting for my approval.

He doesn't need it. My heart already belonged to him the moment he kissed me.

I've always belonged to him, whether he knows it or not. Those nights we spent together forged an unbreakable bond between us that seeped into our very lives. He's mine and I'm his, and even though we've been through hell, there is only one way from here and that's up. I refuse to believe there is only darkness out there. Not when I've seen the light in Angel himself.

He pulled through for us. His heart made it

impossible for him to do what his father wanted; it made him my knight in the darkness. He kept both of us from going insane and made his promise a reality. I live. He lives. And now we can go on together.

When his lips unlock from mine, I want him to keep kissing me, my lips swollen and hungry for more. I grab a hold of his shirt and pull him closer, which makes him laugh.

"Wow, you're needy."

"I'm not sorry," I say.

"I know you want me. You always have, even when you said you didn't."

"Oh, shut up," I say, kissing him again.

"What? You know it's the truth. Even when you couldn't see me, the mask couldn't hide the fact that I knew how to press your buttons, and you fell for me all over again." He grins and cups my chin, kissing me hard.

For some reason, I'm not even mad at what he says. I can't be because that would be as if I denied the truth … he's right, I did fall for him … Again and again. I'll always fall for him. He's the only one who knows me, truly, and who cares more about me than anyone else in this world. He cares so much; he was even willing to sacrifice his own life for me.

He's mine, and despite the fact that we're one messed-up couple with a completely screwed-up past, it won't stop me from finally surrendering to my feelings for him. I won't allow the lies, the shame, or the pain from the past to come between us and our future together.

As he takes his lips from mine, he murmurs, "I love you."

The words shatter me completely.

Make me cry when I thought all my tears had long dried out.

He was right when he said he'd break me, but not in the way we both thought he would.

He broke the iron wall that I'd cast around my heart. He broke through the chains that bound me, broke the shadows that haunted my life, broke the men who ruined me. He broke me … and now he's healed me.

I grab his face and say, "I love you, too."

"Are you sure?" he mutters with a concerned look on his face.

I nod. "I didn't want to admit it, at first … but I can't deny my feelings any longer. It wouldn't be right."

The left side of his lip curls up into a smile. "You've always been mine from the beginning… it was only a matter of time before you realized this. You love the control that I have over your body … the claim that I've staked on your heart," he growls, catching my chin between his index finger and thumb.

I look down at the sheets, wondering how I'm going to tell him this. "There is actually another reason, apart from the sex …"

"I know, I give you more than just sex," he muses.

"No, I mean … there was something I realized when we were in that cell together." I look up at him. "I think I'm ready to have you be part of my life."

His eyebrow rises. "Oh, really now? You're not just saying that because I won't take no for an answer, are you?"

"No," I say, smiling. "I just know, you know? I can't explain it … I just feel it here." I place my hand over my heart.

"All right. But don't think admitting this will make me go easy on you because I won't. I'm still the same old rough, hot-fucking, spanking guy that I was before, and you'd better say yes please to anything I say."

Hiding the blush behind a smile, I say, "I know that … and I wouldn't change it for the world."

"Good." He folds his arms, making himself look big, even though he makes me laugh when he's all bandaged up.

I'm his, whether I like it or not. My heart and soul are bound to him. I love this man … this monster, this raging beast. This fucked-up man I call mine.

EPILOGUE

SKY

A few days later

After a few days, our wounds have healed and we're ready for the world again. There was just one thing I needed to do, and that was a pregnancy test. Not that I was scared, but I just wanted to know what I was in for, considering Angel had sex with me without protection. Luckily, I was in the clear. Angel told me he was sorry for making me worry, which was so unlike him that I just hugged him and told him to shut up, which made him laugh. I forgive him for what he did to me because that's the only thing I can do to move on. He saved me, and that's all that matters.

He keeps saying he has to make it up to me for the pain he's caused, but I tell him it's all right as long as he keeps loving me the way he did ... roughness included. He knows I like his sinful touch and complete control, so there's no need to apologize. I just didn't want to admit to myself that I always had feelings for him. That he was the only one who could rock my world, despite my attempts to suppress the thoughts. I guess it was just meant to be.

We say good-bye to the one who carried us off the streets. Phoenix frowns at us, gazing awkwardly as I walk toward the door with a bag of food and money that he gave us. He seems to be grumpy all the time, but Angel told me it's because he still holds a grudge. But I figured there must still be some brotherly love left ... after all, why else would he have helped us?

"Thank you, bro," Angel says, holding out his hand, but Phoenix won't take it.

"Just go," he says, cocking his head toward the door.

"I mean it," Angel says. "I owe you one. Maybe more than once." He laughs stupidly. "But I'll make it up to you, I promise."

"Right ..."

"Hey ... c'mon, give me a hand. I won't go if you don't." He winks. "We were friends once. We could still be."

"No way," Phoenix says with a sigh, grabbing

Angel's hand and reluctantly shaking it.

But I can still see a tiny smile form on his face when Angel pulls him in for a bro hug. "I know you do. You wouldn't have helped us otherwise." Angel pats him on the back and Phoenix seems to relax a little.

"You're lucky that woman called me instead of the cops," Phoenix says with a shrug.

"We're lucky bastards," Angel muses.

"Lucky, my ass. Next time, I won't be there to save yours," Phoenix says.

I smile at him. "There won't be a next time. I promise."

He squints. "Good."

"Where are you off to now?" Vanessa asks as she walks into the lobby to say good-bye.

"I don't know yet. Sky won't tell me," Angel says with a laugh, grabbing my shoulder and pulling me in for a hug.

"It's a surprise," I say.

"Ohh … exciting," Vanessa says, winking. "Well, I'd love to say I'll see you guys again, but we're constantly on the move as well, so I doubt it."

"Ahh, that's okay, we'll just leave it at 'someday,'" Angel says.

"Thanks for everything," Angel says. "C'ya, bro."

"Thank you!" I say as Angel walks me to the door, carrying the bags.

They wave at us as we leave, and when Phoenix

winks, Vanessa jabs him in the side with her elbow, making me laugh. They remind me of us, only further up in our lives, when things have settled down and all is good.

They seem happy, even though they have to move from place to place, and I can't help but wonder if it'll be the same for me. But then Angel squeezes my arm, looking down at me with a radiant smile on my face that immediately takes away my doubt. Having him and my baby is all I need to be happy. To live. To feel free.

So I step into the rented car with a beaming smile on my face and say, "Let's go."

It takes hours to reach our destination, but every second is worth it. The moment I step out of the car, my feet carry themselves across the road into the forest, rushing forward toward the not so abandoned cabin in the woods.

This is the only place I feel safe. A playground for kids, a happy memory for me.

The lights behind the curtain tell me she's here, right where she should be.

This is where Jamie and I agreed we would meet. A cabin our family once used that nobody knows about except us. Now it's our only safe haven, free of danger.

I can barely contain my emotions as I knock on the door and look behind me to find Angel running, completely worn out. "Sorry, I got a little excited," I say to him, smiling like an idiot.

"What is this place?" he asks.

"A cabin our families used to stay at for holidays, but we haven't used it in years."

When the door opens, Jamie gasps at the sight of me, and I immediately jump into her arms. "Jamie."

"Sky! You're back."

"Oh, god, I've missed you."

"I thought you'd never return," Jamie says, letting out a sigh of relief.

"Me neither ..." I smile. "But here I am."

She hugs me even tighter, holding me as if she thought I was dead. "I'm glad you're okay."

That's when I hear a familiar cry, and I let go of Jamie, letting my eyes search the cabin.

"She's in the crib," Jamie says, pointing inside. She holds open the door, and then her eyes fall on Angel. "Who's he?" she asks.

"He ..." I look back at Angel, who looks at me, giving me permission to tell her everything. For a second, I wonder if I really should. A few words can't sum up what we went through together, and I can't explain my emotions or his to anyone. I could tell her all the bad things he's done, but when I think about it, it doesn't really matter. All that matters is what's left ... him and me.

"He's the guy who saved me," I say.

It's not the complete story, but it is the truth.

She smiles at him. "Well, then you're more than welcome. What's your name?"

"Angel," he says, shaking her hand.

"Jamie. Pleasure to meet you."

"Likewise." He steps inside with me, and the moment I see my baby, I lose it.

Tears well up in my eyes, as I rush toward her crib and pick her up, hugging her tight.

When I hold her, I feel freed of my burden. She's the reason I went through all of this. Why I survived when no one thought I could. Why I persisted and overcame my fears.

She's the reason I still live.

Finally, I have her in my arms again.

"No wonder you wanted to come here first thing. I was already wondering what the hell we were doing in the middle of the forest, but now I understand," Angel muses, looking at me with a smile on his face.

"Jamie saved her for me when the men came to get me. I can't thank her enough." I nod at Jamie, whose face turns completely red.

"Well, of course. I will always help you, you know that."

I blink away the tears in my eyes and look at Angel. "This is the reason I wanted it to be a surprise."

"Do you want some alone time with her? I can go if you want," he says, running his fingers through his hair.

"No …" I shake my head, unable to stop the tears from flowing. "I didn't know how to tell you this."

"Tell me what?"

"When we were in that cell together, I saw your feet and that birthmark, and that's when I knew." I hold up the baby and show her foot.

Angel's eyes grow wider, and he takes a step forward, his hand shaking as he reaches for her foot.

"Angel … I want you to meet your daughter, Lily."

***

ANGEL

My … daughter?

"How do you know …" I stammer.

"When I was recovering, I counted back the weeks starting from when she was born. The conception dates match the exact week we were together, and what your father did to me was weeks after that. I know it's huge, and that it might come out of the blue, but I went over it again and again," Sky says. "There's no question about it. She's yours."

What she says shatters me completely.

I gaze at the girl in her arms, her pristine green eyes staring back at me as if she knew me before I did. My hand tentatively slides across her birthmark, my brain having difficulty processing the truth. The mark is the same as mine, and her face looks exactly like Sky … but also a little like me.

In an instant, I know. This little girl … she's mine.

I lick my lips, uncertain about what I should say or

how I should react.

For days, I believed Sky was fighting for the baby my father conceived, and now it turns out that all this time I was the father.

I'm … a father?

"Do you want to hold her?" Sky asks.

I nod, still unsure about what I should say—if there's even anything I can say at this point.

I'm not just flabbergasted. Utterly destroyed is more like it.

But in a good way.

Almost as if someone crushed my soul and this tiny little human being picked it up and rebuilt it again from the ground up.

When I take her from Sky's arms, good chills run down my spine, goosebumps littering my skin.

"Support her head," Sky says, helping me as she places the baby in my arms.

I feel like a fool, not knowing how to hold her. I feel like I could break her at any time. She's so small. I bring my hand down to hers, and her fingers can't even wrap completely around one of mine. She's so tiny … and yet this tiny human has managed to split my soul in two.

Well, look at me, the big, bad wolf, crying his eyes out over a girl. I'm a killer, a stonehearted monster, and yet I melt when I look at her. It's as if I'm not even *me* anymore.

Tears spill out of my eyes as if I've been cutting

onions, but not because I'm sad.

It's the first time in my life that I genuinely feel good about myself and about something that I did. I'm a bastard only good at killing people, bred for the fight … and still I managed to create such a beautiful thing.

"Hi, Lily," I say, as she closes her eyes to yawn, which makes me smile like a motherfucker.

She's perfect. Everything I want but thought I couldn't have and wasn't worth having.

Am I even worthy of her love? To be in her life? All these questions arise that I don't know the answer to, so I look at Sky, wondering if she knows.

She smiles, blinking away the tears. "Stay with us," she says.

I don't think I can smile any harder than I am right now. "Of course, I will. She's my girl, dammit."

Sky smiles broadly, looking relieved that I said yes.

She probably thought I'd get cold feet. She may be right because this is one hell of a responsibility. However, looking at her now, there is only one possible answer and that's fuck yes, I'm ready for it.

I'm ready to love.

Ready to let go of my past.

Ready to live.

I look down at Lily and imagine all the possible roads she'll be able to take in her life; all the blocks she'll have to face, all the troubles, the worries, the happiness, the good stuff. I can see the houses we'll live in, the mess we'll make, having dinner together, laughing and crying … just living. I see it all and wonder if she's ready for it. Because I know I am. I can see it all, and I know now that I can face anything that comes in my path.

Because now I not only have Sky, but I also have my baby girl, and there's no way in hell I'm ever letting go of either.

"My little girl …" I mumble, cradling her in my arms.

In her, I see the beauty of this world, which I didn't think was worth living until I met her.

My love together with Sky brought her into this world. A little miracle that ultimately pulled us together. The undying connection we felt was there for a reason, like some invisible string pulling us together so we could get back to this little girl and become a real family.

"So … this is my new family now," I mutter. "My Azure Sky and my beautiful Lily."

"Yes," Sky says.

"But … I don't really know how to be a dad," I say.

"That's okay," she says with a laugh. "You're a natural. Look." She points at Lily, who's already sleeping like a princess.

God, it feels like she stole my breath away.

When I was down and out, I thought there was nothing left to live for.

That my only reason for existing was to kill and to be killed.

Sacrifice after sacrifice.

Until I finally became the one to almost give up.

I did it all for her, my Sky.

She leans in and drops her head on my shoulder and together, we shuffle about, admiring the precious girl in my arms. I realize it's a good thing I never gave up the fight.

After I had made the deal to let Sky off the hook, I didn't think I still had a purpose left in this world. I had done my job. I'd fulfilled my purpose. I saved Sky from the pain she had to suffer and then I gave up on myself … just like that.

But then Sky told me her secret.

In twenty-one minutes, I learned the truth behind all her lies.

Her baby … my baby … is alive.

Twenty-one seconds was all it took to bind me to this world, to keep my body grounded but let my heart fly up into the clouds.

This little girl here …

She's my purpose now.

And, along with her mother, I'm never letting go of them for as long as I live.

They'll have to pry them both from my cold, dead hands.

That's how much I love them already.

That's how much they're mine.

Sky murmurs, "We can't go back to my home or yours. Will we be okay?"

I press a kiss on her forehead and look down at Lily, feeling prouder than I ever have. "We'll be more than okay."

I don't know what we'll do or where we'll go. But as long as Sky and Lily are here in my life, I know we'll be all right. It doesn't matter where we settle … as long as we're together then we can do anything we set our minds to.

Love is how we thrive; what pulled us through and made us do the impossible.

I feel nothing but love for these two.

Sky doesn't realize this, but I do … I wasn't the one to save her.

She saved me.

THANK YOU FOR READING!

Thank you so much for reading Twenty-One. I hope you enjoyed the story!

For updates about upcoming books, please visit my website, www.clarissawild.blogspot.com or sign up for my newsletter here: http://eepurl.com/FdY71

I'd love to talk to you! You can find me on Facebook: facebook.com/ClarissaWildAuthor, make sure to click LIKE. You can also join the Fan Club: facebook.com/groups/FanClubClarissaWild/ and talk with other readers!

Enjoyed this book? You could really help out by leaving a review on Amazon and Goodreads. Thank you!

Read on for an excerpt of Stalker, a Dark Romance featuring Phoenix & Vanessa!

EXCERPT OF STALKER

PROLOGUE

PHOENIX

Her skin glistens in the darkness, and my eyes hone in on her like she's a diamond ready for the taking. Pictures of her and Phillip's faces hang above her head, with movie awards stacked on top of a shelf to the side. A perfect shell for an imperfect heart. She's incredible … and she will be mine.

She is all I can think about, as she lies there in her bed, silently sleeping the night away.

She has no idea that I'm lurking in a corner, hovering close to her defenseless body. She smells of roses and expensive wine, and when she rolls over and her chest is exposed, I lean over her and take in her scent. Breathing out hot air on her skin makes her arch up toward my mouth, her mind unaware of what her body desires.

She's so close…all I have to do is grasp, and she's

mine for the taking.

She's a devil in disguise. A vixen. A seductress, but I won't let her beauty distract me from my goal.

I fucking hate her to death.

Literally. I'm going to kill her.

But doing it now would spoil all the fun. She's defenseless and doesn't even know I'm here. There's no fun in chasing an oblivious prey. I want the hunt. I want to feel the adrenaline and smell the fear as she runs for her life.

She deserves what's coming for her, but I'm not going to give it to her that easily.

I'll watch her from a distance; I'll make her sweat and think she's going insane.

And then, when she's at her lowest, I'll strike.

She'll never see it coming until it's too late.

And then, she'll be begging for mercy.

CHAPTER 1

PHOENIX

Six months done, and four thousand five hundred and sixty days left in prison. With a black marker, I write the numbers on the calendar and cross today's date off like I do each day. On the corner of this sheet is a black skull, which I've repeatedly crossed out, punctured, and stabbed to vent my anger, imagining it's her face.

That woman … just thinking about her makes me want to punch holes in the wall I'm staring at.

I hate her to death, in the literal sense. I don't just *want* to kill her … I'll make it happen. One way or another, she's going to pay for what she did. Punishment and pain aren't enough … only death is, and I'm going to bring it to her doorstep.

These walls won't hold me back. Maybe now, but not forever, and when I get out, she'll be the first to suffer. She's lucky these steel bars surround me and keep me locked inside, far away from that pretty little lie she calls life. She thinks she's safe, she thinks she's innocent, but we both know that's not true. She's hiding behind that fake, perfect mask of hers, but all it takes is a snap and it'll crack right down the middle.

I'll make sure to bring the pain when I get out of here. She deserves it.

You might think I'm an asshole for wanting to kill a girl, but this girl has gone pretty far ... further than most girls will ever go to clear their own name. She framed me so she could point the cops at me and put me in jail. That's like cutting the heart out of a man. If I had one, I'd be dead already, especially because I involved myself with the likes of her.

I admit that I'm not a saint. I did some bad shit, too. I killed her husband, but he deserved every ounce of the pain that he received. He was a cheating bastard, and so was she. They both deserve to go to hell.

I reek of fury and rightfully so. All I can think about is making her suffer the way she's making me suffer. Lock her up and hurt her. My fingers twist, grabbing the empty air as I imagine strangling her. I can already feel the bones crack.

She fucking ruined my life, and not just because she put me in jail. That girl is full of secrets, cloaked behind a façade that I'm dying to strip away. Of course, nobody believes me. With my tattoos, piercings, and dark hair, I look like the typical killer, someone whose words mean nothing in the face of a threat. It's always been that way, and I don't expect that to change anytime soon. My life has always been about bare-knuckle fights to claim authority over whatever I deemed as mine. That's all I do, all I know. Fighting in whatever way necessary with whatever means I can gather just to get what belongs to me.

And the worst thing is that I once fought for her.

That's right; she's not just my most hated rival, but she also used to be the object of my affection. I say 'used to', but I'm not so sure if I'll gut her that quickly when I see her face again. I might actually fuck her first, and then kill her. Exes ... I'd rather ax them.

If I could, I would erase every memory I had of her, just so I'd stop thinking about her. Instead, I'm locked up in this cell, reminded of her day in and day out ... thinking of all the ways that I'm going to make her beg for mercy.

"Are you sulking again?"

I turn my head at the sound of the annoyingly sarcastic voice of my cellmate. At times like these, when he says shit like this, I just want to rip his head off. However, the cavity in my chest has reserved a tiny spot for him to the point of it growing on me like a parasite. That's what you get when you spend months in the same room with another guy. Somehow, you are attached to the person just because they're there ... they're alive, and you can talk to them. That alone is enough to create a bond. At least, in here it is.

So, I'll spare him ... for now.

I narrow my eyes at him. "Shut up."

He raises his eyebrow at me, his blue eyes flaring

with curiosity. "I know what you're doing when you twitch your nose, crack your knuckles, and sneer at the wall. You do it every day." He cocks his head at me as he sits on the edge of his bunk bed, his feet dangling close to my head. "You're thinking about her, aren't you?"

"Mind your own business, will you?" I say, shoving his legs aside. "And get those damn feet out of my fucking face. They smell like rotting junk food."

He attempts to rub his socks against my chin, so I pull his leg so hard he crashes to the floor.

"Ow! Fuck!" he yells, rubbing his head as he crawls up. He runs his fingers through his long, dark hair. "What did you do that for?"

"That's what you get for taunting me," I say.

He frowns. "Asshole."

I smirk. "That's me." I flip the pages of my calendar back where they belong and throw it on the table. "Got a problem with that?"

He raises his brow. "Always."

I smile, and so does he. I know this fucker never gets mad at me, and that's why I like him. It's also why he's still alive. Being in a cell with me isn't easy ... if you manage to survive. What can I say? The fucker has grown on me.

Suddenly, something strikes the bars of the cell, and it makes me jolt up from my seat and turn around. It's the guard, flashing a cocky smile.

"Sullivan. DeLuca." With a low voice, he says,

336

"Time to get some fresh air."

I sigh, packing up my things, like we always do. Everything has to be left tidy and neat, so the officers can check the cell with a quick glance. The guard opens the door when we're ready, and he escorts us downstairs where the rest of the inmates gather as well. We always go outside in designated blocks, one block never coming into contact with the other. They do it to separate the racial gangs, which are notorious for starting prison riots.

Me? I don't belong anywhere, and neither does DeLuca, so we stick together mostly. I hate cliques and avoid them like the plague. They have nothing to offer us, and I have no interest in siding with idiots. However, that makes us easy targets, too. That's why the guards are always on their toes whenever they let us out of the cage.

We walk outside with the rest of the inmates and go to our regular spot near the picnic table. It's to the far east side of the premises, close to the fence where the grass is still green instead of soiled by dirty boots. I go on my knees and pluck some grass out of the earth as DeLuca sits on top of the picnic table and leans back to enjoy the sun.

"Fucking fine day it is, Nix," DeLuca muses, groaning as he stretches.

"Mmmhmm," I agree, but I don't want to talk with him right now. Outside is the only place where I can think of other things besides that fucking woman, *and* I can hear more than just his voice. Being confined to a small cell does things to a person. It makes them vulnerable ... weak almost, and that's a feeling I can barely stomach. It makes me want to start a riot just for the sake of regaining my spirit.

I pluck some more grass until I find what I'm looking for—a colony of ants has taken up residence here over the past couple of months. I move a few small stones until I find their nest and just look at it. They crawl everywhere with little leaves and other types of food, bringing it to the nest, as well as carrying the larvae. It's a tiny ecosystem resembling humans, only on a much smaller scale. I just like to watch them. That's all. And maybe help them every now and then, just for fun.

Suddenly, a boot comes crashing down on top of the nest, crushing the ants.

Enraged, I look up at the person who just butchered a whole city worth of insects.

"Playing in the sandbox, are we, Sullivan?" he snarls, spit flying out of his mouth and onto my cheek.

Getting up to my feet, I wipe it off and lean in with narrowed eyes. He checks me out from top to bottom while his buddies gather around us, creating a circle to trap me. This guy is clearly looking for a fight ... with the wrong dude.

Lifting my hand, I smear his spit right back on his own cheek, dragging it along slowly as everyone watches with parted lips and audible gasps. Apparently, now I've gone and done it. Shit's about to hit the fan. Great. Just the way I like it.

When I'm done, I wipe what's left of the goo on my pants and cock my head, waiting for him to make the first move.

"You fucking cocksucker. I'll teach you a lesson." The guy growls and up his fist goes, right into my face. I take the blow like a man, absorbing the full force and letting my body move with his smack. It takes me a few seconds to recuperate. It's a good punch. However, not good enough.

"Is that all you got?" I say, turning my face back to him.

The cocky look he's championing immediately turns into shock, as he probably realizes it didn't hurt me much. When I smile, he screams and his face turns completely red. Before he can lash out in anger, I punch him in the gut.

That's when DeLuca gets off the table and hits another guy in the back, causing him to buckle. Then he gives him a knee to the face and steals his knife. He cuts another attacker's arm, who screams for help, while I fight my attacker until he's down on the ground and I'm on top of him, beating the shit out of him.

DeLuca scares the others away with the knife, stabbing anyone who dares to come close, as I pummel my opponent with no remorse.

"Who's teaching who a lesson now, huh?" I yell, my fists spreading his blood all over his face.

By the time the guards arrive, his face is already split open at various points, and his nose is crooked as fuck. I probably broke a few bones here and there. The guards blow on their whistles and sound the alarm, yelling at everyone to get down on the ground. I stop at this moment, as I'd rather not get a fucking Taser on my ass. That *does* hurt like a bitch.

We lie down, and my attacker is groaning from the pain as the officers swarm in and cuff us all. I'll probably be put in solitary now, but it was worth every punch I gave him.

Nobody messes with my business. Whether it's ants or a kill, it's my fucking business, and everyone best stay out of my way … or I'll take down every last one of them.

ALSO BY CLARISSA WILD

Dark Romance
Mr. X
Delirious Series
Killer
Stalker

New Adult Romance
Fierce Series
Blissful Series

Erotic Romance
The Billionaire's Bet Series
Enflamed Series

Visit Clarissa Wild's website for current titles.
http://clarissawild.blogspot.com

SUBSCRIBE TO

CLARISSA'S NEWSLETTER

To receive exclusive updates from Clarissa Wild
and to be the first to get your hands on her books,
please sign up to be on her personal mailing list!
You'll get instant access to cover releases, chapter
previews, free short stories, and you'll be eligible to win
great prizes!

Link: http://eepurl.com/FdY71

Connect with Clarissa!
Website: www.clarissawild.blogspot.com
Twitter: www.twitter.com/WildClarissa
Facebook: www.facebook.com/ClarissaWildAuthor
Pinterest: www.pinterest.com/clarissawild
Google+: www.plus.google.com/+ClarissaWild

ABOUT THE AUTHOR

Clarissa Wild is a New York Times & USA Today Bestselling author, best known for the dark Romance novel Mr. X. Her novels include the Fierce Series, the Delirious Series, and Stalker. She is also a writer of erotic romance such as the Blissful Series, The Billionaire's Bet series, and the Enflamed Series. She is an avid reader and writer of sexy stories about hot men and feisty women. Her other loves include her furry cat friend and learning about different cultures. In her free time she enjoys watching all sorts of movies, reading tons of books and cooking her favorite meals.

Want to be informed of new releases and special offers? Sign up for Clarissa Wild's newsletter on her website clarissawild.blogspot.com.

Visit Clarissa Wild on Amazon for current titles.

CPSIA information can be obtained at www.ICGtesting.com
Printed in the USA
LVOW10s1337151115

462657LV00004B/334/P